THE
SILVER FANG

Tamara Gray

Paranormal Romance

New Concepts

Georgia

Be sure to check out our website for the very best in fiction at fantastic prices!

When you visit our webpage, you can:

* Read excerpts of currently available books
* View cover art of upcoming books and current releases
* Find out more about the talented artists who capture the magic of the writer's imagination on the covers
* Order books from our backlist
* Find out the latest NCP and author news--including any upcoming book signings by your favorite NCP author
* Read author bios and reviews of our books
* Get NCP submission guidelines
* And so much more!

We offer a 20% discount on all new Trade Paperback releases ordered from our website!

We also have contests and sales regularly, so be sure to visit our webpage to find the best deals in ebooks and paperbacks! To find out about our new releases as soon as they are available, please be sure to sign up for our newsletter (http://www.newconceptspublishing.com/newsletter.htm) or join our reader group (http://groups.yahoo.com/group/new_concepts_pub/join) !

The newsletter is available by double opt in only and our customer information is *never* shared!

Visit our webpage at:
www.newconceptspublishing.com

New Concepts Publishing
5202 Humphreys Rd.
Lake Park, GA 31636

ISBN 1-58608-725-8
© copyright 2004 Tamara Gray
Cover art by Amber Moon, © copyright 2005

NCP books are available at special quantity discounts for bulk purchases for sales promotions, premiums, fund raising, or educational use. For details, write, email, or phone New Concepts Publishing, 5202Humphreys Rd., Lake Park, GA 31636, ncp@newconceptspublishing.com, Ph. 229-257-0367, Fax 229-219-1097.

First NCP Paperback Printing: 2005

Chapter 1

I was alone. A sudden feeling of despair crept into my mind as I perched on the edge of the barn roof, overseeing the landscape below. An eerie fog swirled lazily across the trees billowing down to the yard covering everything in a blanket of gloomy mist. Rolling my shoulders and trying to release the tension and fear, I huddled against myself wrapping my arms tightly around my legs. A mind-numbing chill ran up and down my spine, and the only thing I could feel was my trembling body. Concentrating on survival was the only way to dispel the pending feeling of doom that now inundated my senses. The only hope of escape was inside the barn, and somehow I had to build up the nerve to make my next move. Scanning the area one last time, I reluctantly stood. Taking a deep breath, I leaped into the fog, floating effortlessly through the cool night air. The mist chilled my skin while the long leather jacket I wore flared out around me. Flipping in mid-air, I landed safely with a small thud. Nostrils flared as the stench of the dying creatures mixed with freshly cut grass. The smell of blood and danger mingled in the cool evening breeze causing my stomach to churn with hunger. I shook my head trying to clear my thoughts and forget the flashbacks of the attack. Now what lay before me was silence filled only with the pounding of my heart.

Squatting low to the ground, I peered cautiously into the night. The moon illuminated the gloomy world, causing silver light to dance over everything in its path. Aiming my guns into the darkness, I propelled my power searching for what my eyes could not see. My energy flowed effortlessly, but could only find dead or dying creatures. Dawn was approaching and the moon was descending rapidly. I might actually survive this hellish night.

A bolt of fear jolted through me as a long sharp cry pierced the silence. My power probed the creature nearest me. I stiffened waiting for a possible attack. Sending my energy deep inside the creature, it turned to meet my gaze--its red eyes glowing angrily as he sniffed the air and felt my presence. The werewolf let out a blood-curdling scream, trying to escape my grasp.

"Die," I whispered. wrapping my power around its beating heart squeezing with the unseen force. I watched from afar, as my energy captured its heart, exploding it into a million pieces. The monster's deafening screams and claws slashed at me breaking my trance even as I felt its life slip away. The smell of rotting inhuman flesh and muffled whimpers was the only evidence left of the fight that occurred moments before. I stood, my emotions buried somewhere deep within. The numbness moved across my whole body as the rush of power tingled over every muscle and cell. Smirking wickedly over my triumph and the fact I was still alive and the sun was about to rise, I turned to face the barn doors shoving them open. I cringed as they swung inward creaking and banging into the wall.

"Shoot!" I cursed, knowing that the noise probably woke the dead.

As I entered a wave of stagnant, warm air floated over my face stealing my breath away. The moon's light cast ominous shadows around the barn, but I did not need the light to see my intended target. "God bless you old man." I whispered, thankful the car was parked exactly where he said it would be. Staring into the dimly lit building, I waited patiently for any sign of the creatures that hunted me. *Nothing!*

I bolted for the car and wrenched on the door handle. *Locked!*

My hands were shaking as I raced to the passenger side it was locked also. *Just my bloody luck.* "Who leaves their car keys in the car when it's locked?" I grumbled to myself, getting angrier by the minute. From what I could see, the car looked to be in good condition and the keys were exactly as the old man said, in the ignition. I screamed internally as I kicked the door of the car.

I hated getting messy. That thought made me chuckle softly as I looked down at the cuts and bruises from the battle with the werewolves. I quickly removed my leather jacket while moving back to the driver side, wrapping my arm and gun in its velvety protection. I struck the weapon against the glass shattering the window sending shards of glass onto the front seat and barn floor.

Tossing the gun and jacket into the car, I bent down to unlock the door. That was when the hair on my neck bristled standing on end. Clenching my fists, I swerved around to meet the beast, sensing the evil clawing at my mind. The creature's power engulfed me sending fear pulsing through my veins. Waving my hands, I frantically tried shoving the wicked energy away, to no avail. I backed slowly up against the car and reached in grabbing my gun, never taking my eyes off his amber demonic stare. Gun in hand, I moved away from the car as the beast stalked closer.

Losing my footing, I stumbled back as the monster took another step forward. He mirrored my every move. The werewolf was hideous, eyes glowing red with demonic power and hate. His body elongated standing on hind legs that were once human. Blood dripped from his massive fangs pooling in the hay at his feet. Its claws had chunks of skin and flesh clinging to his long razor-sharp nails, some of the flesh, my own. The smell of death forced me to retreat until I was cornered between the beast and the vehicle. I was trapped, nowhere to go, frozen in horror.

Move, Samantha! MOVE! My mind screamed in terror as I contemplated my options. The thumping of my heart roared in my ears drowning out the growls of the beast before me. As I inhaled the warm musty air, pain shot through my lungs. I slowed my heartbeat attempting to catch my breath while the adrenaline raged unchecked inside my body. The creature effectively blocked the barn doors with his enormous frame. *Samantha, stay in control.*

"Ty, you don't have to do this," I pleaded, hoping he could understand what I was saying. "You have a choice."

The creature only watched oblivious to my pleas. In a whirl of inhuman speed, I darted past the car, heading for my only escape, a ladder leading to the second floor of the barn. The ladder seemed to be moving away from me, rather than closer, as I sprinted toward it. If I could get to the second floor, I would have a clean shot at the beast. Turning, I sent a couple rounds in his direction. He avoided the bullets with ease. Reaching the first step, I leapt up, grasping the rung holding on for dear life. Swinging myself into action, I started to climb.

The monster crashed through the barn following its prey. Crouching directly below my escape route the werewolf lunged into the air. He made it up two steps when he reached for my leg. A warm power tore through me as his claws began to shred my flesh. I screamed as bones snapped, tearing tendons and muscles beneath the onslaught of his fury. My leg dangled as he continued to rip into my soft tissue exposing crushed bones beneath. He jerked me downward and as he did, I dropped my gun screaming from the pain. Blinding white light and dizziness overwhelmed me as I fell back, landing on the ground with a thud. Slowly pulling my body up I tried to crawl away from the monster. I could only move from the waist up, the rest of my body immobile with throbbing pain. My arms steadied my weight as I slid across the floor. Straw stuck to my wound, causing me to cry out in agony.

The werewolf jumped, landing with a loud bang. He remained motionless in front of me watching my painful progress. I screamed as he put his lengthened claws around my neck and lifted me into the air. I dangled helplessly as he held me inches from his distorted face. Excruciating pain shot through my body as he shook me mercilessly.

He was going to snap me in two.

The creature's lips curled back showing his needle sharp fangs. The blood on his breath made me gag while I blinked in disbelief at the repulsive monster. He leaned over my neck taking me into his mouth. I felt warm liquid flood down my neck and chest as he crushed and shredded my muscles, growling with pleasure. With every beat of my heart, the warmth spread over my body.

My sight blurred as I fumbled for my second gun. My fingers shook as I aimed the weapon at the demon's deformed head.

I managed to gargle what would probably be my last word, "DIE!"

I fired the gun over and over until it clicked empty. It released me as it fell, while my torn, limp body slammed to the floor. I had to get to the car. With every ounce of strength, I dragged my body towards the vehicle. The smell of my own blood blended with the straw made me retch with nausea. My eyes hazed over brining on the welcoming darkness. Soon my cries of pain diminished to shallow whimpers as the smell of lilacs filled my nostrils. *Lilacs? I don't remember....*

I was dying, alone and cold. I had never feared death but the thought of dying by the hands of this monster just didn't feel right. In the back of my mind, I knew the end was near. The last few days of my life flashed before me in a blur. So many risks had been taken and for what? I had finally found a purpose for living and now the end was crashing down around me. It had all started with him. He came into my world and changed me forever....

Chapter 2

Betty was a 22-year-old secretary, just out of college, who was trying to finish her masters in theology. She was a cute, blonde-haired woman who always seemed to attract loser boyfriends. I know it really isn't any of my business who she dated, but the fact she talked about each one as if they were going to be the father of her children made it my business. Okay, so I'll admit she annoyed me and maybe that was my problem, but most of the time she gave me good reason to be annoyed. For instance, the fact that a vampire sat in the chair across from me, and two behind him, might be one reason for annoyance.

You heard me right, vampires. Welcome to my wonderful world. The world where vampires are real and things that go bump in the night tend to bump harder than you expected, and if you aren't willing to bump back, get out of the business.

I cleared my throat. "What can I do for you gentlemen?"

I was met with silence, just three pair of sunglasses cocking their heads in unison. Reminded me of a litter of puppies.

So when Betty walked back into the office, smiling sweetly, with a steaming hot cup of coffee, which smelled like heaven, it was a welcome distraction. Even if deep down I wanted to march her right back out into the hallway and beat some sense into that thick skull of hers. She was officially on my hit list for my afternoon surprise of a friendly visit from the neighborhood vamp.

Two of the vampires watched Betty with matching smiles that showed all fangs. She sat the coffee on my desk. "Anything else you'd like Samantha?" The southern drawl in her voice caused one vampire to sway.

Yeah, she was a beauty all right. "No thanks Betty, you have done quite enough." The smirk on the vampire sitting in the chair told me he caught the sarcasm in my voice. Unfortunately, Betty never understood sarcasm and worshiped the ground I walked on.

I gave her a menacing glare. Betty stood for a minute and then slowly backed out of my office, shutting the door behind her.

When I focused back to the group, he leaned forward, and I leaned back, hand reaching for my weapon. He smirked as he slid a manila folder across my desk. I forced a smile, between clenched teeth, at the group. I mentally shrugged as I tried to remind myself they were just potential clients. *Stop being so jumpy!* My right hand strayed to my neck, consciously aware of the pulse that beat wildly under my fingers. I took a deep, cleansing breath and let my hand drop to the folder.

I flipped it open and my eyebrow shot up as I glanced inside. My mind cringed as I shuffled through the pictures. I tried to hide the shock and horror of what I saw, but even a hardened prosecutor would flinch at the grisly display of remains. "You knew the victim?"

The vampire nodded. "He was a close friend." His words were laced with pain.

I nodded, acknowledging his pain, and quickly sifted through the remaining photos. They disturbed me despite knowing the victim was a vampire. I had avoided working with vampires, until now. I'm not normally so judgmental of people, but vampires are different. They are monsters, not humans. I'd witnessed first hand the damage a vampire could cause in a human's life. More than once I had been hired to protect way too many innocent people from vampires, only to find months later they were turned, or worse, missing. Laws were only just recently passed to protect vampires, and give them citizenship in the United States. Under the new law, vampires could own property and were made to pay taxes. This being the New World, we were the first to make such concessions. "Let freedom reign." I sighed.

"Excuse me?" The vampire questioned.

I blushed, "Oh sorry, was thinking out loud."

He smiled.

As usual, my nervousness caused me to say stupid things. Quickly I tried to get back on subject. "It occurs to me," I said, "that your friend might have been killed because he was a vampire."

The vampire leaned closer. "It is possible."

I cleared my throat, annoyed at his curt answers. "Okay, so why our company?" I asked.

He smiled. "Your reputation precedes you."

Two can play this game. I smiled back, "I see."

Guess the reputation I'd earned of being a real perfectionist was something the vampires admired because I had three vampire clients offer me work in the last six months. So far I hadn't taken any of the work, but as vampire numbers increased I was being forced to reconsider my decision not to work with bloodsuckers. Plus, they were wealthy and right now we needed the income. I hated being forced to take on a client I couldn't handle. One wrong decision when choosing a client, and I could end up dead or worse one of them.

"I'll be honest. I don't normally work with vampires."

He rubbed his chin. "So I've been told."

I quickly retreated. "I'm not saying I won't take your job, I just wanted to make sure you understand this would be a first for me."

His power bristled. "This would be a first for me as well. We take care of matters on our own, but this is different."

"Different how?"

"I believe humans are involved, therefore human law takes precedence over vampire law."

"Don't want to get your hands dirty, I see." I mumbled under my breath.

His eyebrow rose over the rim of his sunglasses.

"I've never worked with your kind, but that doesn't mean I don't understand how you work."

Head tilted to the side, he nodded. "It can be difficult to maintain proper relationships with the authorities if we take the law into our own hands."

"If our company does take your job, I need to know everything you know about what happened. I don't like being lied too, and I like things to run like a well-oiled machine." Vampires were known for skirting around the truth if it benefited their cause.

He held out his hands. "Of course, I would expect no less."

I was anal retentive in my work and it showed. The job itself allowed no mistakes. When you made a mistake in the bodyguard business someone died, so perfection was a necessity.

I arranged the pictures across my desk and stared at the men in my office. As if noticing them for the first time, I was suddenly blinded by their auras. They weren't half bad looking either; actually they were gorgeous, even behind sunglasses, which made me leery. The one who appeared to be in charge was especially handsome. Dating vampires was a dangerous game to play. Personally, I never had the desire, but this man would tempt even a saint.

John Wilkins and I started the Eldon Agency over ten years ago. We built a large client base with a lot of hard work, sweat and blood. Mainly my hard work, sweat and blood. John just liked to sit back and boss me around from behind the comfort of his desk. He mentioned a new client coming in today, but neglected to inform me the job was for vampires. *Dang, and a master vampire!* John never excluded important information like dealing with a master. Sometimes John let the money do the talking instead of asking the right questions. Although I couldn't hold it against him since we needed the income desperately.

Despite the group's good looks, it was their auras that surprised me the most. I had a "knack" at detecting vampires, especially lately. Master vampires had been known to hide their true identities, but I felt something in the air when they were around, a power or rift around their bodies as they moved. Vampires give off a certain aura depending on their age and strength and this group was sending a strong vibe over the entire office.

The auras I saw strengthened significantly around vampires, psychics and werewolves. I felt weird telling people about this strange gift, if it was a gift at all.

I gave myself a metal slap and tried to focus on the work at hand. My eyes roamed over the group uneasily and settled on the vampire before me.

"You will take the job?" More a command then a question, but I didn't take well to people telling me what to do.

"I will have to think about it. Frankly I need a lot more information. For instance, I'm not sure what you want me to do that the cops couldn't do for you." I gulped quickly, noticing his two companions watched me as if I might make a good snack. Even as I wondered if they might enjoy having me for a mid-afternoon snack, I noticed how powerful their auras were throughout the room. The vampire who was sitting had to be a master. And he sat in my office, and I had Betty to thank.

He opened his mouth then closed it the first sign of hesitation. "We need someone who can be discreet, and you come highly recommended. We insist you take our offer seriously."

I bit my lip, trying to maintain a professional manner. "Your vagueness isn't going to get me to take this job." I answered, my voice shaking.

"I will tell you everything I know." He leaned back in his chair. "But first, we will need your total cooperation in keeping the media out of our business."

"Vampire business."

"Yes." That one word said with enough conviction, to make me believe he would do anything to keep this quiet. That worried me.

I shrugged my shoulders. "I can't control the media, but you have my word if something is leaked it won't be from my office." I sighed, still annoyed at this situation. "My customers appreciated the fact I am discreet about my work." I paused. "I have various references from some of the wealthiest patrons in New Orleans if you would like a copy." I didn't mention it was normally those same clients that always gave me the most unusual jobs. I continued, tapping my fingers on my desk. "I enjoy a challenge, but there is only so much I can do with limited information." I could tell by looking at the man before me that this vampire would definitely be a challenge I would never forget.

"I understand your concern, and as I stated before, if you choose to take me on as a client we will be forthcoming with everything you need to know." From the tilt of his chin, I noticed his focus was on my breasts. *Brazen son of a gun!* His eyes were hot against my skin despite being hidden behind dark sunglasses.

"I am not going blindly into any situation sir, but I know my place and my job. On many an occasion I have handled the media and never had an incident." A cool chill ran up my spine as he slowly ran his tongue over the fangs now in full view. "You... You..." I was stuttering not accustomed to vampire's advances. "I am not an escort service either." I wanted to take the words back as soon as I said them, but it was too late.

"I know."

The sunglasses hid his eyes and that bugged the crap out of me. There was something about looking a person in the eyes, the doorway to their soul. Not to mention it was rude to wear sunglasses inside, while trying to conduct business. Or maybe I was sensitive because he was a vampire. Maybe it was his sly smile and raised eyebrows that gave him a boyish quality--and that caused a whole new set of problems.

He flashed me a fang filled grin. "I did not mean to offend you. I only thought it was necessary to warn you of the type of press this might cause."

My hand involuntarily moved back to my neck. It felt as if the walls in my office were about to crash down around me. "I appreciate the warning, but I am more than capable of handling the media."

"I am sure you can handle most any situation Miss Houston." The two vampires behind him chuckled.

Vampires were renowned sexual predators. They had the charm and the looks to bring any woman to their knees. I had seen it happen to some of my best friends, and vowed never to let one get close to me. I just hoped this vampire would behave himself. He was undeniably a looker and for some reason I had the feeling he was used to getting what he wanted.

"I can be resourceful when necessary." I replied. Freaky clients were just part of the profession as a bodyguard detective for hire. "But I know my limitations."

"I wish all people were as honest as you are Miss Houston. It is refreshing."

I watched his smile broaden as I leaned over my desk and whisper. "Some would say I am brutally honest."

He chuckled as he matched my motion, leaning forward. "Resourcefulness and honesty have their uses."

"Not all vampires are willing to ask for help. And I have never had a master vampire ask for my services."

He looked stricken, his smile faded. "How did you know?"

I laughed. "It isn't like you are trying to hide it." His power was flooding the room, making it hard to think straight. "I might be unfamiliar with your kind, but I know power when I see it." Clearing my throat I began to take another look at the folder. "What happened here?" Nobody answered. They knew as well as I that the horrific story was told all too well through the pictures I examined.

"That is what we want to know, Miss Houston." Power stormed around the group, explosive. Looking from one vampire to another, I only realized then that I was outnumbered. A cool sweat coated my forehead and I shifted in my seat. Three in one room at once was enough to make anyone squirm. *Calm down Samantha, they won't hurt you.*

A chill ran down my back as I carefully examined the photo that showed the victim strung up like a piece of meat. Silver chains were strung through the victim's body embedded deeply into his flesh. The skin had literally been torn from his limbs and torso.

My eyes widened in horror as I imagined the last moments of this man's life.

"This person has to be stopped."

I jumped at the interruption of my examination. I didn't trust my voice so I nodded my agreement. Hey, I didn't like vampires, but nobody deserved to die like this, not even a vamp.

Tilting the picture in my hand I brought it up for a closer look. "He was alive during this photo." I set the picture down and tapped the man's face, or what was left of it. "From what I can tell, he is talking or screaming, but I can't be sure which." I whispered to myself. "Whoever took this picture enjoyed themselves immensely," I continued, ignoring the man before me, deep in thought.

"How do you know this?" The vampire's deep voice boomed throughout the room.

"Well the photographer took his time documenting the murder from beginning until the end." I turned one picture to show him. "Look, this picture has nothing but charred remains, and this picture shows the victim without any injuries at all." I pointed out, laying the pictures in order from what I thought was start to finish. "See here, his flesh isn't torn." I pointed to picture with my finger.

The vampire winced, closing his eyes for a moment before glancing down at the picture.

"I'm sorry." He was obviously upset over his friend's death.

"No, continue. It just angers me that he died this way. No one deserves to die like this… nobody." His voice trailed off into a whisper.

"My thoughts exactly. If it's too much to handle just let me know." For a brief moment, he seemed vulnerable; I almost pitied him, almost.

"I am fine, time heals all wounds."

I brought my focus back to the photo. "So what I was trying to say was the victim is alive here, and here" I kept lining them up, "and here." I groaned. "They were torturing him for hours."

"It appears you are right."

"I still think you should contact the police." "You know they will not help. Not our kind."

"Not your kind," I corrected him. I knew the cops wouldn't work on the case because it involved vampires. Humans tend to fear that which we don't understand. I was a human so I could relate, the vampires in my office scared me.

I thumbed through the rest of the pictures when something caught my eye. "Wait, what is this?" I pointed to what seemed to be red glowing lights behind the man's body. I brought the picture closer, turning it from side to side trying to figure out what those lights were. I grabbed another picture from the pile that contained the lights.

"You have a keen eye." The vampire chuckled. "I now understand why my master was so insistent we seek you out for hire."

Ignoring his comment, I took a third picture and grabbed my magnifying glass from my desk drawer. Lifting the picture to the light, I placed everything in front of me. I looked up, mind swirling with curiosity. "It looks like eyes."

The vampire extended his hand and I slid the photo to him. He looked at it carefully, stiffened suddenly, and then placed it face down on my desk. "Indeed they are eyes."

"Werewolf?" I mumbled, shaking my head in disbelief. I had no idea what was going on in the vampire community, but lately they seemed to be in a lot of trouble with werewolves. Most people still denied the existence of Lycans, but not me.

The pictures had me seriously freaked out and my suspicions of the vampire who sat across from my desk had me instinctively reaching for my gun. I scooted my chair away from the desk and leaned nonchalantly back in my seat. He could already have killed me if he wanted to, but one could never be too careful. Paranoia kept me alive this long, and it might keep me alive a little while longer, if I was lucky.

I watched him and his buddies warily. He was tall, at least six feet, with dark shoulder length hair that curled in ringlets around his face. Sunglasses hid his eyes, making him appear mysterious and deadly.

From the view at my desk, his broad shoulders tapered down to a slim waist and long legs. I always did admire tall men. He sat back in his chair like he didn't have a care in the world while I assessed him. His chest rose softly with every breath, giving me a hint of his well-defined muscles, from beneath his clothes. He wore a black button down shirt with black pants. The dark color seemed to emphasize every movement he made with his powerfully built body. Most of the vampires I had interviewed were on the smaller side, but this vamp had a large frame and nice build. My eyes moved back to his face, handsome, not pretty like the majority of vamps I had seen. Actually, he was down right breathtaking. There was definitely something different about this vampire and the two men with him. I just couldn't understand why a vamp this powerful would need my protection. If he wanted to take me down, he could in an instant, and if he could take me down he could most certainly protect himself from the vampire haters in the world. I was a force to be reckoned with, but even the great Samantha Houston had her limitations.

I managed to relax and gave the vampire my most professional smile. "Who found the body?" I asked, and then quickly corrected myself. "Or ashes?"

Waiting patiently for an answer, I contemplated my next course of action. He seemed to flinch at my question and the men behind him looked uncomfortable.

His accent floated sensually over the room. "The pictures were delivered to us on Monday in an envelope."

"Someone is playing games." I said.

"Miss Houston, we want you to find out who killed my friend, and to protect my family from further attacks."

"This isn't normal." I shook my head.

He reached across the desk to grab my hand, and I pulled it back before he made contact. His hand stayed rested on the pictures. "I need to know if you will take the job? My master is insistent that we secure your help." He paused before asking, "Do you accept?"

"I need to. ..."

He interrupted me. "I have been very patient, but you seem preoccupied. If this is too much for you to handle, then we will seek alternative support." His smile was rigid and his words were laced with a hint of irritation.

I hated vampires, the arrogant son of a gun.

The more that I thought about his annoyance. the more annoyed I became. Somewhere between fear and fantasy this vampire had thrown me off course. My fingers tapped lightly on the desk as I watched him carefully. "Who is the man in the picture?"

He lowered his glasses. "His name was Leonardo Darius. His friends called him Darius."

His eyes were a piercing shade of green. Stunning was the first thought that popped into my mind. What bugged me even more was his air of arrogance. If there was one thing I hated more than vampires, was a man who was arrogant. Now I faced an arrogant vampire man.

"Well, Mr.?" I stopped waiting for him to fill in the blank.

"I am sorry--how rude of me, my name is Siön Baptiste." He nodded and held out his hand.

I ignored his outstretched hand. His grin widened as if impressed with my bad manners. "I was under the impression your secretary had informed you of my name and our arrival?" His voice echoed through the office deep and masculine. This time he stood, hand held out giving me no choice but to comply or look childish.

He was much taller than I expected. Gritting my teeth, I reluctantly grabbed his hand and to my surprise, it was warm. I found myself closing my eyes as the warmth moved up my arm and slowly pulsed along my skin. The heat spread quickly as my hand began to tingle. My stomach lurched as waves of pleasurable electricity washed over my entire body. I tried to pull back, but his smile broadened as I struggled to pry myself loose. His eyes held mine. My mind screamed, "run for your life," yet my hand and body didn't budge. My eyes opened as my knees buckled. I let out a breath and tried to gather my composure before I nearly tumbled back. He released my hand grudgingly, his middle finger sliding over my palm as he let go. I plopped back down in my chair, disgusted with my reaction to his power. It was scary and felt good, all at once. He continued to stand, looking from his hand, to me, and back to his hand again. It was his shocked expression that made me feel better. He looked as dazed as I was. Good!

The green orbs swirled and rotated, his pupils growing in size, the black almost completely engulfing the green. "What did you do?" He asked.

I just stared at him breathlessly as he returned lazily to his seat. "The question is what did YOU do to me?"

He huffed crossing his leg, leaning on his hand watching me. "I assure you, it was nothing I did."

This was the exact reason I avoided vampires. They could force their will on you. I had a hard enough time submitting to authority, let alone being controlled by a power hungry vampire. I straightened in my seat. "It wasn't me, either way keep your mojo to yourself. I don't like mind tricks and you pull that stunt again and I'll have you booted out of here faster than you can say, crazy." My voice trailed off as he began to laugh.

I had never succumbed to a vampire's powers before, but this guy had me swooning. His laughter sent a second wave of spine tingling chills over my entire body. "Let us put this aside for now. I like what I see." He smirked. "I know you can help me." He grinned wickedly.

There was an undercurrent in what he was saying and I saw right through it. "Help you solve this case and offer you the services of our best body guards." Vampires possessed the ability to control most people with their words and there was no doubt in my mind this vampire could do just that.

"Not just any body guard, I want you." Alluring eyes highlighted his handsome face making him even more daunting. I gazed into his lovely eyes trying to decide on the color. Never had I seen eyes that shade of green, but I knew behind the beauty, hid a cold-hearted killer.

He smirked at my perusal of him.

I want you as well! SAM, concentrate!

A warm blush raced up my neck and across my face. *Busted!* This guy was cocky. He was so sure of himself, and his accent was starting to grate on my last nerve. Sexy voice, sexy accent, and it irritated me for some reason. Could it be he was getting under my skin? *Jerk!*

Using his vampire charms on me wasn't going to get him anywhere. He wouldn't get away with it, not with me, not ever. I bit my tongue, hard enough to draw blood. The pain immediately cleared my head, and my sudden burst of anger helped to further clear my thoughts as I began to contemplate my next course of action. Whatever I was going to do, I had to tread carefully. This vampire was very powerful.

Forcing my eyes from his, I set my sight on the two thugs beside him. "I could lose my license if I don't turn the guy who murdered your friend into the cops. I need to know that you guarantee that nobody will harm him, and that you will let the law handle the situation once the time comes."

Siön Baptiste leaned over to the man at his right whispering quietly to him. I strained to hear what he said to the man, but he spoke quietly. I could only catch bits and pieces and he was speaking French. I think he was asking them to leave, but I wasn't sure.

The man on Siön Baptiste's right looked around the room nervously. He appeared torn between leaving Siön Baptist alone with me, or facing Siön's anger for not obeying him. The big lug shook his head and led his overgrown buddy to the door, exiting the room. Before shutting the door, they both glanced back solemnly. What was little ol' me going to do to the big bad vampire sitting across from me? *Jeesh, some people and their pets!*

Turning my gaze back to Siön Baptiste, it became apparent just how alone we were. His power surged over my body, heating the air around me. I slowly scooted up to my desk. No sudden movements. As he watched me, I maneuvered my right hand on my gun, which was neatly strapped to the belly of the desk. "I will have Betty type up a contract by the end of the week. You can discuss the financial terms with John." I removed it the gun gently out of the harness, I placed it carefully in my lap.

"We have already worked up a contract. I will bring a copy tonight for you to review," he said.

I gripped the gun until my hands went numb. "We will use our contract." The gun wouldn't kill him, but it would slow him down enough for me to make a run for it. Filled with silver bullets, my weapon would seriously wound or kill a werewolf. Vampires were different. Unless you hit their heart repeatedly, or cut their head off they would survive any gun wound I could inflict. Actually I had only witnessed one vampire's death and it wasn't by my hand. One minute the creature was hissing and showing fang, the next just a pile of ashes.

Siön Baptiste rubbed his chin, raising an eyebrow. A devious grin crept across his mouth as if he already knew what I was about to do. With one smooth motion, he slid his chair nearer to my desk. As he moved forward, my heart leaped into my throat, the movement causing me to gasp. I wondered if he sensed my body tighten. His masculine scent filled the room, inundating my senses. His eyes watched me as if he were caressing my entire body. I frowned, shuddering at the thought of any vampire, let alone this hunky hulk, touching me. I focused my gaze on the blinds instead of his face. Even with the blinds closed and lights dim, I could still see his perfectly chiseled features. He was a good-looking bloodsucker, and he knew it.

"Ahem... Ahem..." Clearing his throat, he drew my attention back to him, only to notice a smirk cross his face. He knew how uncomfortable I was looking at him. He was so self-assured and arrogant. His confidence seeped through every pore, floating effortlessly into the air. "We will use our contract." He grinned like a cat ready to pounce on a mouse.

"No, we will not." I whispered, cursing quietly at how weak my voice sounded.

My gaze roamed to his mouth, curious if his full lips felt softer than they appeared. His smile was magnetic and terribly appealing. I shook my head, lowering it to hide my feelings. *He had to be using some type of hypnotic vampire powers on me. Vermin!*

Concentrating on his face, I moved my gun into position, watching for any advance warning. "Forget the contract for now--you can take that up with John. How long had the victim been missing?" I asked, pointing at the pictures. I couldn't help but notice it was getting dreadfully stuffy, almost claustrophobic.

He was genuinely surprised as one eyebrow lifted showing an amused expression. "I guess that means you are taking the job?"

"I need somewhere to start. Where did he live, who did he hang out with?" I asked.

He started laughing and as he continued laughing, I became increasingly uneasy. "We can fill you in on details tonight. But we have our suspicions who might be responsible for his death. We were hoping you could help in this matter."

"I can help if you cooperate." I grumbled. "How old was he?"

"Who, Darius?"

"No, the other dead vampire in the picture." I wanted to take it back as soon as the words left my mouth. His lips thinned and it sounded like he was growling deep within his chest. I couldn't be sure.

He flexed his hand as if trying to maintain his beast and continued. "He was 250 years old." He sighed. "In the prime of his life, cut down too soon."

I wanted to laugh, but I kept myself in check. If I were really lucky I'd survive to see 50, and he had the nerve to complain about 250 years? Must be nice. "Once again I'm sorry for your loss." Trying not to sound annoyed, and failing miserably.

"Darius was a good man."

The sun peeked through the shades from behind him. The light appeared blindingly bright against his dark silhouette. He almost looked angelic, with a shiny halo behind his head. I knew better than to assume this man could be an angel, maybe a fallen angel. *We all know where assuming gets us--in a crap load of trouble.* The thought ran through my head bringing a smile across my face.

Siön Baptiste shifted in his chair, bending forward while the sun crept across the contour of his features. The moment the light hit his skin I nearly jumped out of mine. My mind repeated what I refused to believe. *He was a vampire out during the day.* My heart somersaulted within my chest, climbing into the back of my throat. Why hadn't I noticed this important fact previously? I tried to stay calm, but I feared the pounding of my heart and perspiration sliding down my face would give me away. If I panicked, I might never see a sunset again. How was this possible?

Don't let him see you sweat, I thought to myself wiping my face with my hand.

He shook his head whispering as if he read my mind. "Don't look so shocked, you know I am a vampire. I will explain myself tonight after your visit with Nicholi." He was pleased at my stunned expression.

Visit with Nicholi? "Just who do you think I am visiting tonight?"

He smiled. "My master would like to meet you personally to extend our offer."

I never thought vampires could be so happy. He had a permanent grin on his face while his eyes teased, and infuriated me beyond the point of reason. My nerves were frayed; this was exactly why I didn't mess with vampires.

"I really do not find any of this funny. How are you out during the day? I need answers." I stood slowly, hand moving to my back slipping the gun in the waist of my pants. *I was brave yes, smart not always.*

"Take the job and I will tell you."

"You can't force me to take this job. And stop using your vampire tricks on me." I tried to sound like tough girl, but my voice was squeaking. The shock of what sat before me overwhelmed my senses. A vampire out during the day? "Just because you are good looking doesn't mean you can come in here and boss me around. Vampires are rude, and arrogant and you should really keep your mojo in check."

"Mojo?"

"Yes, mojo, powers of persuasion." Laughing aloud, he slapped the desk with his hands. Moving swiftly and effortlessly, he leaned closer grabbing a pen from my desk and began twirling it between his long fingers. He spun the pen like a toy and I had the feeling he was definitely toying with me. "I assure you, I am not using my mojo on you."

"I have this feeling you are holding back on me Siön Baptiste, and I don't like it one bit. Tell me everything."

Lifting an eyebrow while grinning he said, "My master would like to hire you to find who killed Leonardo. Our family has had several threats." He continued to play with the pen. "We need someone to investigate Darius' murder and protect our family. You came highly recommended." He sighed obviously annoyed at explaining himself. "He would like to discuss details with you in person tonight." His voice was so soothing and controlled, I almost believed him. He flipped the pen and it flew across the room hitting the wall behind my desk. Happy with himself he grabbed a second pen from the cup on my desk sporting a devious sparkle in his eye.

"I don't know what you think you're doing but stop playing with my pens."

"Meet me at 8:00 at the Silver Fang and we shall discuss this further. Nicholi is looking forward to meeting you tonight," he coaxed, tilting his head sideways. The second pen went flying across the room landing somewhere near the filing cabinet. His smile broadened and ignoring my warning he reached to grab another pen.

I quickly slapped his hand away from the penholder. He pulled back snickering. I had an overwhelming desire to wipe that grin off his smug face with another slap. Instead, I glared menacingly at him. "I am glad I can entertain you Mr. Baptiste, but what makes you think that I want to meet your master and that I will take this job?" I raised my voice as I spoke.

He appeared taken aback by my response, but obviously he didn't know me that well. Siön Baptiste shook his head, mumbling quietly in French. "Because you are intrigued and won't be able to help yourself."

"Don't be so sure."

His long fingers caressed his chin while watching me. "Madam, do not disappoint us this is of an urgent matter. It is never wise to disappoint Nicholi."

He waved his hand aggravated, "And put that silly weapon away, it will do you no good against me." His last comment sounded like a warning.

My mouth dropped open, "How did you know?"

"I can smell the silver and you just cleaned the gun this morning." He smiled. "I could bend you to my will if I chose to, and your gun would not save you."

My training was taking over and I decided, for once, it was better to be polite. I placed the gun carefully on my desk. John always handled the clients. I wasn't patient enough for them. I would never win a Miss Congeniality award, but I was good at saving lives. I glanced around the room looking for an escape route if necessary. I tried to read his perfectly masked expression, but it was blank.

With the most determined look I could muster, I abruptly told him, "I don't work well with threats Mr. Baptiste and especially threats from a bunch of bloodsuckers like you." I felt my face redden with anger as I spoke.

Leaning forward, he placed both hands on my desk. "Madam, this is no threat, just a request. All we want is to catch this killer and ensure our families safety. I would think the financial gain alone would influence your decision. A great sum of money has been offered for your services. We agreed on six figures minimum."

He smiled and I could feel the heat rising as his electrifying warmth continued to swamp my office. He had another pen in his hand by the time he nonchalantly sat back in his seat. I hadn't even noticed him take it from my cup, but I knew it was my pen. What male vampire would carry a purple pen with pink hearts?

He pushed the pen in and out of his fingers rapidly. The movement was embarrassingly sexual. His face flushed and his accent became more prevalent as he mindlessly maneuvered the pen between his long masculine fingers. *He thinks he can push me around. I'll show him. Two can play this game.*

Clearing my throat, I replied coyly, "I don't remember agreeing on taking your money or your job."

His head shot up, and he started to speak.

I lifted my hand to silence him. Pausing for just a moment I took a deep breath and continued. "I will however agree to meet Nicholi if you get out of here."

I stood, making sure to use my height to my advantage. "No funny business. The minute you or your boss gets out of line, you can forget hiring me. Do you understand?"

With the last statement, I fondled my gun one last time before walking to the door. Standing impatiently, I hastily pointed to the exit. "If you want to see me tonight you had better leave now."

Siön Baptiste gradually rose to his feet, looking very smug. "I think we are done here." I turned to escort him out of the office, except he stood directly next to me. "Until tonight." I whispered blinking, confused at his sudden movement and my body immediately tensed at his nearness. Vampires move faster than humans do, but I had never seen one move like this before. He just appeared out of nowhere. Towering over me with a smirk on his face, I was immediately aware of the sheer size of him. While he sat in the chair across from me, he seemed tall but not that tall. Siön Baptiste smiled, making sure to show me every inch of his fangs.

Jeesh, they looked sharp.

By the expression on his face, he didn't act as if he appreciated being treated like a child. His eyes swirled with anger. "Madam," as soon as the word came out I flinched. He spoke very quietly. "Madam, I assure you, you will be safe tonight. No 'funny business.' " Pausing for only a moment, he continued. "You intrigue me, which is a rare event for a vampire as old as I." He chuckled, causing me to recoil further away from him.

Countering my retreat, he dipped into my body while his legs brushed up against my legs. A low noise escaped my mouth as heat spread between my thighs. Moving his head to my hair, he sniffed softly, sending vibrations over every nerve. I was frozen, engulfed by his power. The tingling sensations moved in waves as his breath skimmed my cheek. He brushed his soft lips lightly against mine pressing his hip into me. I stood, unable to coax myself to move as my traitorous body reacted to the tender strokes of his hands on my arms and the lower half of his body now perfectly molded to mine.

Clenching my fists, I dug my fingernails into the soft flesh of my palm. The pain quickly brought me out of the obvious spell he cast over my senses. My knees buckled as I shoved my now bleeding hands between his chest and mine. Every move I made he countered, propping up against me, sending tremors through my body. The fire moved over my skin like a warm breeze on a cold night as I struggled to get free of his hold. I pressed his chest as hard as I could, feeling his heartbeat rapidly against my hands. My struggles only seemed to excite him as his strength captured me completely. His eyes dilated with an animal hunger, warning me that I was in grave danger. I immediately ceased my fight and froze in fear.

Trembling, I reminded him, "Like I said earlier, either you leave now or the meeting is off." Even as the words came out, my body leaned into him as if my mind had control of my voice but not my will. His breath and soft lips caressed my neck, his tongue flickering wet and moist against my throat.

"And put the pen back," I gasped.

My body burned, shaking with fear and something else I didn't recognize. He had to be using his power over me to get me to react this way. He ignored my pleas, and slid the pen down my face. I shut my eyes to evade the heat from his gaze. "You are resisting me, why?" His sensual voice slithered down my spine.

"You have until the count of three; one… two…."

He moved his lips over my ear whispering, "You drive a hard bargain, Samantha. We will see you at eight." His lips swept over my neck resting on my pulse. He inhaled while groaning softly.

"Three." I suddenly felt chilly as I opened my eyes and he was gone.

Taking a deep breath, I let out a sigh. "What a cocky son of…" I screamed in anger. If he had still been standing in my office, I would have hurt him. No doubt, my bum would be on the way to jail. He made my blood boil. Even though his eyes were the most amazing green I had ever seen.

Get a grip Samantha! "Jerk!" I mumbled to myself, closing the door behind me.

I walked toward my desk and that was when I noticed the purple pen on my chair. "How the hell did he do that?" I yelled louder as the anger surged through my veins. "JERK!"

Just then, Betty walked into the office, her hands up in the air. I glared at her angrily as she started to explain what happened.

There are three rules I strive to follow throughout my life. I never demand of others what I'm not willing to do myself, I never get involved with clients, and I try not to care too much. My rules had been easy to follow, so far.

Chapter 3

After a long, heated exchange with Betty, I left the office taking the gruesome pictures the vamp had left behind with me. The time had come to gather information regarding my potential clients. "Know thy enemy," came to mind.

My best friend since high school, Trevor Alexander, worked as cop and always offered to help with my cases if needed. I loved him like the brother I never had.

Rubbing my aching temples, I plopped down on my bed holding the phone to my ear with my shoulder. "Trevor, Trevor, pick up the phone. I know you're there!" I hollered, hoping he would pick up.

Trevor slept all day after working the streets of New Orleans at night. I had patience normally, but I really needed to know more concerning my special clients.

I normally stay away from people I love because they end up hurt, or worse, dead. Trevor understood my hang-ups and yet he still loved me like a sister, so heck, it worked for both of us. He was a typical All-American man, full of himself and life. Despite Trevor's good looks and personality, I was never attracted to him. Right off the bat, we both new we were too much alike to date. The friendship made things easier, and most people thought I was nuts for not pursuing him. Dating him would be like dating a younger brother, just not natural or right. We both knew it would never work. My role in his life was that of protective older sister who chased off more than one tramp in my time. And his role in my life was annoying younger brother who did nothing but tease and torture me. I really did love him, except when he didn't pick up the dang phone.

"Trevor, get your butt out of bed. Pick-up the phone or I'll drive over and personally yank you out of bed." I hoped he heard the frustration in my voice. I wasn't angry with him. It was the dang vampire who had me riled up. Siön Baptiste had left me in a bad mood.

Just as I started to hang the phone up, a sleepy voice said, "Sam, I am going to kill you. It is only 5:15 p.m. and I worked until 11:00 a.m. this morning."

"Sorry Trev, I'll make it quick, I promise. It's important or I wouldn't have called you. Do you know a vampire by the name of Siön Baptiste or Nicholi?" Realizing quickly I had forgotten to get Nicholi's last name. *I was really out of it this afternoon.*

He yawned. "I think so, why?"

"Well, he came into the office today looking to hire me to solve a murder and protect his family."

He paused, the silence deafening. "Did you say Siön Baptiste?"

"Yes, Siön Baptiste and Nicholi. I do know that Nicholi is Siön's master." I sighed, wrapping the phone cord around my fingers hoping he would know something.

"Sam, they are nothing but trouble. I thought the names sounded familiar. Working with them is like getting involved with the vampire Mafia, if there is such a thing. They are ruthless and they'll use whoever and whatever to get what they want. What do they want with you?" He half-heartedly laughed until he heard silence on the other end.

"Please don't tell me you are taking a job? They will chew you up and spit you out. I know you're a tough girl, but you don't want to mess with the *Al Capone* of vampires." He paused. "I have a very bad feeling about this." His voice sounded as if he'd had the wind knocked out of him. "Besides, they should use the cops and I'm not saying that because I am one. The vampires in this community think they can weasel their way around the justice system. They can't get away with murder Sam, and they will do whatever they can to use whomever they can."

Before he could continue to preach I interrupted. "Take a chill pill, Trev. I will be armed and it's a public place. We are only meeting to discuss the job. I don't have to take it." I was trying to convince myself they were harmless, but my own internal alarms screamed, run.

"All they want is for me to find out who murdered their friend and protect the family." I sighed, giving into the fact I would take the job because we needed the money.

"I don't like it Sam, just be careful. Vampires can't be trusted."

"I know they can't."

Since vampires had become a worldwide phenomenon, it was now illegal to go around killing them, unless it was in self-defense. Vamps had their hands in politics, banking, and real estate. You name it they owned it. Most strong masters were wealthy and very influential. They bought their freedom and victims. Nobody totally understands the vamp's hierarchy, but many a reporter had died trying to find out. People were fascinated by evil. What could I say? Rumors of a group of powerful demonic beasts ruling over the vampire race had only surfaced in the last ten years. They were still very secretive when it came to vampire politics. Money was what made the temptation of taking vampire jobs so appealing. Vampires were filthy rich, at least the masters were, and in my case, we really needed the cash.

"Why your company? There are bigger fish in the sea, Sam."

"Trevor, they offered six figures," I replied, wondering if he thought I wasn't capable of doing the job.

"Holy crappie, you're kidding right?" He asked. "It sounds too good to be true." Trevor was a cop by nature so he always questioned motives.

"Nope, they were dead serious." Chuckling I said, "Get it DEAD serious." I couldn't stop laughing. It never hurt anyone to laugh aloud once in a while even if it was at his or her own stupidity.

Trevor was silent for a moment before he added, "You have a sick sense of humor, Sam."

"Okay, I do, but it doesn't change the fact that this is a huge job."

"I still don't think it's a good idea, Sam, six figures may not be worth it," he explained.

"Just remember my rule, Trevor; nothing is worth dying for especially a vampire."

"You and your stupid rules, Sam." He mumbled.

"Don't worry about me, I can take care of myself." Although the words had not been spoken aloud, I knew deep down that, if it came to protecting a client I would willingly sacrifice my life. It was who I was as a person, and why I was so good at my job.

He sighed, as if giving up talking me out of going and then simply added, "I'm going with you."

"Okay, but make sure you don't get in the way. I'll pick you up at 6:15!" I hung up before he could answer. I wasn't going to sit around arguing, because once Trevor made up his mind there was no changing it. Plus, I could tell by his voice that he wasn't going to take no for an answer. He was a big boy and very capable of taking care of himself. Sometimes I wore the role of protective older sister too well for my own good.

Standing slowly, I stretched my weary body and looked around the room. The only place I could relax anymore was in my bedroom. My safe haven from the violent world I was exposed to daily. My house was located in a quiet area of New Orleans. It was a five-acre plantation that had been in my adoptive parent's family for over 50 years. I loved being far enough from the city to enjoy a quiet secluded life. My home was just isolated enough to forget my work and charming enough to allow me to remember a simpler time. More importantly there were no local vampires. The vampires stuck to city life. I guess the wide-open fields and werewolf-ridden forests didn't agree with their kind.

The sun would be setting in about an hour. I've been attuned to the sun setting and rising everyday for the last two years. Like an internal clock telling me when to watch my back.

Walking around my bed, I headed to the bathroom, stopping in front of my balcony. My room had a huge bay window with a door that led to a massive pine deck that overlooked a spacious yard and an in-ground pool. Lilacs surrounded the garden along with elegant weeping willows. The grounds were stunning. Adding a certain historical factor was the cemetery in the back of the plantation. It was one of the only cemeteries in New Orleans still underground. All new cemeteries were required to be above ground because New Orleans was below sea level and the ground tended to get really saturated when it rained.

I watched the willows blow gently in the wind, as I recalled my childhood desire to have my real mother in my life. That would never happen since she died when I was born. Sighing deeply, I reluctantly turned away from the window and my dreams. For the most part I was happy, the only thing missing in my life now was a man.

My problem was the lack of time or patience to deal with men. Men were just too needy and I couldn't keep up with their egos. Trevor just happened to be my only male friend and even then I couldn't commit to a relationship because he was just that, a friend. If I only knew my real mom and dad, I think my whole life would have ended up differently. God knows I wouldn't be so independent and so darned hard to be around sometimes.

Strolling to my closet, I snatched my favorite black outfit and heels. I wandered wearily into the bathroom and started a shower. I definitely didn't have enough time for a bath, but oh well.

Thirty minutes later, I put on my black stockings attaching them to my garters. I strapped my gun with silencer, to my inner thigh. *What more does a woman need between her legs?* Slipping my black skirt over my garters, I buttoned the matching silk blouse. I glanced in the mirror one last time, and decided I looked presentable enough.

Rubbing gel into my hands I gingerly ran my fingers through my hair, scrunch and done. A little black eye liner to emphasize my amethyst eyes and some gloss for my lips. I'd always thought my lips were huge, but the fads these days were fat lips, and I was definitely in style.

My two cats, Beanie and Koko were lying on my bed watching the whole show unfold. The only two males I'd let in my bed lately.

I gave them both a kiss, ran down the stairs, grabbed my keys and bolted out the door. The sun descended gradually out of sight as I drove to Trevor's downtown apartment complex. The   clouds   billowed around the last bit of the sun's glare and, if only for a moment, the world seemed at peace. Without warning, a sudden feeling of dread overwhelmed me. It felt like someone had followed me. Like the feeling people get when something isn't quite right. I looked in my rear view mirror. There was not one car behind me or in front of me, odd for this time of night. My knuckles were white from the firm grasp I had on the wheel. In the back of my mind I knew I had to get off this street. I pressed my foot to the pedal and accelerated. Turning onto Main Street I swerved recklessly in and out of traffic. It wasn't until I pulled into Trevor's apartment complex that I loosened my grip on the wheel. I shifted the car into park and turned to see if anyone approached from the darkened alley near the building.

My head facing the street I flinched when the car door opened and Trevor jumped in. "Hey, you okay, Sam?"

"Yeah, I'm fine." I glanced in the rear view mirror, and waited for whatever was out there to make their presence known. Nothing happened.

I sighed and glanced back over to Trevor, trying to mask my worry.

"Are you sure you are okay?"

"Yes." In an attempt to change the subject, I smiled. "You look good Trev." The hair on my back stood on end. I shuddered.

"Something is wrong Sam. What is it?" Trevor watched me, the worry plain on his face. It still amazed me how tan he was in the middle of October. He had his hair pulled back, the sandy blonde color accenting his tanned skin and honey brown eyes.

"Really, everything is fine." Trevor was the only steady friend I'd had over the last few years. He'd stuck by me through thick and thin. I watched him in the dim light of the car; I realized he meant more to me than anyone had in my entire life besides my parents. My dad practically adopted Trevor into the family. He was tossed from foster home to foster home, until my father took him under his wing. When my dad died I had to comfort Trevor more than myself.

"Think Betty will like?" He joked, lifting his shirt to show me his gun.

"Oh please, Betty likes anything with a Y chromosome, or is it X?" I laughed back, hitting his arm.

He snorted. "You are asking me? I have no idea what you are talking about."

"Never mind." The car moved forward as I eased off the breaks.

"So, we get to meet the big cheese tonight?"

I nodded; one eye watched the alley behind me.

"Why would Siön Baptiste hire your company?"

I kept my eyes on the street ahead as I replied, "Money."

He laughed, "Sam it is always about the money with you."

With that, I pulled out and onto the highway. The car rolled to a stop at a red light. "Why wouldn't he hire our company?"

He raised his hands defensively. "Hey I'm not saying they shouldn't, I just wondered is all. I know there are larger firms, and he can afford the very best."

I sniffed, annoyed at his comment. "Who said we aren't the best? Just because we are smaller doesn't make us any less professional. We steal large clients from those big firms all the time."

"Guess you are right, it just seems odd. You do realize as a cop, it would be my obligation to turn in any illegal activity that happens tonight."

"Nothing illegal is going to happen." I left the murder out of the conversation. Maybe it wasn't a good idea to bring Trevor along, but it was too late now.

"Just promise me one thing, whatever happens tonight you keep to yourself. If the cops get a hold of anything that is discussed tonight it will more than likely be leaked to the media. Until I have a better grasp of what is going on, that isn't going to help me do my job."

"Don't hold it against all of us cops because of a few greedy buggers who tipped the media off on your last case. That wasn't my fault, and we eventually caught the guy didn't we?"

"Yes, but you know vampires won't stand for any leaks to the media."

"I can't imagine what they would do if something did get out. Could be a war."

"Possibly, they want to keep their wholesome image so they can get in with the politicians."

"They screwed your father over, they will screw us all if we aren't careful."

The memory of my father's demise stung, even years later. He helped set up laws to protect vampires as citizens. Some vampires, old ones, didn't like the responsibilities that came with the new laws. They killed him and my hatred and anger toward the vampire community was born from the loss of my father.

I glanced over at him, "Trevor, if anything bad happens tonight, you make sure to get your bum out of there."

"Bub?" He laughed.

"No, bum!" I scolded.

"Sam, you need to stop watching those foreign flicks. What exactly is a bum?" he teased.

"Trevor, drop it, you know exactly what I meant. Bum, Arse, Butt... need I say more?" I huffed, and blew a curl out of my face. "Besides, this guy is dangerous and we need to take the job seriously. One wrong move and we are dead meat. If things get out of hand, I want you to take off." Dangerous because he was a vampire and they couldn't be trusted.

He turned and watched the street venders on the corner. All jokes aside, he said, "Let's get one thing straight. I will never leave you Sam. I would die before I let anything happen to you. You have been the only family I have ever known." He paused taking a deep breath. "I owe your father, for everything he did for me."

"He loved you Trev, you were his only son."

"Are you sure, you want to take this job, considering who you will be working for?"

I let out a breath, not realizing I had been holding it while he spoke. The serious tone in his voice made me nervous. I was flattered he cared; yet I knew Eldon Agency needed this job and the money. We trusted each other enough that if things got out of hand, we could handle ourselves. God knows Trevor could handle anything, but we both knew neither of us could handle losing each other. He turned his gaze toward me. We gave each other a nod as if we understood perfectly. I ignored his comment and ignored the fact he was right. I wasn't sure I could handle protecting the very creatures that killed my father.

"It's gorgeous out. I love the fall." I whispered as I studied the splendor of the city I cherished so much. New Orleans was far from perfect. It had its share of problems, which included a high murder rate. It appealed to vampires and the supernatural alike, but they were only half the city's problems. There was an increase in werewolf sightings and those monsters were the real danger. No one messed with the wolf clans.

I sped up, making my way in and out of traffic. "Do we have time to stop for dinner?" Trevor asked. "My treat."

"Well gee, if you're paying then yeah, we have time," I laughed. I had wanted to get to The Silver Fang early so I could scout the place, but I was hungry.

The French Quarter was the heart of the city, filled with tourist attractions, sounds and the appetizing smells of New Orleans. The cuisine here runs the gamut--from po' boys to classic pizza, but it would take a lifetime to hit every restaurant. We decided to stop at Galatoire's Restaurant on Bourbon Street. I loved their food and since Trevor was buying, we went all out.

We parked a few blocks from the restaurant. Nothing like a walk to wake you up on a cool fall evening. New Orleans was getting ready for the many autumn festivals and the excitement was like nothing else on Earth. Popular vampire books and jazz put New Orleans on the map, but it was the local life that kept it there. Now that the world knew vampires existed, the popularity of New Orleans only grew.

Trevor offered me his arm and I gladly accepted. I practically dragged him down the sidewalk, my stomach growled loudly with hunger pains. Trevor held the door open and we entered the elegant, century-old restaurant. I stopped dead in my tracks. Galatoire's was beautiful. The dining area was tiled with mirrors everywhere. All the staff was dressed in tuxedos. The beauty of the decor and busy staff wasn't what prompted me to stop. Sitting at the first table, I saw the devil himself, Siön Baptiste. He dipped his head and saluted us casually as we shuffled past his table. The host sat us a few tables behind him. My face flushed from anger, embarrassment, or both. Why did I even care, it wasn't like he was someone important.

I jumped when Trevor interrupted my brooding. "Hey, Sam, isn't that...."

I waved my hands frantically. Vampires had great hearing and whatever Trevor was about to say I knew Siön Baptiste would hear it. "I know, just drop it," I growled.

"Fine." Trevor grabbed the menu and busied himself searching for a meal.

I caught myself staring at Siön Baptiste as he casually sipped red wine, the green of his eyes brighter than I remembered, watching me above the rim of his glass. His lips looked so sensual, folded against the glass. He pulled away from his drink and ran his tongue luxuriously against his bottom lip. My face flushed at the thought of that same mouth over mine. A young woman strolled over to his table and sat down. She was gorgeous. I could tell she wasn't a vampire because her aura was weak. She had two fresh puncture wounds on her neck. *Manwhore, I thought to myself as he leaned over and kissed her cheek.*

"Vampires need to eat too, you know, Sam," Trevor reprimanded, aware of how disgusted I was with my potential client.

"Yeah, but they don't have to do it in public. Come on Trevor, you know as much as I do, a vampire's bite is addicting. The poor girl is probably hooked like a junkie."

"No different than your addiction to chocolate."

Okay, he had a point there. "I don't trust them."

"You mean you don't trust him." Trevor corrected.

I nodded. "I'm not sure why, but I have this feeling there is an ulterior motive to why they want to hire me. It's like this warning in the back of my mind, not to trust him."

Trevor took my hand in his. "Sam, maybe you should reconsider." He looked over toward their table and I followed his gaze.

The woman laughed as Siön Baptiste leaned over and whispered in her ear. Her eyes locked with mine, and she covered her mouth, hiding her smile. It was a look a woman gives another woman, when they feel superior, or above them. I wasn't sure why it bothered me so much, since I had only just met the man. Who cares what his floozy thought of me. I had to give him some credit, he sure did attract attention. All eyes in the restaurant were on him and his little tramp. He had a certain air about him, arrogant.

A handsome young waiter came to our table. "Can I get you some wine? We have a fine Barlow," He asked, his voice trailing off in my mind.

I ignored Trevor while he ordered our drinks. I was too busy watching Siön Baptiste play footsie with his blood bank. The girl leaned back and continued to giggle like a schoolgirl, while he spoke quietly in her ear. She was absolutely besotted with the freak.

"Sam? Hello? Are you going to order?" Trevor interrupted my irritated thoughts.

"Oh, I'm sorry."

The waiter stood anxiously, waiting for my order. Even though he was busy, he very politely gave me plenty of time to decide.

"I want a big juicy steak. This one please." I pointed to the item on the menu.

"Very good choice. One of our finest cuts. It is rather large, would you like the petite cut?"

"No, I'm hungry enough to eat a cow." I snickered.

The waiter nodded and ignored my comment. "How would you like that cooked?" He asked, pen moving rapidly writing down my every desire.

"I'd like it to moo." I smirked. He looked shocked. In the age of vegetarianism, I was a rare commodity. What could I say, I liked beef and I liked it juicy.

"Umm moo?" He chuckled nervously.

"Yep, I want it to squeal when I cut it."

Trevor coughed into his hand, mumbling under his breath. "Squealing would be a pig." Then we both laughed outright, as the waiter appeared very uneasy at my request.

He nodded and asked if we wanted anything else, and then quickly departed.

"Sam, you're so savvy." Trevor chuckled hitting my arm.

"You can dress me up, but can't take me out."

"Hey, don't you have to meet him in two hours?" Trevor asked pointing at Siön Baptiste.

"Yep." I nodded.

"Well if he hangs out with women like that all the time, no wonder he's the most eligible bachelor in New Orleans."

"What?"

Trevor watched the couple and lowered his voice. "You didn't know? He was GQ's most eligible bachelor in the south. The article said he could have any woman he wanted; yet he never dates. Of course, they must have been wrong. It looks like a date to me."

"Well I don't care if he's the most eligible bachelor in the world, he's not my type."

"Nobody is your type, Sam." Trevor chuckled, and squeezed my hand. "You know, maybe someone like Siön Baptiste would be good for you."

I ripped my hand from his; angry he would even suggest the idea. "Over my dead body." I growled. "I don't mess with vampires, and especially the likes of Siön Baptiste."

Trevor stared behind me, no longer hearing my words. I turned to see what Trevor was looking at and found that Siön Baptiste stood over my shoulder, smiling down at me.

"Good evening, Samantha." He ignored Trevor, watching me with his fiery gaze.

Dag Nabbit!

"Hello." I couldn't believe that was all that came out. He probably heard the whole GQ conversation. *Dangit!*

He grinned. "If I had known you visited our end of the world, we could have met over dinner." He paused, the silence awkward. Leaning down he whispered quietly, "Unless you do not enjoy, how did you say it? The likes of me?"

I blushed, his breath hot against my skin. He pulled back, and gave me a look of pure condemnation.

"I would never want to take time away from your personal life." My voice was surprisingly calm.

"I only get out once in a while, and tonight I am celebrating.

Trevor interrupted our conversation. "What are you celebrating?" He asked.

Siön Baptiste ignored Trevor and kept his eyes on me.

"I do venture down this way from time to time." Trevor grabbed my hand, as if he sensed my growing agitation. Siön Baptiste glared at him as he moved closer. "And who is your charming friend, Samantha?" His voice glided sensually over my skin as he spoke.

I wanted to say none of your business but instead replied, "Trevor is a close friend of mine." I turned to Trevor. "This is Siön Baptiste."

Trevor lifted his chin, but didn't say a word. He appeared to be in a trance.

Both men were tall and predatory. The only edge Siön Baptiste had over Trevor was his power, which currently sifted all around us. As far as looks, they were opposites. One was tall, dark, handsome, and scary as the devil himself, and the other tall, light, and sweet.

They eyed each other up and down. "Samantha is like a sister to me." He draped his arm over my shoulder. "If anything happens to her." He warned.

Siön Baptiste moved closer. "I assure you, nothing will happen to her on my watch."

I interrupted. "Well, I guess we will see you in an hour or so."

"You surely will." He bent down and kissed me on the cheek. The immediate heat of his lips against my skin made me pull back. "Good evening." He bowed and walked away, leaving a trail of energy floating through the room.

I sat motionless, the lingering feel of his lips on my face made the hair on my neck stand up. I put my hand up and felt the heated flesh as Siön Baptiste strutted confidently away. The patrons in the restaurant couldn't help but stare at the man. I couldn't help but stare. He demanded people's attention with his predatory masculinity.

The waiter returned with our meal, mumbling under his breath. "Gorgeous isn't he? My favorite customer. He tips well, too. I had no idea you knew him. Have you known him long?" He smiled placing our food on the table. "He is good to our community, always donating money to the needy. What is he like?"

Trevor and I sat in silence willing our waiter away. After we ignored his question, the waiter shrugged his shoulders and left.

"I really don't like this," Trevor said. "If he hurts you in any way, shape or form, I can't promise what I might do."

"Don't worry about it, Trevor. I can handle myself." I lowered my voice watching for any sign of Siön Baptiste.

Trevor leaned into me grabbing my arm almost painfully. "You need to be careful, Samantha. You are the only family I have." His eyes locked on mine in a silent battle then he smiled. "I can tell you like him."

"Oh shut up." I smiled as we both fell back into silence and finished our meal. The waiter came back and said the bill had been paid. I thanked him and we left a tip.

"Dang, he paid for our meal didn't he?"

"Yep."

"I don't like charity hand-outs." I grumbled.

"Sam, he wants to hire you so of course he's going to try to impress you. Then again, the way he looked at you, he might want more than just to hire you."

"Not funny. Besides how many times do I have to tell you, not a vamp, not ever."

"Never say never." He warned. "Tell me you don't get a vibe from him?"

Maybe he was right, either way I didn't trust Siön Baptiste. The whole thing stunk like a set up. I would find out eventually, just hope I wasn't in too deep when the crap hit the fan.

We left the restaurant happy to be on our way to the club. Both of us remained quiet until we arrived at The Silver Fang. Why exactly they called the club the Silver Fang, I have no idea. Rumors were circulating online that the manager of the club had silver heated and poured into a cast of his fangs. If werewolves attempted anything funny, one bite mixed with the silver would enable the vampire to kill the wolf. Who knows really, but we were about to find out.

Chapter 4

The Silver Fang was located in the club section of the city, just off the north end of Bourbon Street. Vampires were sensual beings by nature and they had their hands into businesses that promoted sex. It was what they did best. They owned every strip joint and club from here to Pittsburgh. The werewolves owned the north and vamps and wolves just didn't get along, so they usually stayed clear of one another. Until recent rumors had acknowledged that werewolves were expanding their territories.

Ultimately the Lycan and vampire wars were not my problem. Tonight my problem was a troublesome sexy vampire. I pulled into the lot and parked in the VIP reserved parking, as instructed per Betty. I hoped that girl got something right. She once sent me to a client and her instructions almost got me killed.

"Enter without knocking, whatever you do don't knock," she had warned.

They meant don't enter without knocking. I was about two seconds away from having a bullet put through my skull. Betty appeared to be innocent, but just maybe she was trying to get me killed, now that's a thought.

I flinched when Trevor interrupted my thoughts and said quietly, "Sam, it's not too late to say no. You can always quit this job and get another. Maybe look into a safe job, like being a cop. You would make a great cop." I could feel him staring at me.

Laughing, I replied, "Trevor, you've been shot three times, not to mention 25 broken bones over eight years. Hello? Safe?"

"You know I just care way too much for your smart bum." He smiled.

"Bum?"

"Yeah, why not." He replied.

"Trevor, bum doesn't work. If you're going to pick up my terminology at least get it right. Smart arse would have been better." My laughter echoed down the alley and throughout the parking lot.

"Hey, I tried." He shrugged his shoulders. "Can't blame a guy can you?"

"I can blame you all I want, but remember one thing I don't quit, ever." My mind and heart were still contemplating what he had suggested. The only word that came to mind scared me. *Quit, never!* Fear gripped me and I prayed that my voice would hold up. My neck was sore, and my shoulders were so tense from this completely crazy day. I lowered my head trying to ease the pain. "My work is all I have."

"You have me."

"I know and I appreciate your friendship." I said.

He nodded and sighed. "Something about this Siön Baptiste I like, and then something that scares me." He paused, as if he sought the right words to say. "I want to scream don't take this job, yet somehow I think it might be a good chance for you to get over your fear of vampires."

"I am not afraid of vampires."

"You can lie to everyone else Sam, but I know you hate them. It's in your eyes when you look at them."

"Everything I was told as a kid that wasn't real in this world, is just that, real. It makes me wonder what other kinds of monsters are out there that are hiding in the shadows or in our closets. I had horrible nightmares when I was a kid. Stuff kids should never worry about, and yet I was dreaming in full color."

"Sam, not all vampires are alike. Some are really decent citizens."

"Maybe that is what I fear the most, accepting the monsters as one of our own kind."

"You know Sam I have your back, no matter what you choose."

I couldn't face him as the tears threatened to fill my eyes. I couldn't tell him the horrible nightmares I faced as a kid. They were so real I'd wake screaming, sheets soaked with sweat. God knows I hated to cry and especially in front of people. Crying was a sign of weakness in this business. *Get a grip, Sam!* I scolded myself. I felt weak as a tear slid down my cheek. A scream threatened to escape my mouth, but I quickly choked it back down, and took a deep breath to calm my nerves. I took his hand and squeezed it gently and he squeezed back.

"Your decision is going to change your life, I can feel it. There is a reason Siön Baptiste walked into your office the today, I'm just worried that I might not be able to handle that reason."

My foot tapped nervously as I struggled to say, "He is a vampire who can stand the light. Did you know that?"

"Yes, there have been rumors. According to Jeff at work there are only a handful of vampires who can stand the light. Guess he has the best of both worlds."

"I guess he does." I whispered.

"Just don't let him use you." He squeezed my hand.

I shook off the dread that hovered over me. "Okay, let's get this over with." We both got out of the car. As I walked to the club, I heard his footsteps behind me and I couldn't help but wonder what I would do without Trevor in my life. We had been each other's rock when our families died. I closed my eyes, and wiped the thought from my mind. *Don't go there Sam, he's right here alive and well.* Yet the nagging feeling haunted me, that something bad was about to happen.

We passed the line of people waiting to enter, and headed straight toward the ape at the entrance. The girls in line watched Trevor, jaws dropped and eyes popped out of their heads. I just smiled politely and released his arm, giving him space. Trevor dated on and off, but had fallen in love with a co-worker. She didn't even know he loved her; heck I wasn't sure Trevor knew he loved Tanaya. It was written all over his face when he saw her walk into a room. My goal over the next few months was to hook them up on a date. Tanaya helped me get into the business, other than Trevor she was the only person I talked to on the force anymore. I watched the women stare at him, and I couldn't help but feel like a proud sister.

The security guard was doing a good job keeping the peace. He escorted people into the building, checking ID's as they entered. The line to the club wrapped around the building filled with young kids seeking vampire thrills.

The big goon eyed both Trevor and me from head to toe. He sniffed the air and smiled wickedly. "I smell cop," he growled. "Get in the back of the line." He sounded menacing or at least attempted to play the part.

I couldn't help but smirk. "Wow, big boy can speak? I am impressed. You will let us into this nice club because we are here to see your boss." He just stared straight ahead void of expression. "Let's try this again, my name is Samantha Houston. I am here to see Nicholi." I slowed the last sentence down so he could understand, but he didn't seem to get the joke and he wasn't happy about it either. *What a beefcake.*

Sometimes I couldn't help but be a pain in the arse, it felt so natural.

"Well miss you aren't on the list, so you will have to get in line."

"Forget this." I turned and walked away.

Trevor ran up behind me. "Sam, what are you doing?"

I huffed. "I'm not going to stand in line for two hours to meet this guy. Forget it, I don't care if he's the President of the United States."

"What about the money?"

"Screw the money." I growled, annoyed at myself for even agreeing to meet Siön Baptiste and his Master.

Trevor grabbed my arm and yanked me back. "Ouch." I hollered.

"Listen Sam, just stop a minute." I kept walking despite his painful grip.

"Sam!"

I stopped slowly facing him. "What?"

"Go back to the car, I'll go find out what the mix up is at the club, okay?"

"It won't do you any good Trev, they won't meet us, we aren't good enough for the likes of them."

"Just let me go try again. If I come back and they still won't let us in, then we will leave."

"Fine." He headed back to the club. "I don't know why you are so set on getting me this job," I growled.

"Because he knows your company needs the money." A silky smooth voice offered. I looked up, and Siön Baptiste was leaning casually against my car. He had a folder tucked under his arm.

"What are you doing here?" I asked shocked to see him.

"I was waiting for you." He pulled the folder out from under his arm and handed it to me.

I hesitated before taking it from him. "What is this?"

"You will see." He smiled.

Opening the folder, I peeked over the top at him. He was looking past me toward the club. He wore a long leather jacket, down to the ground. I couldn't see what else he had on, but was surprised that I even cared.

I forced my attention back to the pages inside the manila folder. "A contract." I whispered.

He nodded. "Indeed. I hope the amount is enough to acquire your services?"

I blinked, and read suspiciously through the contract. Gulping I answered, "Yes, this is too much if you ask me."

"I did not ask you."

This was way more than my normal asking price; actually it was three times my normal asking price. "Why so much?"

He pushed off the car and stood in front of me. The warmth of his body was way too close for comfort. He leaned closer, lips dangerously close to my mouth. I closed my eyes, his breath brushing against my skin.

He whispered, "I want this murderer caught and punished. I need someone I can trust, and despite your lack of trust in me, I do trust you to do your job, and do it well."

I was lost in the feel of him so close. Fighting the urge to wrap my arms around him, I bit my lip. My voice came out breathy, "I will do my best."

"I expected as much. Meet me inside in five minutes, I will introduce you to Nicholi."

When I opened my eyes, he was gone. Circling madly he was nowhere to be found. He just vanished. "Holy cow."

I opened my car and set the contract inside. It was enough money to get the new office John wanted. I had to take the job there was no choice. And if this was how vampires paid, I could kick myself for not offering my services earlier.

"What took you so long?" Trevor took my arm as he escorted me into the club.

"Nothing. Thanks for getting us in the club."

"Oh no problem, just explained to the dude that we were expected. Sometimes Sam, you need to relax and work some charm. You are a good-looking woman, why not flaunt it?"

"Just stick close Trev." I tried to distract my roaming thoughts of worry for Trevor's well being as I scanned the club. "He said he'd meet us inside." My heart was beating wildly, half excited about the money and worse, excited to see Siön Baptiste again.

The Silver Fang was packed with both vampires and humans alike. A wall-to-wall orgy with men and women making out, and God only knows what else they were doing. The music pulsated through the building, thumping in our ears. Mist floated up from the floor enhancing the image of danger. Americans loved their vampires. Clubs like the Silver Fang were growing in popularity.

"Mama Mia," Trevor's eyes were wide as pancakes.

"Put your tongue back in your mouth." I smiled at him.

Movement in my peripheral vision caught my attention. A vampire latched onto a woman's throat. *Yuck!* The woman had her hand down her skirt pleasuring herself while the man drank from her neck. *Double Yuck!* The vampire met my gaze, the woman's blood dribbled down his chin. She took her finger, wiped his mouth, and began licking it seductively. Another sick vampire hang out.

Trevor took my hand in his, "Finger licking good."

"Disgusting," I said, grimacing at the thought surviving on blood alone. "How do they do it?"

Before Trevor could answer someone standing in the corner of the club drew my focus away from the couple. The man turned and caught me staring at him. He loomed over the crowd. His hair was white, held away from his face in a loose ponytail down his back. There was an unnatural animal shine in his eyes as the pulsing lights streaked across the room. I quickly looked away as his eyes turned to me illuminated from across the dance floor. I couldn't help but wonder if every vampire in New Orleans hung out in this club.

"Keep your eyes peeled for Siön Baptiste, Trevor." I said, tugging him nearer.

"Sam, I'm not helpless."

I shrugged my shoulders and raised my hands frustrated with the idea of spending all night in this club while we waited. "I know, but I'm not sure what is going on here, and I don't see Siön Baptiste, so he'll surely send someone to escort us. Probably another one of his dumb pets."

We both inspected the club, readying ourselves for any sign of our associates. My hand instinctively reached for my weapon. Having a gun in hand was always soothing. Most women would find comfort in a man. Not me, my Beretta will work just fine.

I tightened my grip on my gun through the material, just as fingers slid over my shoulder grasping me. Trevor's expression told the story as I slowly turned around. I was now face-to-face with the man who stood across the club earlier, and I backed up. Looking at his hand, which was still securely attached to my shoulder, I gave him a stare that would scare any vampire. He released his grip immediately.

"Miss Houston, Nicholi is waiting for you downstairs." He pointed toward a door that said, "Employees only." He waved his hand leading the way. "Follow me, please."

I didn't even get to answer and he was already rushing off toward the exit. The vampire moved easily through the dance floor as the sea of bodies parted for his large frame. His eyes scanned the room, gleaming fluorescent yellow. He just plain freaked me out.

Trevor hooked my arm in his as we maneuvered through the gyrating bodies, heading for the door.

When we finally reached the vampire he held up his hands and said, "You must leave him here. He is not allowed past this point."

I shook my head. "No, if he doesn't come, I don't come." My voice sounded steadier than I felt at the time.

He ignored me and crossed his large muscular arms over his bulky chest. "Miss Houston, we cannot allow him past this door. My master has many enemies and he will have to stay or you both leave." His voice sounded deeper and if I didn't guess wrong, I would say I heard a low deep growl coming from his throat. This vampire was used to getting what he wanted.

I turned to Trevor. "Stay here. I'll be back in 30 minutes. If I'm not back by then break the door down or better yet, call the cops." I wanted to make sure the big guy heard me. I didn't think the vamps would appreciate the fact that I'd brought a cop to our meeting, so I left that little tidbit out of the conversation.

"No, I'm coming with you." Trevor insisted pushing me behind him.

"No, stay here. I saw Siön Baptiste in the parking lot and everything is fine." I slid past him. "I'll be fine. Thanks for coming. Keep your eyes peeled, lots of vamps here and who knows what else."

He ignored my last comment. "You saw Siön Baptiste already?"

"Yes, and everything is fine. Just stay here I'll be back in no time." I nodded at the big guy. He opened the door and I exited the booming dance club into a darkened stairwell. I could hear Trevor cursing as the door shut and locked behind me.

I hesitated. If I wanted to leave, now was my chance. I took the first step as if I was walking through quicksand. The atmosphere in the bar was nothing like below the club. A staircase spiraling downward was encased with stone walls the entire length of the stairway. Only lanterns lit the way down.

The big man followed me closely as if to say, "don't try anything funny."

As I continued down the steps I asked, "So, what is your name?"

I was greeted by silence. He didn't say a word. I twisted my skirt as we continued down the stairs, so I could reach my gun with minimal hesitation. I'd learned early on in this business you hesitate, you die, or your bread and butter dies. I felt goose bumps prickling down my neck and arms as we headed further into the club's underground basement.

At the bottom of the steps, I could see a bright light at the end of a long hallway. The club didn't seem this long from the outside. A thick film permeated the air the closer we got to the door, reminding me of a sauna without the steam. I couldn't catch my breath, making it feel like I'd hit a brick wall. The light blinded me and for just a moment, I felt fear, but suppressed my desire to scream and run.

The room had white walls, white furniture even a white bar, adding to the blinding brightness. I turned around to ask the big guy a question but he was gone. *Vampire tricks, you've got to love them.*

"You may take a seat on the couch, my dear," the voice echoed in the room as a cool wind blew down my neck. I knew it was Siön Baptiste by the accent and the cocky tone in his voice. My blouse was sheer with a low front, revealing just enough cleavage. The voice seemed to crawl inside my clothes, washing over my skin.

Peering around the room, I couldn't see anyone. Walking cautiously to the middle of the room, I answered the voice. "I prefer to stand, and who am I talking to?" I asked making sure it was Siön Baptiste.

He laughed a touchable, caressable laugh, making my body shudder. "You forget so soon?" He asked. "Take a seat Samantha, my master will be but a minute."

The cool, soothing voice collided into me causing a small gasp to escape my lips. I could have sworn I heard the voice from the corner of the room. The feeling of his power lingered, stimulated my body as if he spoke from within. *This can't be right.* "No vampire trickery or I leave." I whispered, trying to regain my composure.

"Madam, please sit." He said softly.

I swiveled to see the other side of the room and when I did, I felt a hand on my back. I turned back around and Siön Baptiste stood directly in my path. *Son of a biscuit....*

I was about to tell him exactly what I thought of him, using a few choice words when he gently put his finger on my mouth grinning. "Now, now, a lady should never curse."

I retreated slowly from his heated touch. The leather jacket was off and he wore a black silky shirt with the top two buttons opened. The material pulled back revealed a smooth flawless chest. My eyes roamed over his body, taking in its masculine beauty. His black leather pants looked as if he'd poured them on. His hair was down around his face with little strands covering his forehead. He looked like he just woke up, but in that sexy just out of bed way. If possible, his eyes seemed greener against the black.

I took another step back from the sexy vampire in front of me. "It isn't very nice to sneak up on people." I could control my emotions better than any vamp, but he unnerved me. I knew he could read it in my eyes and body language.

"Samantha, you have the most marvelous eyes I have ever seen on a woman." His voice caressed my body as he advanced closer.

I stood my ground. "Thank my mother. I hope your master shows better hospitality than you have shown here tonight. One minute you are here, the next you vanish? It's just plain rude." You could hear the bitterness in my voice.

He nodded. His gaze swept over my body as he slowly circled me. I was a deer caught in headlights. "Samantha, I do apologize for the location. I am sure my master will clear up any questions you might have." He bowed, grasping my hand. His lips brushed softly over my wrist moving slowly up to my palm. As he released me, his tongue flicked slowly over my skin. My knees buckled as his mouth took my breath away.

Warm butterflies fluttered in my stomach moving down my legs and up my chest. I blushed, yanking my hand away. The temptation to slap him almost got the best of me, but instead I wiped my hand on my skirt. "What was that? Don't play games, Siön Baptiste, or I'm leaving," I croaked, his heat still swarming my senses.

He acted as if wiping his kiss was an insult, but then his expression went blank as quickly as I had seen the emotion. "Madam, Nicholi will be here shortly. Would you like a drink?" He turned and moved fluidly to the bar.

My mouth dropped as I watched him move, immediately appreciating the wonderful view of his butt. He was gorgeous in leather. I reluctantly tore my gaze away from his bum and decided to look around the room again. A fireplace on the opposite far wall escaped my notice earlier. I always checked out my surroundings, planned the best and safest exit route, if needed. I saw two doors, the one I'd entered and another door near the fireplace. How did fang boy get in the room?

Out the corner of my eye, I could see Siön Baptiste pouring himself a drink. He was mumbling under his breath in French. He ran his hands through his thick hair, pulling it back from his face. His face was flawless, breathtaking.

Gulping, I cursed him silently while watching his body flow effortlessly. "Siön Baptiste, I don't mean to be rude, but where is your boss?" As soon as I said boss the lights went out. Darkness completely engulfed us. My heart beat rapidly against my chest loud enough I could hear the thundering in my ears. I fumbled down my thigh and retrieved the gun from between my legs. Took the safety off, and crouched low to the floor.

"What is going on?" I could barely hear my voice over my heart. As soon as I spoke, someone took hold of me. I shoved the gun into the side of the person.

The man stumbled back but still held on. "My sweet, it's Siön, Samantha, it's me!" I heard alarm in his voice.

I made an effort to withdraw, with my elbow hitting muscle, but his superhuman strength held me tightly. "You almost got yourself killed and if you try anything funny, you will." I attempted to sound calm as the dark swallowed us both.

Stuck in the dark, encircled in the arms of a vampire, wasn't my idea of a good time.

Chapter 5

"Madam, we must go at once." He released his hold, and placed his hand in mine, uprooting me as he spoke.

As soon as our hands touched, lightning heat spread up my arm over my whole body. It calmed me and excited me, all at once. I never realized a vampire's hand could be so warm. He led me gently through the room.

"Shouldn't these clubs have emergency lighting?" I asked. No sooner had I said it, we were out in a hallway with emergency lighting.

Siön Baptiste bowed and waved his hands pointing at the lights. "Your wish is my command, my sweet."

I shook my head, my temper getting the best of me. "As if you had anything to do with the lighting, you..." I stopped before I finished, "Don't call me your sweet again." He was such a pompous, cocky son of a gun. I fully intended to shoot him the first opportunity I had. Just one wee little shot to the bum, nothing too harmful. I smiled to myself at the thought. You could kill vampires if you shot them enough, but one shot would only sting just a bit.

He answered while he yanked me down the hallway. "Are you always this difficult?" He looked back only to laugh. "And I did help design this club, including the lighting, my sweet."

He laughed at me. Demonstrating my anger, I squeezed his hand as hard as I could, but his expression remained blank. Just as I let up on his hand I could feel his grip tighten on mine. I flinched, but tried to mask the pain. We rounded a corner just as he eased up. *Ouch!* I wasn't going to give him the satisfaction, but I knew there would be a bruise in the morning.

He stopped at the bottom of a long set of stairs spiraling up into the dark. "I'm sorry for hurting you." He said.

"You didn't hurt me." I mentally rubbed my hand.

Leaning against the wall, he folded his arms watching me curiously. "Ladies first, ma petite beauté." An odd look crossed his face as I moved past him. His accent lingered on my body like the warm touch of his hand.

I swirled around, only to notice him covering the smirk that washed over his face. "Don't get any ideas and what does that mean? Ma pet... whatever... you know what I mean." I asked.

Shrugging his shoulders nonchalantly he flashed me a sexy grin.

"What does what mean, my *beau l'orage?*"

His voice was so bewitching, and I cringed to think he might be using it to seduce me. It wasn't going to work. *He can have his fun toying with me.*

Siön Baptiste held out his hand. "Why are you so angry? I have done nothing wrong." He smiled wickedly.

"Forget it, let's just get out of here." As we started up the steps, I remembered Trevor still waiting in the club. "Wait, Trevor! We have to go back and get my friend."

Siön Baptiste looked lost for a moment, and then he shook his head. "We cannot go back, it is not safe." He pushed me up the stairs. "You will not die on my watch, *beau l'orage.*" His voice whispered over my skin.

I turned wide-eyed to him. He looked very serious, yet seductive. He cocked his head, smiling widely, causing my face to burn with anger. My heart hammered loudly in my throat as I moved closer to the edge of the steps. "I am not going anywhere without Trevor. And please stop using vampire tricks on me!" My voice was steady and calm, but I wanted to scream.

He watched me carefully and replied. "Then I will be forced to carry you, beau l'orage." With one sweeping motion, he effortlessly picked me up and headed up the stairs. "Oh, and I am not using my powers on you, beau l'orage. It is just my amazing charm and good looks wooing you." He laughed as he continued on his way. "You are beautiful when you are angry, little storm."

Flashing a livid glance his way I continued to struggle in his arms. He just smiled holding me tighter against him. *At least I still have my gun!*

As if he read my mind, he grabbed my gun and stuck it in the back of his pants. *What the... nobody takes my gun.* I started to wiggle, hitting his chest as I tried to get out of his strong grip. He was so damn sturdy. The whole time I fought him, he grinned mischievously at me.

"Put me down!" I could feel the anger mounting as I took a deep breath and calmly demanded. "Put me down or I won't take this job."

He shrugged his shoulders. "Your boss already agreed you would take the job."

I gasped. "He did not."

"He did."

"Put me down, NOW!"

He pressed me closer. His hand slipped under my skirt, grasping my thigh in his palm. "Samantha, if you stop moving, it will make this a lot easier on all of us. Please, Samantha. I swore no harm would come to you. Stop struggling or you will hurt yourself." He slid his hand slowly to my butt, as he continued to walk effortlessly up the stairs.

I bit my tongue as my mind roared in anger, mumbling every profanity known to men. I tried to push him away as the heat built everywhere his body touched me. My response to his touch made me angry with myself. "Get your hands off me, you bloodsucker." We finally reached the top of the stairs, and the last thing I wanted to do was plummet down those same steps killing myself. I would be patient and wait for the perfect moment, and then he would pay. "Please put me down." I begged.

He ignored me, like every other man I knew. With a quick flick of his hand, the door before us blew off its hinges and flew into the alley with a loud bang. The noise was deafening as we headed through the opening and outside. People screamed in horror and sirens howled all around us.

"What is going on?" I smelled smoke. "We need to get Trevor."

When Siön Baptiste didn't respond to my pleading, I began to struggle. "I will not leave him," I screamed and kicked more fervently, trying to break his hold on me.

A thick dense smoke floated through the air as Siön Baptiste knelt and put me in a limo. Before I could escape, Siön Baptiste managed to slide in beside me. "GO!" He yelled, hitting the front of the car.

"STOP!" The man behind the wheel seemed to hesitate.

Siön Baptiste asked, "Where is your friend and what does he look like?"

"He is tall, and his name is Trevor."

"Stay here." He warned, getting out of the car. "I will get him."

"Thank you."

A few minutes later the door opened and Siön Baptiste slid in next to me. "He is safe."

The driver nodded. As the car pulled out of the alley, I could see the Silver Fang on fire. People ran from the building while the smoke poured from every opening. Tears filled my eyes as I gritted my teeth together trying to force them back; I would not cry.

Clutching his arm, I shook him violently. "Where is he?" I fought back the tears, struggling to open the door. Siön Baptiste's large body wrapped around mine, holding me. He prevented me from escaping and the determination in his eyes pierced my skin as he held me against him.

He took both of my hands, drawing them against his chest. "Samantha, if I take you back and harm should come to you, I will be killed. If we go back, we might both die. What would that accomplish? I must get you to my master. Your friend is safe." Frustration laced his words.

I shoved him away. "Let me go." I felt the warm trickle of tears running down my face. I kicked the door with my heel, trying the handle again with no luck. "If Trevor is harmed in any way, you will pay! Maybe not now or tomorrow, but I will hunt you down." I retreated as far away from him as I possibly could.

Siön Baptiste nudged me back towards him, lightly pressing his mouth to my head. "My sweet, I cannot take you back. I am sorry. Your friend will be fine," he said quietly.

"I can take care of myself." I growled.

He showed no emotions, his face was totally blank while he glared at me. His lips rose ever so slightly, showing me his sharp fangs. Both eyebrows lifted in amusement and surprise while he mumbled under his breath. "You are stubborn."

"And you are a selfish creep. Don't you ever lay a hand on me again, do you hear? You disgust me." A slight vibration interrupted my ranting. My cell phone. I quickly put my hand down my blouse, and retrieved the phone from between my breasts.

Siön Baptiste spoke quietly, "You continue to surprise me, Samantha."

I answered the phone. "Sam, its Trevor. Are you okay, are you out?" I heard the panic in his voice.

Watching Siön Baptiste, I answered carefully. "Trevor, I'm okay, I think. Are you okay?" The tears now fell freely from my eyes.

"I'm fine. Someone helped me get out just in time. The place was crazy, the wall caved in as I was getting people out. I'm lucky I got out alive. The guy was strong, picked up part of the wall and flung it, next thing I know I'm sitting on the ground. Paramedics all around, and then whisked off to the hospital." He paused. "Stay at my place. They are going to admit me into the hospital and they won't take no for an answer. I will call you as soon as I find out what is going on."

The connection began to break up as I said, "Trevor, be careful."

I wasn't willing to lose Trevor and the thought tore a hole in my heart. Placing the phone on the seat, I lowered my head and cried. "Thank you."

"For what?" He asked.

"Saving Trevor."

He sighed. "It was the least I could do, since I put you in danger."

"They were after you weren't they?"

"Yes, werewolf assassins sent to kill my family."

"I'm getting in way over my head." I mumbled. "At least Trevor is okay, thanks again."

Siön Baptiste thoughtfully considered my reaction before he said, "Madam, where do you need to go?"

"313 West Boulevard, Welche's Place." I could hardly see. My eyes burned from the tears and my mascara ran down my face.

Siön Baptiste's body stiffened and I shifted uneasily in my seat. What had changed from just a moment before? His voice sounded flat and cold as he spoke. "I will stay the night to protect you, Mrs. Houston." He rubbed his chin as if in deep thought. "And tomorrow night we will meet Nicholi."

Correcting his mistake immediately I replied, "It's Miss Houston and I don't need your protection. Need I remind you I am supposed to do the protecting?" I took a deep breath, my body suddenly feeling very weary.

He faced the window turning his back towards me. "That was not your husband on the phone?" He asked, curiously.

"No, and even if it was, it's none of your business. I don't need to explain anything to you." I suddenly wanted to be anywhere but around Siön Baptiste. "John agreed to take the job, so I'm stuck for now."

Siön Baptiste acknowledged my irritation with a smug nod. "Madam, I am sorry if I offended you, I meant no harm."

"Sorry? You knew the werewolves were out to get your family and you let on it was a human. So you can take your sorry and shove it where the sun doesn't shine."

"You cannot rule out that there is not human involvement." He said angrily.

"All you vampires are the same. Trying to make humans out to be the bad guys. Trust me, no human would be involved in this crap."

He slid closer, eyes flashing angrily. "Why do you hate my kind? What have we ever done to you?"

"Its what you do to the million of innocent people who fall under your spell. It's the vamp addicts who kill themselves or the hundreds of women who disappear in the city. You have no soul. You are evil and it goes against everything I ever believed in."

His fangs glistened in the shadows. "What do you believe in? Your people have managed to destroy our world. We gave you power for thousands of years and you wasted it. Everything you humans touch is destroyed. Our kind is back to make the world a better place. And what Samantha are you here on earth to do?"

"Bite me!" I knew as soon as the words left my mouth that it was the wrong thing to say. I angered a master vampire and I was a dead woman.

Siön Baptiste quickly closed the gap between us, sliding across the seat. He hovered over my ear so close I could feel his breath against my neck. "My pleasure." His tongue flicked tantalizingly against my skin while his fangs scraped over my pulse.

I froze in panic as his mouth worked its magic. I was in some kind of trance and couldn't move. I felt a small pin prick then a wave of pleasure as his fangs sunk into my neck. His mouth hovered, lips pressed against my skin. It was so good I cried out as wave after wave of hot liquid lava pumped through my veins. He slowly pulled his fangs out, and licked the pinholes he left closed. I was floating above and out of my body.

I wiggled away from his mouth and moved to the opposite side of the seat. A warm blush crept up my neck, covering my face. My body sizzled at the burning sensation caused by his touch. I felt very uncomfortable; I wanted to jump out of the car. "You... You... Your teeth were in my neck!"

He shuddered, his voice husky with desire, "Yes, and that is just a taste of what I can offer you. Did you not ask me to bite you?" His eyes were dilated and fangs were elongated.

The car rolled to a stop and I immediately recognized the street corner. I tried opening the door, but it wouldn't budge. "Let me out. I can walk the rest of the way!" I was tired and my voice shook with anger and frustration. "Let me out!" He bit me! I struggled with the handle and I sensed Siön Baptiste drawing closer. He reached across my lap, grabbed the handle, and gently opened the door. I slid out and started to shut the door, but Siön Baptiste stood towering over me before I had a chance to walk away. *He was too smooth, too fast for me.*

I waited, hands on my hips, while my foot stomped furiously. "Oh no you don't, get back into that car." I pointed angrily at the limousine. "You are not coming anywhere near me. You bite people!" I screeched the last words out, feeling my face redden in anger. He was really starting to piss me off, so much I couldn't think straight.

"You enjoyed it, did you not?" He smiled fangs still elongated.

I stuttered, "Nnn no, I didn't."

His hands held out to his side. "Madam, my master will be very angry if anything happens to you. I must stay to make sure you are safe tonight. The wolves have many ways to find us." He pleaded, holding his hand out to me moving closer. I backed up and when I refused to take his offer, he simply shrugged his shoulders. "You are a spoiled brat, Samantha Houston."

"A brat?" I chuckled. "You have no idea. Give me my gun now."

"Why?" He asked.

"Oh no reason at all other than I WANT TO SHOOT YOU." I hollered hands on my hip.

He put his hand down and shook his head. "No, I do not think that would be wise in your present state of mind." He looked around the empty sidewalk nervously. "I will not flash a gun out in the open when there is no need. Besides it will not do you any good, you cannot kill me. Come with me, Samantha." He pleaded.

"Enough bullets in anyone's heart and you are dead, vampire or not."

He smirked. "True, but it would take more fire power than what you have here in this little gun. Not to mention you would fail your mission if you did kill me."

"Forget the job, you can't just bite me!" I didn't give him a chance to finish before I started hurriedly down the sidewalk.

"But I did." He chuckled loudly.

I cursed him under my breath repeatedly. The nerve of him, to bite me and then act as if he owned me. I refused to turn back to see if he was following. I just wanted to get to the apartment so I could call Trevor.

A brat, how dare he. I got half way down the street and something halted me in my tracks. I tried to move and I couldn't.

"You can run my darling, but you cannot hide. You are part of me now. Come back to me."

"GET OUT OF MY MIND, YOU FREAK!" I screamed. I ran to the apartment complex. My car was still parked at the club along with my keys to get into the building. I had an annoying habit of leaving my keys in the car. I kicked the brick wall and pounded my fist into the building. *Ouch!* This night couldn't possibly get any worse. I marched up the stairs to the door.

I rang Mrs. Fields' call button. "Mrs. Fields, can you let me in? I forgot my keys." I turned to the dark empty street sensing a strong rift in the cool evening breeze. "Mrs. Fields, are you there?"

Starting to feel a little frightened, I reached for my gun and realized Siön Baptiste still had my weapon. Looking down the dark street, I thought I saw a shadow larger than Siön Baptiste heading in my direction. "No, No, this night can't get any worse."

I rang Mrs. Field's call button repeatedly. "Please, Mrs. Fields pick up."

That was when I felt a weird sensation crawl up my skin into my mind. Someone was watching me and it wasn't Siön Baptiste. I whipped around only to notice a man dressed in black stalking me from across the street. He smiled and his teeth flashed white against the dark shadows behind him. The aura was inhuman and dangerous. He was a werewolf. I choked back a scream as he took a step in my direction. It was the same feeling of dread I had when I left to pick Trevor up at his building. This Lycan had followed me earlier.

He stopped moving as Mrs. Fields voice came over the speaker. "Sammy, is that you?" As I stood on the sidewalk in the dark, I was relieved to hear her sweet old voice break the deafening silence. I was just one step away from safety. I slowly exhaled releasing the breath I hadn't realized I was holding.

"Yes Mary, it's me. Can you buzz me in? Quickly, Mary." My voice was shook as tears threatened to stream down my face. I was afraid to look back in the direction of the werewolf. "Hurry. Hurry." I begged.

"Of course, sweetie. Tell Trevor I said 'Hello.' "

With a buzz and a click, the door unlocked. I just wanted to get inside away from the creatures of the night. I knew with the bloodsucking vamp on my arse and now a werewolf, I was in genuine danger. Her voice trailed off as I started to enter the building. Before I could move, a long arm reached over my head and pushed the door open.

Frozen in fear, my eyes followed the hand up to the arm. I turned to see Siön Baptiste with a very smug look on his face while he held the door. He wasn't around a minute ago and this disappearing and reappearing act had to stop before I lost it and started shooting things. The werewolf was gone.

"You look pleased with yourself." I shook my head furiously causing my hair to whip around my face, but I was truly relieved to see the vampire. "Siön Baptiste, you have to leave. I am not letting a vampire into my friend's home to bite his neighbors." My voice was stern, as I turned to face him.

He leaned up against the door with his hands folded over his broad chest. "Would you rather I invite the werewolf to spend the night with you? His bite would not be as pleasant." He was so confident that I couldn't resist him, but he was dead wrong. "I cannot leave you to that fate or Nicholi would have my head."

I waved my finger in his face, finally shoving it into his firm chest. "I am so sick of hearing your sob story. Get over it. You're already dead, nothing new." I walked into the building and as soon as he slid in behind me. "Oh no you don't." Using one of my self-defense moves I pushed him up against the wall and grabbed him firmly around the neck. "A girl can only take so much, Siön Baptiste. You are dangerously close to pushing my last button." I said.

"Has anyone told you how lovely you are when you're angry?" He held my gaze with his eyes. He smiled but the fire burning behind those beautiful green globes held dangers I could only imagine. Sneering he said, "I would very much like to push your buttons, my beau l'orage."

"If you so much as lay a hand on anyone in this building, you will regret it." As I spoke, I raised my knee, pushing it into his groin. "Do you understand?"

He coughed and nodded. "Oh, I think I get the point." He mumbled in French as he watched me. I didn't understand a word he said and it only further fueled my anger. I walked to the elevator and waited. After all the steps tonight in heels, I was going to take a shortcut.

"I am the one who is supposed to protect you, not the other way around."

"It might help if you *push* the button, my sweet." He whispered in my ear, emphasizing the word push. Taking my finger, he guided it to the button. Warmth spread up my entire arm with his gentle but strong touch. He forced me to push the button, the movement of his hand over mine prodding me forward. "So let me stay the night, protect me from the big bad wolf." He teased.

I couldn't take the heat from his gaze or touch so I pried my now tingling hand away from his grasp. Pushing past him, I entered the elevator embarrassed by my stupidity.

"You can protect yourself." I grumbled.

"First you want to protect me, now you want me to protect myself. You are a confusing girl." He followed me into the elevator. "What floor?"

"Seven." I sighed, finally realizing he wasn't going anywhere.

As he pressed the button, he turned with a devilish grin, "Madam, does that include you?"

I looked at him puzzled, "What?"

"Can I lay a hand or two on you tonight?" He smiled, eyes twinkling as he ran his hands through his hair.

He was so infuriating I wanted to scream bloody murder. "Are you going to force me to take my frustrations out on you? Because if that occurs I can't promise you what might happen. I really don't want to hurt you, especially because you are worth so much to me alive." I scoffed.

His smile quickly faded as he moved to my side. Purring in my ear he said, "I do believe you will hurt me someday, Samantha, but not physically. As much as it pains me that you only take this job for money, I am willing to take a chance on you." He paused, blowing teasingly over my neck. "But I dare you to try and take your frustrations out on me. It will not be as easy as you think, my beau l'orage." He moved his arm over my stomach. My double-crossing body wobbled from the nearness of his warmth.

My stomach exploded in a sea of arousal under his heated gaze and smoldering touch. I lowered my eyes pleading with him and my body to cease and desist. "Why don't you just leave? What do you really want from me? Why did you bite me?" My voice just a whisper.

"I don't want to leave, I want you, and I wanted to. Does that answer your questions?"

"You are a pain."

"I try." He smiled.

Despite the horrible night and weird events of the day I found myself smiling. He was kind of cute in an annoying, I'm-going-to-bite-you vampire way.

"What is this?" He wrapped his fingers in the soft silk of my blouse, and lightly tugged on the material. "Hmmm... Soft." His voice knotted my insides. He moved his hand under my blouse and over my stomach below my bra and paused, rubbing his fingers against my skin.

My voice was lazy, "Don't touch me again or else."

I felt powerless in his embrace, unable to move or protest. He brushed my nipple with his knuckles and I gasped. My heart rumbled in response to his caresses as he lowered his hand past my waist to my thigh leaving a trail of fire over everything he touched. "Or else?" He asked. With the pressure of his fingers, he forced my legs apart. I felt warmth all over, melting away my resolve.

"I'll kill you." I gasped. His hand glided across my leg to the now empty holster hidden below my skirt. "Samantha, you are without your precious weapon. What could you possibly do to me without your gun?" He said softly along my neck as he slid his hands further up my thighs. My lower body trembled as his hand moved dangerously close to the soft heat between my legs. His long, magical fingers brushed against my opening, causing me to groan softly.

He responded to my pleasure in a low husky voice. "Beautiful storm."

My world swam in streams of colors, heat and desire, threatening to consume me. I could barely breathe. He murmured lowly in French, causing me to flinch and pull back further. I felt the sharp scraping of his fangs against my neck and fear-rushing adrenaline brought me back to my senses. *I have more control than this, what was my problem?* I pushed his hand away, swiftly lifting my knee and striking him in the groin. He doubled over for a few seconds, cursing quietly. I stood and watched him carefully, waiting for him to react. He sat up and in a blink of an eye, and grabbed me by the shoulders, lifting me up into his arms, cradling me against his chest. I had no time to react--it all happened so rapidly. The elevator stopped and he exited. I fought the hold he had over me, hollering and hitting the whole way. He strutted to the apartment door and with a flick of his hand, it opened while I continued to kick and scream.

I stopped yelling only to ask, "How did you know this was his apartment?"

He just stood there holding me against him tightly. "My little storm, what am I to do with you?" He laughed that sexy I-am-going-to-eat-you-for-dinner mind-shattering laugh.

"I'll tell you what you're going to do. Let me GO, you ignoramus," I growled.

"Madam, please settle down before you get hurt." He pleaded with those gorgeous eyes as if he was concerned for my well being.

I knew better than that, he only cared about his precious master and the job. His cologne floated over me dark, deep, and sensuous. His hand slid over my butt, moving closer to my inner thigh. I would forever wonder why I picked tonight not to wear underwear. The thought of his hands touching me sent tremors up and down my body.

The lights came on as we entered the apartment. "We are here, Madam, and all is well. No one is dead or bleeding." He paused. "Yet." He said, eyes twinkling mischievously.

I pressed my hand further between us trying to grab onto something. "Put me down, put me down now." He smiled and released me. I hit the floor with a thud, looking up at him. "You bastard." He put me down all right. He dropped me on my arse in the living room then threw my gun to the floor.

Peering down at me, he smiled seductively. "Madam, keep the gun, it will do you no good to shoot me. It is like a warm teddy bear that cuddles with you at night, but doesn't protect you from the devil." He held out his hand to help me off the floor.

I knocked his hand away and stood on my own. Taking my gun, I angrily shoved it in my holster. *Shoot him! Shoot HIM!* I wanted so badly to listen to the voice in my head, but jail time wasn't in my cards. There must be a better reason for killing someone other than just being a pain-in-the-butt vampire, who just happened to take a bite out of me and also who dropped me on the floor. And besides because he was stronger than most vampires, I wasn't even totally sure shooting him would kill him. I would bide my time and if he made one false move, he could kiss his pretty bum goodbye.

I was relieved to be in Trevor's apartment since it was such a homey, familiar place. His apartment was much smaller than my house but it still felt like home.

I pointed to the door. "You can leave now. You have worn out your welcome!" I grunted. "I rescind your welcome, be banished."

He laughed, raising an eyebrow and folded his arms over his broad chest.

"Be gone." I tapped my foot nervously. "Vanish from my presence!"

Siön Baptiste didn't budge; he just stood there smiling. I thought I could revoke his privilege or something from entering, but I guess it was just another vampire wives' tale. He looked so dang good and he knew it. I had a sneaking suspicion Siön Baptiste wasn't accustomed to rejection. Good thing I didn't care. "Do you ever listen to people? I want you to leave." I smirked.

He lifted an eyebrow and nodded. "If I go now you will lose your money. Or worse, the werewolf who has been following you will find you, and kill you. I cannot protect you if I cease to exist." He sighed as he moved to the door.

"I am SUPPOSED to be protecting you, not he other way around. Why the sudden concern for my well being?" The anger that had been building up since The Silver Fang was ready to break free. I couldn't promise anyone's safety if that happened.

"My concern for your well being started the day I met you."

"That kind of line might work on other women, buddy, but not this woman."

He looked stricken. "I do not use lines on women."

"Sure you don't." *I had enough!* "I would like you to leave." I said calmly.

He ignored my question, but opened the door, apparently admitting defeat. Standing completely still, with his head cocked to one side, he looked as if he was analyzing my reaction and question. He then proceeded to leave as abruptly as he had entered. Finally, I had won the battle. I walked over to lock the door and as I started to shut it, he grabbed my hand, swung himself around, and slammed me into the wall. He pressed against me until the swell of my back hit the doorknob. Leaning over, he locked the door. He took both of my hands, and shoved them harshly above my head with only one of his. His muscles flexed as he held me. I'd never met a vampire this strong.

He hesitated a moment, and I fought the urge to look him in the eyes. "My sweet, I will not die for your stubbornness tonight," he hissed the words. "And I will not stand by and watch you die, not tonight, not ever."

With his free hand, Siön Baptiste grasped my chin, forcing me to face him. I refuse to lose tonight. Samantha Houston never lost. This vampire was dangerous and I didn't trust him. He had already bitten me once tonight.

"Get off me!" I yelled.

"Do not struggle, my control is weak." He gasped.

I had heard this from many friends that vampires liked the chase. The more you avoided them, or struggled the more vigilant they became in their pursuit. I looked into his eyes, searching for an answer to why me. I choked on my words, as I was soon lost in his gaze. His eyes were simply gorgeous, like the rest of him; they swallowed me with his desire. He held my gaze with a hot, lustful stare, sliding his tongue slowly over his sensuous lips. My pulse quickened and my knees buckled as he moved his mouth over mine. This time he didn't stop, pushing his lips into mine, he penetrated my mouth with his tongue. He gently caressed my lips, sending feverish warmth through my body. I tried to struggle, but he was too strong and it felt too good. My body throbbed with pleasure as he crushed his hips into mine. He felt wonderful against me, and the feeling of his heart thundering against my chest made me gasp. We molded together perfectly. As soon as the noise escaped my mouth, he took my breath. My body melted into his and I felt myself return his passionate kiss. His grip lessened, as he slowly released my hands. I dropped my gun to the floor and with it, any hope of him leaving.

It was hard to think, let alone talk. My whole body scorched, writhing under his kiss. He slipped his fingers tenderly through my hair, down my neck, bringing me closer to him. My hands dropped around his back, grabbing his shirt. He wrapped his arms around my waist, snuggling me against him. He pushed his legs against me, and moved his thigh between mine. The leather pants were much softer than they looked. I was effectively trapped, as he laughed in my mouth, soft and low. The sound tickled my body, tightening my nipples, moving downward to other hidden places.

He picked me up without any effort, never losing contact with my mouth. Moving with ease through the apartment, as if he owned the place, he managed to find the bedroom and placed me gently on the bed, releasing his mouth from mine.

Siön Baptiste stroked my hair, and that one gentle touch brought my face to his. How could a monster be so gentle? I gazed at his angelic face and the smooth line of his body. He had the look of a man wanting something forbidden, yet not caring. The heat in his mesmerizing eyes brought a low groan to my throat. He lowered his mouth toward mine, and slowly licked my lower lip. He was so hard, so firm against my hips that my hands moved instinctively towards his pants.

"I want to taste you, my sweet," he muttered, nuzzling closer.

Taste? Fear boiled up the back of my throat, I shook my head and pushed him away. "No." I couldn't believe my own ears.

He moved his mouth to my neck, sliding his hand up my leg to my thigh. We were burning with desire--our bodies begging to be one.

I fought the feel of his mouth on mine, the feel of him in my arms, trying to say something. I only managed to say, "No." This time I my voice was stern, as I attempted to push him off me. My breath came in shallow pants while my body quivered from the inside out.

Oh, God, the things this man did to me.

"You are not enjoying yourself??" His voice husky and his eyes gleamed with need.

I shook my head, moving my hands to his hard chest. "No, I can't do this. You are a client, it's just wrong." He lifted me up off the bed and began unbuttoning my blouse. I froze, held by his hungry gaze.

He yanked my clothes off with one quick sweep of his hand. I was almost completely naked and the look in his eyes was desperate. Captivated by the sheer power of his presence, I couldn't move. I watched helplessly as he caressed my legs, leaving a trail of heat touching just high enough to tease, without touching too much. My hips lifted begging him to reach further. He removed my stockings one at a time and slowly pulled off my garters. He threw the covers back and placed them gently over me. Turning out the light, he pulled the shades down and sat on the edge of the bed.

I rolled away from him, bringing my legs into my chest, feeling a cold void from where his body no longer touched me. The taste of his kiss still lingered as I held onto my knees. Immobile with fear, excitement, or both, I stared into the darkness of the room. I attempted to catch my breath as my heart continued beating erratically.

"You can't sleep in here."

Reality smacked me in the face and I jolted straight up. For some reason I had no control over what Siön Baptiste did and this frustrated me. The feeling of helplessness pressed against my chest.

"I will not leave you alone." he replied, sounding sure of himself.

"Who, and what, are you?" I whispered, afraid to hear the answer. "You are just too powerful for a normal vampire."

"Does it really matter what I am?" He asked.

A tremor traveled through my body. "Yes, it does." It mattered because I needed to know what I was up against.

He chuckled softly, sending my body into defense mode. "I am older than anyone you have ever encountered. Does that answer your question?" He remained calm, not revealing any emotion other than his soft laughter.

"No, it doesn't. Are all vampires this vague?"

I only knew he was laughing because the bed was shaking. "No."

"I want you to leave. I'm not sure I want this job anymore." I hope he didn't hear the fear in my voice.

The bed moved. I felt a warm whisper of his breath on my neck. *Oh God, I didn't want to die like this.*

I barely managed to croak the words "do not touch me again." I knew he wouldn't hurt me, but his touch was intoxicating and I needed to be able to think clearly.

"My sweet, I will never let harm come to you while I am alive." He sounded sincere.

"Stop calling me your sweet." I was feeling better, much better. "I am not sweet."

He grinned in the dark as he swept his tongue seductively across his mouth. "You taste sweet." He moved his hand down my back, stopping above my hips. "I will stop if you do not enjoy my touch." The room carried his voice all around me... like a cool blanketing autumn breeze, like basking in the sun on a cold day. He made me feel so hot with need and yet the chill of what he could do threatened to devour me.

"Please stop," I said it with determination and strength.

"As you wish, my sweet."

"Don't you need a coffin or something?" I asked.

His laughter resonated off the walls, down my spine, and through places no man should be able to touch. "You are quite a find, my darling."

"If you don't leave, I will." I started to get up and realized I was completely naked and in order for me to leave the room, he would see me totally exposed. Was it really so bad sleeping with a vampire? I lay back down, and pulled the covers up around my chin. "Touch me once and I'll have your head on a platter," I warned.

"My dear, don't make promises you cannot keep." He was angry and with that, the room fell silent.

Great, piss off an already dangerous, sexy, biting vampire. Not good, Samantha, not good!

Chapter 6

I stretched under the covers, and opened my eyes slowly. I had a sneaking suspicion Dorothy wasn't home anymore. I wanted my red shiny shoes and I wanted them immediately.

Sun penetrated the cracks in the blinds, casting shadows and light over the entire room. *Was it all just a bad dream?* Pulling the covers up under my chin, I turned toward the nightstand. The alarm clock glowed bright neon red in the shadows. It was already 10:00 a.m. I tried rolling over and realized quickly that a long arm stretched lazily over my stomach, pinning me to the bed. It hit me all at once--nothing about last night was a dream. Everything I'd imagined truly did occur, even Siön Baptiste.

I lifted myself off the bed using my elbows, and squirmed under the warm pressure of his arm. A warm sensation swirled deep inside as the inviting arm moved gently across my skin.

I almost had to stop because it felt so good. Then I remembered he was a vampire, and they can never be trusted. "Get off me," I screamed, pushing his arm away. Siön Baptiste's masculine arm slid down the side of his body as he slowly moved, taking most of the covers with him. My mouth dropped open in surprise, he was naked. *How dare he!* His long muscular thighs and back were uncovered giving me a wonderful view of his body. *Get a grip, Samantha!* Watching the movement of his muscles with every breath he took reminded me of his soft kiss. A warm blush spread over my face. Even asleep, he somehow managed to look smug and happy as a lark.

I sat up quietly and began to shuffle toward the side of the bed. I wasn't about to wake sleeping beauty since this beauty was a deadly vampire. My feet hit the soft plush rug and as I turned to replace what was left of covers I noticed his butt was still unfortunately covered with the sheets. *What a shame.* The temptation to yank the covers off overtook any rational thought as I stared longingly at the good-looking vampire before me. My stomach fluttered, sending sensations of lust and sex through my body. I took the sheets in my hands. I could pull on the covers lightly enough to expose what I knew had to be a great bum. *Yes, what a great idea, a little peek never hurt anyone.* I gently tugged at the sheet and just as I got a good grip, he rolled over. I jumped back as the smug handsome bastard smiled knowingly, sending heat to my face and other places. My body crashed into the nightstand. The collision sent the lamp, me and the alarm clock all flying through the air. I tried to break my fall by grabbing the sheet and pulling it with me. I landed with a thud on the floor and the lamp fell behind me. Everything happened so quickly. Before I realized what hit me, I was on the floor, the sheet still in my hands. *Graceful, Sam!*

I shook at the sound of his voice. "My sweet, if you wanted a peek, you could have just asked." He started laughing, almost a giggle. "You did not need to go to all this trouble, my little beau l'orage."

I sat on the floor while the heat from his gaze washed over my entire body. How embarrassing. Anger soon replaced my embarrassment as his smile deepened to a knee-slapping laugh. *I didn't have to put up with this bugger.* I got up and without looking at him or the bed, I threw the covers around me and stomped to the bathroom. Slamming the door shut, I grimaced as the pain from my fall and embarrassment enraged me.

I moved away from the door only to stop dead in my tracks. The sheet was firmly embedded in the frame, not allowing me to lock the bathroom door. No way would I take a shower with the door unlocked while a sexy, dangerous vampire waited in the next room. I gathered the sheet and shoved it back through the door into the room. I slammed the door and locked it. I listened to the mocking laughter from the other side. Leaning my head against the door, I heard Siön Baptiste slide out of bed and head for the bathroom.

"I am taking a shower, so bug off, fang face." The last word came out with all the hatred I felt at the moment.

"You're not going to allow me to tag along?" He said cheerfully through the door.

"I am serious batman, bug off. I've had to put up with enough of your crap for one night." I hit the door with my palm. Leaning my forehead against the frame, I moved my ear over the wood straining to hear what he was doing. I knelt down and peeked through the keyhole, but couldn't see anything. *Darn!*

I stood as he rested his head against the door. His finger traced heated circles near my face. I felt the warmth of his body even through the space between us and quickly backed away.

He very quietly insinuated, "But my sweet, it was a night I will always remember."

I stepped further away, my heart beat nearly out of my chest. Did I forget something else about last night, something important? No, he was just playing his vampire games.

"Just let me shower in peace, we can talk about the job after I'm done, okay?" He didn't answer. With that, I walked over to the shower and turned the water on. Trevor always left spare weapons and a fresh change of clothes in his bathroom closet. I opened the closet door and sat on the toilet while I pulled out a large plastic container.

The bathroom was set up so that the door was on one side of the tub and the toilet, sink and closet were on the other side. Anybody walking in would only see the white porcelain tub. The tub was an antique pedestal with a curtain on all four sides. There was a small window over the toilet that let in enough sunlight to make the bathroom seem more spacious.

Opening up the plastic container, I removed a gun and throwing stars. Trevor, thankfully, picked up my habit of being a little paranoid about werewolves and vampires. He had these weapons made for an undercover gig a few years ago. As a little girl, I'd watched Bruce Lee movies and always wanted to learn to throw Chinese fighting stars. Last year I'd earned my black belt in judo and eventually trained in using the stars as weapons. I even had a halter that held both guns and stars. I fumbled through his container and found a harness. "Awesome, great minds do think alike." He had a pair of sweat pants and a large t-shirt. I was going to drown in them, but I wasn't going to go back into the room for my clothes. For now it would have to do.

I placed the weapons on the toilet next to the tub. Easy to reach in case I needed them in a hurry. In the cabinet above the sink, I found some men's deodorant and cologne. "It will do."

"Hope you don't mind, Trev." My heart began to ache at the thought of Trevor in the hospital alone. I had to find a way to ditch fang face and head over to pick him up, today if possible. I knew it wasn't going to be easy to get away from bat breath, but there was no way I would jeopardize Trevor's safety. Siön Baptiste seemed bent on making my life miserable. I took a deep breath determined to set things right. "Samantha, you idiot," I scolded, angry at my lack of control over the situation. I always tend to complicate my life more than it needs to be, and the vampire in the next room was one big complication.

Shutting the cabinet, I stared at myself in the mirror. My hair was a mess and my eyeliner was smeared all over my face. Was this what I looked like last night? I resembled a close relative of a raccoon. I managed a little laugh and walked to the tub. The whole room was engulfed in steam. I always did like a hot shower.

I washed my hair and rinsed it. Stretching down to the shelf near the tub, I grabbed some conditioner. My hair was long, ash blonde, curly and without conditioner, unruly. I reached for the bottle when I felt something behind me. I stood still while the water hit my face, holding my breath.

Maybe if I didn't move maybe it would go away. I jumped as a strong hand slid around my waist. The hand caressed my breast teasing my nipples between his fingers. My nipples reacted to every stroke, growing and hardening. I felt myself being turned around and up against a naked erect body.

I tried to open my eyes, but the conditioner stung, forcing me to keep them closed. I groaned softly as the hand left my waist and clutched my chin. I struggled to break free, but he held me tightly. Warm lips brushed against my cheek and moved further down my jaw finally resting on my lips. One minute I was trying to get free, and then next, melting into a kiss that would wake my dead grandmother. His lips parted mine with the slightest of pressure. When his tongue caressed my tongue I deepened the kiss sliding my hands up muscled arms. He stepped into me, the slick hardness of him pressed firmly against my stomach. The minute he slid over stomach I was jolted back to reality. Rubbing his hands up my arms and over my shoulders, he rested them on my hips lifting me closer to his shaft. I shivered, moving back slowly. I leaned out of the tub and slowly reached for my gun. A cold gust of wind hit my backside. I shifted around and to my surprise nobody was there. I splashed water into my face so I could see, and blinked. To my shock nobody was around.

My pulse vibrated with both fear and excitement. I could still feel his touch even though he wasn't there. What was happening to me? "Siön Baptiste, are you in here?" I asked. No answer. I quickly finished and toweled off. The sooner I solved this murder and saved his arse, the better off I would be. I'd had my share of mind games before, but nothing like this. Was I dreaming? The door was locked no one could enter. "I must be spooked, that is all. Get a grip, Sam," I spoke quietly to myself.

I was wrapping my hair in a towel when I heard a knock at the door. I just about jumped out of my skin. "What do you want?" I hollered. I could feel the anger begin to replace my fright. I was going to blow and nothing was going to stop me.

Siön Baptiste's voice floated into the bathroom. "We have a guest, Samantha, and we need to talk."

"I'll be done in a minute, JUST GIVE ME A MINUTE." I always internally growl at people when they piss me off, but now I almost heard a faint growl as I screamed.

I could still taste the kiss on my mouth from the shower. Siön Baptiste had a sweet sensual minty tasting kiss, filled with promises of untold pleasure. The memory of last night brought a warm sensation below. It couldn't have been real, it must have been a dream. Could I have slept while I took a shower? I checked the door and to my astonishment, it was still locked. I had never heard of a vampire walking through walls, but then again I'd never met a vampire who could live in the light either.

Finished drying off, I slipped some boxers on, from Trevor's stash, along with gray jogging pants and a white t-shirt. I stuck the gun in the front of my pants and shoved everything else into the closet. I ran some gel through my hair and wrapped it back up in the towel.

When I entered the bedroom, I could smell coffee. Was our local vampire domestic also? I headed out to the living room, looking for our visitor. I found a big burly guy sitting on the couch. He sat completely still with Siön Baptiste standing behind him hands on the guys shoulders. The man looked at me with cold brown eyes. He was bald, except a neatly trimmed goatee. His shoulders were huge and you could see the muscles under his tight tee-shirt bulge in rhythm to his heartbeat. I had to remember he was a potential client and I had to keep myself under control. *Act like it's no big deal, Sam. There is a big burly dude in the living room eyeing you up like you are a piece of candy.*

"This is my--"

I cut Siön Baptiste off before he could say a word. "Hey to each his own, if you like it both ways that is totally your own business." Ralph tried to stand up, but Siön pushed him back down.

"Ralph, stay." Siön Baptiste ordered him.

"Yes good boy Ralph." I mocked.

I headed for the kitchen, intent on getting a hot cup of coffee. "So I guess this is your breakfast?" No answer.

Siön Baptiste grabbed my arm. "Let go of me."

He pulled me to him. "I think you offended Ralph, and if you know what is good for you, you will apologize." He squeezed my arm dragging me over to Ralph.

I stopped standing before Ralph. "Ralph, I am sorry."

Siön cocked his head in surprise. Ralph's eyes widened.

"Sorry you have to deal with a butthead like him." I shoved Siön Baptiste back and walked away.

"We need to talk and I refuse to talk to you if you are going to suck on this guy's neck."

Siön Baptiste gritted his teeth, and Ralph dropped fangs and cringed.

"I do not suck on males."

"Sure you don't." Ignoring his anger I held my hand out to Ralph. "Nice to meet you, Ralph." I know they heard the suspicion in my voice because as soon as I said it, Siön Baptiste lifted an eyebrow and

Ralph chuckled. For a tall, burly, mean looking dude, he had a nice laugh and smile. I gave him a smile back and he took my hand.

"Nice to meet you Ma'am." Ralph shook my hand firmly.

"Nice to meet you too, Ralph. So how long have you known Mr. Baptiste?"

"All my life Ma'am." Polite too, how cute.

I turned to Siön Baptiste who chuckled quietly. "Listen, Siön Baptiste, if I'm going to protect you, I need to meet the men closest to you. I want to question everyone, not just humans or wolves. I need to rule out that someone close to you doesn't want you dead."

Ralph stood and quickly took up the space in the room. I looked up at his angry expression. "I would never harm my master." He growled. Siön Baptiste grabbed his arm, holding him back.

His eyes flashed angrily. I stood my ground lifting my hand. "Whoa boy, I'm not saying you would. I just have to check everyone out you catch my drift?" I backed up thumbing my gun. I secretly hoped I didn't have to shoot Ralph; he seemed nice enough for a vampire.

Ralph looked at Siön, confusion written all over his face. "I don't understand Ma'am."

"I meant, in order for me to do my job, I need to check out everyone even his closest friends. It's nothing personal. I am just doing my job."

"She is smart isn't she, Master?"

Siön Baptiste smiled, never taking his eyes off Ralph. The tension slowly faded from the room. "Yes, she is very smart. It is why we hired her." He turned to me releasing his hold on Ralph, but never fully taking his eyes off of him. He handled him like he was dangerous animal, and from the looks of Ralph he had the potential to be dangerous. "Speaking of hiring you, did you sign the contract?"

"I left it in my car."

"I have a copy here." Ralph pulled out a copy from a bag sitting on the couch.

"How convenient." My eyebrows shot up as I took the contract from Ralph, unable to hide the sarcasm.

"Does this mean you are taking the job?" Siön Baptiste asked.

I placed the contract under my arm, and hesitated for a minute before nodding my head. "Yes." This could be the biggest mistake of my life, but it felt right at the moment. Ignoring me Ralph spoke to Siön Baptiste. "I brought clothes for you, boss." Ralph handed Siön Baptiste the black bag.

"You can use the shower, I'm done. Ralph if you just sit here and be patient, I need to get something to eat. Anyone need anything?" They both looked at me and shook their heads no.

Siön grabbed Ralph's arm and whispered lowly, "She is off limits, and do I make myself clear?"

"Yes boss."

"Good, do not let anyone touch her and if they try, kill them."

I laughed. "It is okay Ralph, I can take care of myself."

Siön Baptiste took off toward the room and just as he entered the bathroom, the phone rang. I walked over to the kitchen and picked it up while keeping one curious eye on my new friend.

"Hello?"

"Hi Sam." I could hear a sense of relief over Trevor's voice. He was going to be just fine.

"Trevor, when can I pick you up?" I asked and wished it would be immediately.

He laughed nervously on the other end and then he coughed. "Are you going to lose a lung, Trevor?" I joked.

"No, I am not going to lose a lung, but I will be in the hospital for two more nights. Can you believe this crap?" He barked over the phone. "Did you feed my fish at least? And I know you are eating my food. Jeesh, Samantha try not to eat me out of house and home at least."

The reason he gave me a key in the first place was to feed his fish when he had long assignments. I contemplated not telling Trevor about last night and then looked over at the bedroom and decided to tell him everything. "Trevor, someone is here in your apartment with me. Last night in all the confusion Siön Baptiste brought me home." Somehow, I felt guilty about what I had just said. I paused, "He's still here." I knew he could hear the hesitation in my voice.

There was cold dark silence. Finally, he asked, "Did he hurt you?"

When I didn't answer, he spoke again, "Samantha, did he hurt you?"

"No," I answered calmly. Unless you count setting me on fire with desire as hurting someone, then I am in a world of trouble.

"Did you sleep with him?" He chuckled.

"No and yes."

"What?"

"He slept in your bed, but he didn't touch me."

"I see. Well I'm not happy he's at my house. Hey, I don't dislike the guy, but I don't totally trust him either. Change my sheets before you leave."

"Oh come on, it wasn't like that."

He chuckled and then the phone went silent. "Did he hurt you? Like bite you? Are you now a vamp groupie?"

He was joking but my heart was beating widely in my ear. "No, he didn't hurt me, everything is fine. He wouldn't stop talking about his master killing him if he let me out of his sight." I started to ramble when I got nervous.

"You could have at least asked for a raise."

"This isn't a joke Trev, I'm in serious trouble here."

"I told you Sam to only take the job if you thought you could trust him."

"No you didn't."

"Yes I did."

"Whatever, either way I'm about to sign the contract."

"I am sure you will do what is right Sam."

His confidence in me warmed my heart, but I wasn't sure I would do what was right at all.

"Listen, I've got to go. The doctor will disconnect my phone if I'm on any longer. I'll give you a call tomorrow."

My voice croaked as I thought about him lying in a hospital alone. "Trevor?" I paused. "You are going to be okay?"

He took a deep breath. "I'll be fine, you be safe okay?" He coughed. "Just be careful."

I hung up the phone and pulled out the contract, and leaned over the kitchen counter. I felt confused and unsure of myself. I grabbed a pen from Trevor's junk drawer and started reading through the contract. It was fairly simple. I protect his family and get paid a ton of money. No fine print, and no tricky wording. I laid the contract down and decided to call my partner in crime for a second opinion.

I dialed my boss, John Wilkins. I dreaded the thought of talking to John, but I had no choice. I was afraid of what he would say about our client staying the night. To him it would appear unprofessional and he couldn't help but be careful and protective of me. I wasn't looking forward to speaking with him.

A cheery voice came over the line. "Eldon Agency, may I help you?"

"Is John around, Betty?" I asked, trying to mask my irritation at her for letting Siön Baptiste into my life.

"How are you, Sammy?" She was always so annoyingly cheerful.

"Patch me through to John, please, Betty."

I heard someone yelling in the background. "If that is Samantha put her through, NOW!"

A beep then silence. "Samantha, nice to hear back from you after dealing with our biggest client all year." He was yelling. "Where have you been all night? I tried your cell, your home, and the police." He was still screaming. "There was a huge fire at The Silver Fang, and you didn't have the courtesy to check in?"

I could almost feel him gripping the phone as if ready to rip it out of the wall. John always did overreact. Watching the bedroom door, I pleaded with John, "Calm down. How did you know about the fire?"

"It was all over the news. Is our client okay?"

Oh yeah, I'm fine, thanks. "Yes, our clients are fine. I have to meet with Siön Baptiste's master tonight."

"Good, I signed the contract this morning. We are taking this job Sam."

I wasn't surprised he signed. "No hello, Sam, how are you doing today? Are you okay? Hope you didn't get hurt in the fire. And by the way, why didn't you tell me our client was a vampire? Hello, JOHN, are you slipping in your old age?"

"Do not get sarcastic with me young lady, it might work on Betty but it won't work on me." He raised his voice. I could hear his erratic breathing over the phone as if he was about to hyperventilate.

John always worried about me. He loved me as a father does a little child and sometimes it really annoyed me. After my father's death he taught me the business. I loved him, too, in my own disturbed way. His wife of 22 years divorced him last year and he hasn't been the same since. I felt sorry for him and if he knew, he would hate me for it. I appreciated his fatherly advice and friendship, but he needed my help as much as I needed him.

I looked around at Trevor's kitchen wondering what kind of mess I was getting into. I let John ramble on for a few minutes and then interrupted him. "Listen, they want to use their own contract, did you know that?"

I heard his voice trailing off in the background. "Someone brought a copy by this morning. It doesn't look much different than ours, so I approved it. Listen, Sam and listen good. You better behave like a professional. I should have been called in on this meeting. The money they are offering is enough to keep our budget in surplus for the entire season next year. And you make sure to sign that...."

Before he could say any more, I cut him off and hung up. This was going nowhere fast. He would ramble forever and I didn't have the time or the patience to be patronized. He might stay mad for a while, but he'd get over it eventually.

I was so busy dwelling on the conversations with John and Trevor, I hadn't notice the big guy was no longer sitting in the living room. Great, where did he run off to?

I heard someone in the bedroom. The door was still closed. I put my cup of coffee on the counter and tiptoed quietly to the door, straining to listen. All I could hear was humming. I didn't recognize the song but the humming was unnerving. I had never heard a vampire hum before.

Of course, I'd never spent the night with a vampire either. It was eerie. I knocked on the door.

"Come in Samantha, I was just getting dressed," he said cheerfully.

I slowly opened the door and peeked in. Siön Baptiste was sitting on the bed, buttoning up a black colored shirt. He looked up at me smiling. "I assure you I am dressed."

A happy vampire, who'd imagine?

Peering around the room past him to the bathroom, I asked, "Where is your friend, the hulk?" My eyes were drawn back to Siön Baptiste still sitting on the bed. His black hair fell in soft curls around his shoulders, covering his ears. He was dressed in a black silk shirt that left little to the imagination. His skin looked lighter against the contrast of the black during the day. His pants were simple black Dockers, making the long lines of his body look even longer than they'd appeared earlier that morning. I couldn't help but watch him as he buttoned the last button on his shirt. He left the two top buttons undone showing just enough of his smooth chest. I remembered the feel of his skin in the shower. It had felt so real. I watched his chest moving with each breath he took, and I shuddered.

He turned to me as if he sensed my reaction to his body. "I sent him home, my sweet, so that we may talk alone." Those last words were hardly innocent. "We need to leave to meet Nicholi, shortly. The ride is longer since Nicholi was forced to flee the city.

I sighed. "I'm sorry to hear that, but I should head home to change."

"I really must insist we leave shortly."

"Fine, under the circumstances I can understand." I entered the walk in closet, and glanced around. Trevor had women over, there was bound to be something I could wear in here. Toward the back of the closet there were several feminine outfits hanging. I grabbed the black skirt and a red blouse. The skirt looked a little small considering how tall I was, but it would have to do.

Siön Baptiste stood and walked over to the window, gently pulling back the blinds as I emerged from the closet. He leaned his forehead against the window with his arm over his head as if in deep thought. His shoulders were broad, but it was his face that caused my body to tremble. He was a poster boy for male sexuality. He emanated masculine, good looks. He was truly spectacular. I had never seen a vampire, much less a man, quite like him. I felt a warm breeze run through me. He was powerful and his energy filled the room washing over my skin. A low noise came from my throat. I felt drawn to him. A desire to run my fingers through his hair and taste his mouth swept over me, forcing my gaze away. I put my clothes on the bed and plopped down in the chair next to the window. I couldn't help staring at his astonishing body. He stood motionless in a sexy "come hither" stance. I drank the sight of him in and my body tightened at the wonder of it all.

He turned to me and those eyes said everything. "I am worried about why my master wants to meet you tonight," he whispered, as if afraid someone would hear.

"Why? I need to find out why the werewolves are out to destroy your family." My mind swirled with the information he'd just given me.

Siön Baptiste shook his head, resting his gaze on my eyes as he spoke. "My father, Nicholi, married my mother. She died during my birth." His voice was very careful.

I stopped breathing for a moment trying to understand his words. "I am going to meet your Dad?" I asked.

Shocked to the core, I exhaled. Never had I heard of vampires giving birth or procreating. I'd admit I wasn't exactly a vampire expert, but never in my wildest dreams did I think it was possible. Rumors were one thing, but the ability to produce offspring was scary. "Amazing, he really is your Dad?" I repeated.

He made a small-exasperated sound. "My master and father are one in the same. He wishes to meet with you tonight to discuss the attack on the Silver Fang and the murder. But the murder is no longer of any concern. We know who was responsible, don't we?" He stood motionless as he watched my face.

I just stared blankly into his beautiful eyes. "The werewolves." I acknowledged under my breath.

"Yes, and they will pay for their treachery."

"It is possible the Lycans weren't working alone, so don't go off on a rampage. I have a lot of work to do before we truly know who is responsible."

He nodded. "We will wait to examine your findings."

My mind still stuck on the fact he was born a vampire I decided to pry some more. "So was your mother a vampire?" I asked.

"My mother was human and my father a vampire. I was raised as a vampire, and because I am immune to the sun I am called a Daywalker. I can live in the light where normal vampires will be burned, or worse, die in time."

"Puberty must have been a real b…" I mumbled under my breath.

He paused raised an eyebrow at my sarcasm and continued, "I have powers that vampires do not normally posses." His voice trailed off as he looked dreamily out the window as if trying to think of what next to say.

"How does being a walker in the light work?" Did he have a soul?

What powers did he have? My mind was spinning with question after question.

"How does being a human work?" He smiled as he took a step closer. His gaze swept admiringly over my body. He slanted closer and sniffed breathing softly against my neck. "My sweet, I can hear you breathing." His voice was just a whisper against my ear. "I know you are fearful of me. Tell me what I can do to ease your fear?" I swayed, the accent buzzed against my skin.

I moved into his body, my breath ragged. "I don't fear *you*, Siön Baptiste, I fear what you can do to me." Realizing what I said, my face began to burn.

I took a step back and quickly changed the subject. "I still don't get why a strong vampire family can't protect themselves, but I will do what I can to find the murderer." He walked over to the chair, kneeling before me. His eyes were a swirling sea of green, saturated with lust and pain, the kind of eyes that could easily swallow one's soul. His arm stretched across my lap, as his body filled the void between my legs. My heart felt as if someone held it in the palm of their hand and squeezed. Sweat beaded at the base of my neck, as he smiled. Lost in the moment his lips moved closer, hovering over mine as if he was going kiss me.

A mixture of panic and awe struck me as he unleashed his power. It met me in a rush of pleasure and I both wanted and didn't want to pull away. I tried backed up but Siön Baptiste drew me closer, one hand rested against my neck and the other on my leg. Everywhere his fingers touched electric warmth played havoc with my senses.

"I have never met a woman like you, Samantha." His voice was soft, just a whisper against my mouth.

I blinked hard, and then closed my eyes. The sensations grew stronger, without my site. His power sparked every nerve in my body, sending lightning sparks dancing between us. There was no hesitation in his kiss. It was like velvet fire that seeped into my skin and through every nerve. His tongue slipped into my mouth and moved in slow languorous caress over mine. I gasped, and breathed him in. The taste, the smell, the feel of a hot male body pressed intimately against me. I relaxed in his hold, returning his kiss with as much passion. My stomach tightened as his mouth, hot and moist, claimed mine fully. Groaning from somewhere deep inside, I ran my hands through his damp hair, losing myself in the silken strands. The kiss deepened, and then his warmth and mouth was gone. I slowly opened my eyes. The blood rushing to my face as I realized how completely entranced I was by him.

He stood by the window, hands clenched into tight balls, like a man fighting for control. "I cannot promise that my father's intentions are honorable. He is a deceitful man who causes much pain and delights from it."

Way to spoil the moment. I licked my lips the taste of his kiss still present.

He continued ignoring my frown. "I would not hold it against you if you did not take this job, Samantha." His face was earnest. "I apologize for my behavior. It was unacceptable." His voice was husky with yearning.

It was me who was wrong for letting him touch me, not that I could have stopped him from taking what he wanted, but still, he was a client. I shook my head angry that I hadn't displayed more control.

Even if I could speak I wasn't sure what to say. I stood, and faced him. Mesmerized by his grace and presence, the heat of his power buzzed against my mind.

"I am not sure I like the way you look at me," I blurted out loud, taking a deep breath and continued. "I really don't like you using your powers on me." Even as I spoke, the air electrified around us. "I don't care if your master and father are one in the same. I have a job to do either way, and the more information you provide up front the easier my investigation will be." I somehow felt at ease with this vampire. It felt very natural being in his arms and that frightened me.

He nodded as he rubbed his hand through his hair. He cursed under his breath. "You do not understand what is happening here, Samantha." He smacked his chest with his hand and then waved it in my direction. "You were meant for me, I can feel you inside of me."

The words he spoke hit me somewhere deep, but I wouldn't admit it, not today, not ever. "This is just a job for me Siön Baptiste, nothing more or less." I gave him my fake professional smile. "Sit in the living room until I'm dressed and ready." It really was more of a plea than an order. I knew he could do whatever he wanted, and I couldn't stop him. He terrified me more than anyone had in the past and I didn't quite grasp why.

Twenty minutes later, I was dressed and angrier with myself then I've ever been. I strode into the living room, with a renewed hatred of vampires. I wasn't going to let a vampire influence me, good looking or not. I adjusted my gun strap so it wouldn't chaff my breast. I casually adjusted my bra and holster, which got a strange look from my new vamp friend.

Siön Baptiste glanced at me without saying a word, a blank expression on his face. I broke the silence with a simple question. "Are you ready?" My voice even sounded cold and distant to me.

"We are ready now if you are?" Siön Baptiste answered just as cold.

I'd managed to land the biggest gig of my life, sleep with a vampire, and break every rule I'd ever lived by all in one night. I found new determination to hate this vampire with all my heart. "I would have been ready hours ago if you hadn't used your mojo vampire powers on me." I tossed my hair out of my face.

Siön Baptiste's face tilted to one side as he stood. "Despite your mouth, you are still very beautiful."

I brushed past him. "My mouth has many talents, Siön Baptiste, that you will never experience."

Realizing my admission, I cursed myself softly. *Crap.* I could feel the color rush to my face and once again, I'd managed to put my foot in my mouth. He didn't make a crude comment or even flinch. Either he hadn't noticed the slip up or he didn't care.

Taking my hand in his, he led me out into the hallway, entering the elevator in total silence. I peeked over at him but he seemed to be avoiding my gaze. I settled on checking my outfit. My blouse was just right for the occasion. It wasn't too low or tight, just perfect for concealing weapons. The skirt came to my knees, yet the slit ran up the side exposing my leg up to mid thigh.

Siön Baptiste coughed, drawing my gaze to his. I glanced up at him and the instant our eyes met the pulse of his heartbeat throbbed against the palm of my hand. Something about this vampire made every movement, everything we did so natural it disturbed me on every level. He drove me nuts, made me crazy with fury. I wanted to hit him, not kiss him.

We both finally turned away as the elevator opened. We exited and I jerked my hand out from his as I walked in front of him. Just outside the door, my car was parked next to a black limo. I turned to Siön Baptiste. "Who brought my car?" I asked.

"I had a friend drop it off this morning, but we will be taking the limo," he added the last statement carefully.

Ralph stepped out from the front of the limo and opened the door for us. "The trip will be about two hours. Let me know if you need anything, Master." He nodded in my direction and smiled. Holding my arm as I entered the limo, he squeezed gently and repeated, "Anything at all Ma'am."

I scooted along the edge of the leather seat and turned back. "How about a wooden stake?"

He watched Siön Baptiste expression and when the vampire didn't react he smirked. "Enjoy your ride," and slammed the door shut. I could hear him laughing outside and still when he started the car. Siön Baptiste just sat with a smug smile on his face.

Chapter 7

The ride was quiet for the first 20 minutes. I periodically glanced at Siön Baptiste, trying to read his expressions. His face was blank, his thoughts hidden behind a wall of pleasantry. The only evidence of his tension was the occasional clenching of his fist. Why did I care that he was nervous? Maybe because it made me feel uneasy to find someone so powerful show emotions. Not every human would be so tuned to people's emotions, but I was taught to read emotions so I could protect those who hired me. A twitch of the eye, and tick in the jaw, lack of eye contact could all reveal true intentions of any individual. It bothered me that Siön Baptiste hid those emotions from me. Why would anyone be so apprehensive about a simple meeting? I opened and closed my mouth ready to ask, but decided to let it go. Maybe I really didn't want to find out why he feared his father.

Siön Baptiste interrupted the quietness in the car first. "Do you remember your mother?" He whispered the word mother.

His voice startled me and his question shook me to the core. I answered him as I bowed my head, "my mother died when I was young." It pained me to speak about her and I knew it showed on my face.

"I am sorry." He said.

My mother died while she gave to me, but I didn't feel like sharing my whole life story.

His face mirrored my pain for just a second before he turned away. He chuckled low in his chest. Waves of energy slid across my body as he spoke. "I often smell her on a spring day like I can still feel her in the wind," he said, his laughter changed to anger, energy sizzling my skin, while his voice carried through the car. "Why does God presume to take whom he pleases, when he pleases? Who is he to take life?" His voice trailed off as if thinking aloud.

In the ten years I've been in the business, not once had a vampire shown so much raw pain and emotion. He had gone from an arrogant, to a hurt child in just a few moments. I rotated my legs around, and tucked them comfortably under myself. What possessed me I don't know, but I grabbed his hand. I saw the pain in his eyes and knew all too well the hurt he was feeling. I felt sorry him, felt sorry for myself. For a moment, my annoyance and malice towards him slipped away.

Guess vampires had feelings too, who knew?

My eyes swelled threatening to spill tears. I rolled down the window and let the cool fall air refresh my heated skin. The warmth of the sun cascaded over us shimmering throughout the interior of the car. A flash of light against the car door caught my attention. I turned around to find its source. Light reflected off a silver ring on Siön Baptiste's middle finger. I suddenly wanted to know how talented those fingers might be. I shrugged off the thought, blushing at my thoughts.

"That is a beautiful ring," I said. The detail of the ring was exquisite.

He smiled, pride filling his voice. "It is our clan symbol. Vampires belong to clans, or as you would call it a family. The rings or jewelry we wear represent what sect we belong to." He played with the ring, rolling it around his finger. The ring had a snake head eating its own tail.

"Incredible detail." It was beautifully crafted, my finger brushed across it as I spoke. "About your mom, I think God has a perfect plan for everyone. He cares for those who believe and damns those who don't. See I know someday I will see my mother again." I could feel the tears in my eyes and turned my gaze toward the window.

I released my grip on his hands and he seized my arm. "If you couldn't die and knew you would never see her again, what would you do, Samantha? What would you do?" I could hear the bitterness as his last words slithered over my body.

Capturing his hand I gently removed it from my arm, and placed it on my lap. His eyes were damp with unshed tears. His power was so intense I forgot he was still a man, a man with feelings. I was so busy hating him, the thought that he might be hurting never entered my mind. I massaged his strong hands tenderly. I could barely hold one of his in both of mine. All I could do was shake my head and quietly say, "I don't know, Siön, I just don't know."

An unseen pang of hopelessness sifted through the vehicle. I released him and turned away. We sat quietly each of us looking out the opposite windows. I had to get my mind off my mother and concentrate on the job at hand.

At least the weather was nice this time of year and fall had always been my favorite season. My whole body began to relax at the thought of a cool evening with the fireplace burning, and Siön Baptiste holding me in his arms…

I stiffened. *Wow, where did that come from?*

It was the weather; it had to be the weather. I always felt more alive this time of year. The leaves were turning deep autumn colors, ushering in the season. Siön Baptiste's lips over mine as we picnic by the river…

AHHHH!!! There I go again. I growled.

"Everything okay?"

"Ummmm, just enjoying the view. I like the colors of fall." Leaves the shade of red, orange and brown blanketed the forest waiting to drop to the ground.

"As do I."

Those three words held such promise. His spicy scent filled my head and my thoughts drifted. Making love in a blanket of sun-warmed leaves in the forest. I nearly moaned allowed at the thought of his body over mine.

"A cool breeze on a warm day, bundled up for a hayride, and Halloween treats. Even I as a vampire enjoy autumn."

I nodded, he named some of the best things about fall. October was just around the corner and festivals that surrounded Halloween were incredible. With the partying came added responsibilities and usually this time of year was the busiest at the Eldon Agency.

As I stared out the window in the gloom of the car, I reflected back to the days of my childhood. My memories seemed foggy now and with each passing year, my identity was fading. I understood Siön Baptiste's dilemma because I also longed to see my mother, desired to know the truth. Sitting here in this car so close to a vampire who had a similar tragic story brought a realization of things I'd never thought I could share with the undead. We had a mutual desire to know our pasts while being haunted by our dreams.

I was startled unexpectedly when Siön Baptiste put his hand on my shoulder. "My sweet, it is necessary for you to be blindfolded for the last leg of the trip. It is safer for you if you do not know the way." With that, he drew my hair back from my face and removed a black cloth from his jacket. He very carefully wrapped it around my head. I took hold of his hand and he stopped.

"Samantha, it is necessary." I released my grip, slowly letting my fingers slide down his hand to his bare wrist. He made a quiet noise under my touch and then quickly tied the cloth behind my head. He grabbed my waist, pulling me closer. I tensed and then relaxed as his arm went around my shoulder caressing my back. I trusted him. I shook my head at the new revelation. I trusted Siön Baptiste not to hurt me. The feel of his body against mine sent every nerve burning with awareness. I trusted him and I wanted him. *This couldn't be good.*

I calmly asked, "You know it's hard to trust someone who doesn't trust you?"

He nuzzled his mouth to my ear. "Yes, but it is not you I do not trust. Others might harm you to find us, our enemies I do not trust." His voice was breathy and hot against my flesh, stoking memories of his kiss. I shook in his arms and he drew me closer. "Do you understand?"

My mouth opened but no words came out, only a sharp intake of air as he nibbled below my ear. All I could do was nod, the limo closing in around us. I found myself relaxing further into his arms, swayed beneath the power of his touch. "I will never let anything hurt you, my sweet," he promised. Desire sparked between us, the crackling current bending me to its will. Never in my life had I wanted someone as much as I wanted Siön Baptiste. The want scared me almost as much as the vampire himself.

We were both jostled as the limo made a sharp turn onto a gravel road. Siön Baptiste's teeth grazed my neck as we bounced. I tilted my head, baring my neck to him. I wasn't even aware I had done it, until he nipped the curve between my shoulder and neck. Now blinded, my senses seemed more alert than before. Heightened by darkness everything seemed so clear, even the slow methodical beating of Siön Baptiste's heart. His tongue swept over my skin, as heat pooled deep within me. My clothes clung to me, restricting my motion as I rocked back against him. He mumbled, "so sweet." I felt the first prick of pain, then only white searing light. He pulled away faster than he had bitten me. I was panting, unable to catch my breath.

"I cannot, I am sorry."

To my surprise I wanted him to bite me. Find my release in his power. The limo began to turn and rocks pelted the undercarriage of the vehicle as it slowed. The bumps in the road snapped me out of whatever hold he had on me. "This is a job, Siön Baptiste. Nothing more or less."

"I understand." He tensed his voice distant even from close quarters. The road seemed to go on forever and then it curved sharply. Attempting to hold onto the side of the seat for leverage, I was tossed wildly around the vehicle. Despite his fight with control, Siön Baptiste steadied me throughout the bumpy terrain. He rubbed his hands over my arms, and let them settle softly on my stomach. Butterflies swirled under the heat of his hands. We crossed what sounded like a wooden bridge, and then a couple minutes later the limo came to a stop.

Siön Baptiste seized my hand and commanded, "Don't move until I get back. Keep the blindfold on until I say. It could mean your life."

He scooted over the leather seat exiting the limo. I sat in the car and waited for what seemed like forever. I jumped when the door opened. I heard nothing, just felt a hand pull me gently out of the car. Whoever it was wore a glove. It couldn't have been Siön Baptiste. I stood up outside and felt soft grass under my feet. The smell of lilacs floated in the air reminding me of home. Lavender and white lilacs surrounded my house and the scent was intoxicating. You knew it had to be September in New Orleans when you smelled lilacs first thing in the morning.

The hand led me across the lawn and carefully helped me up a set of stairs. I wondered what John would think about the whole job. These were definitely the strangest clients the Eldon Agency had ever commissioned. Despite my fear of the unknown, the voices in my head reassured me that everything would be okay. I wasn't afraid of death and Trevor often argued that I longed for death so that I might see my mother. Maybe he was right, perhaps in some sick way death would resolve any unanswered questions I faced during life. I craved the opportunity to sit and talk with my mother, hoping to uncover what happened to her in death. How? Why? When? It was the fear of losing people close to me that kept me in this world.

My shoes clicked noisily as we walked. My guide came to an abrupt stop. This was just a job and when it was done, I would put everything behind me including Siön Baptiste. John committed us the minute he signed the contract, but as far as I knew Siön Baptiste was not aware that he had signed. He was still trying to convince me to take his family on as a client. More than likely, he thought using his vampire mojo on me would help convince me. Realistically he was probably acting a part trying to get me to do his will, but that thought alone gave me a new resolve to thwart his advances. Normally, I was great under pressure. I did whatever necessary to impress clients, but I would have to drawl the line with Siön Baptiste. If I wasn't in control he would use me up and spit me out. I was obligated to be at my best or someone would get hurt. I was going to be strong and take charge from here on out.

With new resolve I stood quietly next to the person who was lead me, I could feel the sun fade out of the sky. Guess we traveled a little more than two hours. I would soon find out. I had to grab my skirt to fight the urge to peak out from under my blindfold. I remembered Siön Baptiste's warning and decided to wait.

My heart raced as a door creaked open. A cold breeze ran over my body. Goose bumps rose along my arms and neck. As soon as the door shut behind us, I was silently ushered into another room. My shoes echoed even louder as I walked over a stone floor. I had to be alert these were vampires. They would get no trust from me. Every movement, every sound I waited for a possible attack. I spread my legs shoulder width apart, ready to fight. My arms dropped to my side. We walked through the hallway and into a carpeted room. The guide ushered me to a chair and then spoke, "Please have a seat." The voice was a deep and accented French. He placed my hand on the couch so I could sit without falling.

I heard him move about the room and then depart. The room was so quiet, yet I couldn't tell if I was alone. Concentrating with all my might, I tried to sense an aura. A warning went off in my head, but not one thing came up on my radar. Warmth saturated the room. With the rise in temperature, the hairs on my neck stood on end as if an unseen power coursed through the room.

Suddenly I was itching to be as far away from this place as possible. I jumped as an icy hand touched my shoulder. I swallowed the scream in the back of my throat and tried to remain professional. The hand loosened the blindfold and it fell to the side. My eyes strained as they adjusted to the dim lights. I turned around to see who was behind me but they were gone, disappeared into the shadows.

A small lamp in the far corner lit the room. Shadows cast across my sight hid the overall contour of the room, only outlining the silhouette of the walls. Unable to see anything but a lone light, I strained to adjust my sight. Finally details came into focus. I moved in a slow circle taking in every little feature. The room had stonewalls and a decorative fireplace. A vaguely familiar painting hung above the mantle, but the room was still too dim to make out everyone in the photo. I recognized one handsome face immediately. The room was cavernous and even breathing seemed to resonate against the walls.

Lights started to come to life. The shadows disappeared completely. The room had a pool table in one corner and a bar in another corner. There was a couch directly in front of me and behind it was a wall decorated with weapons. From what I could tell, they looked to be silver. Fascination overtook reasoning, and I strolled around the couch to get a closer look. I ran my finger down the sword. "Ouch," it was sharp. My hand pulled away the blood already seeped from the fresh wound. It slowly dripped down my finger to the floor. *Crud, that was going to leave a mark!* I felt a warm breeze as I raised my finger to my mouth. I reached out to suck the wound and to my surprise, someone snatched my hand and held it tight, almost painfully.

I let out a gasp as the hand burned into my wrist and the length of my arm. I turned to meet my assailant face to face and readied myself for attack. The sight before me sent butterflies dancing in my stomach. My free hand moved closer to my skirt and gun. The invader gripped my hand before I could reach my gun, holding it in a tight grip. The man had long auburn hair flowing over his broad shoulders. His eyes were a sparkling emerald green. He reminded me of Siön Baptiste. He was a little shorter and his face more delicate. His nose perfectly shaped and his mouth a flawless heart shape that looked both red and moist. He smiled. He was dazzling. The heat from his hand spread little by little through my entire body. He was using his power on me. "What are you doing?" I croaked.

A slow roll of magic pulsed through my body. "Stop!" I screamed. Pleasure pulsated deep inside. My legs began to tremble, half fear, and half magic induced pleasure. This was different than Siön Baptiste; I could feel the energy as he weaved his magic around me. A pressure built as he continued to stroke me with his energy. I felt helplessly drawn to his eyes and to his mouth. I struggled but found my legs immobilized. He moved slowly against me, his long muscular body pressed against mine. Pulling me closer, he dropped my left hand. He brought my bleeding finger up to his mouth he began to lick the wound. The cut pulsed red hot as a rush of pleasure washed over me. I shook my head as I tried to resist the trance he weaved around me. This was how vampires fed they manipulated the mind. He was going to drink my blood. I panicked, my mind screaming to run my body powerless to obey. He licked my finger in tiny circles as his wet soft mouth moved over my wound. His eyes were hypnotic. I was held in his stare as it sent a jolt of pure ecstasy through me. With every lick, I cried out. His tongue and mouth embraced my finger. It felt as if he was licked deep between my thighs. My back bowed as he continued short quick strokes. My blood oozed into his mouth. He was biting down as he groaned quietly. He gradually inserted my finger into his mouth and power from below thrust within me. His tongue rolled over the wound as he brought it further within. His energy entered my body. I was captured completely under his control. I cried out, throwing my head back, and my hands grasped for something to hold on to. I fell into darkness, riding a wave of bliss as I gave myself to him. Forced to do his will. He continued to lick and caress my finger. The energy grew moving deep inside. My stomach tightened in response to the waves of orgasms that ravished my mind and body. The stranger held me with one arm preventing me from collapsing. I wanted the power to take me forever. I understood the darkness was swallowing me, yet I didn't care.

He was taking my blood; my soul and I wanted him to have it all.

Chapter 8

"Sevastian! SEVASTIAN!" The voice carried through the room and seemed to come closer. It brought me back from the edge of darkness consuming my mind. I collapsed in the arms of my captor while he slowly released my finger.

"Get off her, you son of a bitch!" The voice drew nearer.

My head spun as the man swept me into his arms, and carried me to the center of the room. He gently set me on the couch. I sat completely still as I collected my thoughts. My eyes weren't focused and dim lights danced across my vision. Pleasure still drenched my senses as I looked up at the man before me. He turned from me, a smirk on his face to greet the man who yelled. I took for granted the man who held me was Sevastian. I couldn't make out the other figure advancing quickly towards us.

The voice roared loudly in my ears. "If you touch her again, I will kill you!" I felt the anger sweep over my body as the voice trailed off. The power stung against my sensitive nerves.

"I was just having some fun, brother dear," Sevastian said.

The energy in the room seemed to steady my spinning head. The man doing all the yelling stood over me. He placed his hand in mine. Almost immediately, my head began to clear. My sight slowly returned. Siön Baptiste was knelt in front of me, concern etched in his face.

"Are you all right, Samantha?" he asked, rubbing my arms.

I nodded suspiciously watching the man who loomed behind Siön Baptiste. He acknowledged my angry gaze, flashing a smile that made my heart skip a beat. As he grinned, my finger tingled. He marked me as if he'd left a small trace of himself in the cut.

I glanced back at Siön Baptiste. "What just happened?" I asked, concerned that if it happened again, I would not be able to control myself.

Releasing my hand, he stood and faced Sevastian. "You have no right." He clenched his hands at his side while he walked closer to him.

The two vampires stared furiously at each other a silent challenge to each other's powers. I expected them to kill each other but they just stood motionless. Siön Baptiste broke the silence. "Sevastian, you cannot use power on her, Nicholi has forbidden it! He will hear about this." He raised his voice while he watched the door as if anticipating someone entering.

Siön Baptiste's comment made me wonder if he had ever used powers on me or did he honor his father's wishes. What if he hadn't used his powers? What did that mean?

Sevastian backed up as if Siön Baptiste had slapped him in the face. "I will not take orders from you, brother. Our father will understand my temptation at such a delightful treat." Sevastian laughed, a low roll that teased my skin into a hot fever.

I just sat still not able to speak, walk, or move, but anger cleared my mind. The laughter continued and the vibrations stirred low inside. I choked on a gasp from the feeling.

Siön Baptiste glanced back at me and then lunged for Sevastian. My eyes could not follow their movement, they moved so rapidly.

I struggled to get up but some invisible force held me to the couch, something I couldn't see but felt. "Let me go!" I cried. The power released its hold on me and my body began to relax.

The lights flickered and the side door flung open. A wind flew through the room knocking over everything in its path. The unforeseen force threw Siön Baptiste over the couch and Sevastian into the wall. The wind swirled like a mini tornado tossing my hair and skirt. As quickly as the storm started, it settled and a man floated through the door.

"How dare you go against me, Sevastian!" The voice hit me like a million fire ants running over my skin.

Siön Baptiste and Sevastian now stood and glided humbly to the man who had entered. The group stood together for a moment each taking their turn to glance in my direction. The man moved past them with ease and sauntered across the room towards me. Were his feet on the *ground?* It looked effortless like an angel moving through the clouds. I could smell sweet lilacs as a cool breeze blew through my hair. Everything moved in the wonderful fresh wind except the creature before me. His aura shone bright red emanating demonic power. I could only stare, held helplessly by his gaze. I felt his beast wash over me, as it probed my soul, tearing at my mind.

Before I knew what was happening, I stood and walked to the man. I shook my head stunned at the effect this new powerful vampire had on me. I didn't like being messed with. I squeezed my hands into fists, pressing my nails into the meat of my hand until I could feel the skin give way. The pain cleared my head. "You must be Nicholi." I gritted between my teeth. I'd had enough of the games. "I don't know what just happened but you can kiss all of this goodbye if it ever happens again." I growled. I had killed vampires for less than what these three had done to me today.

He cackled and the sound roared in my ears. "Siön Baptiste was right, you are a beautiful storm indeed." He took my hand, gave it a kiss, and then released me.

Stepping away, I eyed him cautiously. I waited for his first move. If it wasn't the right move, it would be his last. Even vampires could be killed, with enough bullets to the head or heart.

With room to maneuver I got a good look at Nicholi. Nicholi had long black hair that billowed down to his hips. He was pale, as if he hadn't seen sunlight for centuries, but gorgeous. His eyes were a dark blue, piercing my skin as he surveyed me. He was as tall as Sevastian but much thinner. He didn't have the muscular build of the two men behind him, but he was powerful and you could sense his strength over everything in his wake. He was older than both men--

now just how old was anyone's guess.

Nicholi waved a pale hand to the couch. "Madam, please sit and we will discuss business." His voice caressed the air around us. His magic was stronger than Sevastian's, but different then Siön Baptiste's. He was formidable, but Sion's aura grew stronger as his father approached me.

I sat down on the couch with a thump. Professionalism left at hello, when a bloodsucking vampire decided to yet again bite me. Twice in two days, amazing. I checked my back looking for a sign that said bite me. Betty would have thought it a hoot to pin something like that to my blouse.

The creepy old guy walked across the room and stood by the mantel. He rested against it with his arm. "We are in need of your protection for the next three months," he said.

I smoothed my skirt down my legs trying to hide the gun still strapped to me. *Let the games begin.* "Yes, your son informed me of your needs. But..." But I don't want this job, I thought.

He nodded, glancing suspiciously at Sevastian and Siön Baptiste. "You will protect me and my family from our sworn enemies, the werewolves. The hit at the Silver Fang was one of many attempts on my life and the lives of my sons." His face was void of emotion as he fondled the mantel with his long pale fingers.

"Why are the werewolves after your family? I haven't had any clients in the last three years needing protection from the wolves. Are there any clans active in this area?" I asked.

Siön Baptiste strolled closer to me as if to try to warn me. He glared at me, eyes clouded. His face was full of emotion but none I could read.

"The werewolves see Sevastian and I as a threat because of our special talents. They fear the vampires are trying to create a master race to take over the world," he said.

"Special talents, meaning you can be in the sun?"

"One of a few." Sevastian chuckled, eyebrow raised.

Siön Baptiste gave him a look of pure rage. "We are capable of reproduction, for one. This is why they fear we will destroy the food supply. Take over."

Food supply! My face paled. "Are you?" I asked as I gulped back a silent scream. My eyes floated back and forth trying to read the expression on each of the men's faces, but all were blank. They just stared at me as if I had the answer to all their problems. I had an eerie feeling they were leaving a lot of information out of this conversation. One way or another I'd find out what was going on.

Nicholi ignored my question. "I am sure you have many friends in the business who can take this job for the money we offer. I can handle the werewolves to an extent but need a shadow for both my sons."

Something in Nicholi's expression caused me to wonder if he had more to say. Was he holding back information on what he really wanted? As if he could read my mind, he proceeded. "There is something even more urgent than their protection. If you should accept our offer, your life will never be the same. Siön Baptiste and Sevastian are brothers who both can live in the light."

"I know."

His head spun around magic pushing at me. "Do you?" He moved back to the couch and Siön Baptiste moved to the side. "I have one son who is already infatuated with you, my dear, and the other seems to be on his way." He looked at both Sevastian and Siön Baptiste, nodding his approval. "I would offer myself, but I am afraid my son would be jealous." He cackled.

Offer himself? Sevastian's face was unreadable but Siön Baptiste's held a hint of alarm as he stood near his father, watching him and then turned to me.

What did this have to with me? I broke the silence. "I am flattered that you think your sons are infatuated with me, but this has nothing to do with the job. If it does, then I am bowing out and my associate will take the case or you can find another agency." My voice was shaky as I glared at Nicholi.

Nicholi held out his hand to mine. "Oh no, my dear, only you will do. Everything depends on you." He laughed, a deafening sound that shook the very foundation of the building, and the walls shook as if they would collapse.

I took his hand, not sure why but I felt compelled to do as he asked. I stood stationary as an uneasy feeling grew the more Nicholi spoke. I moved my hand over my skirt so I could reach my gun if needed. "Why does everything depend on me?" Better question what depends on me? This guy was really starting to get annoying.

"You have no idea why you are here, my dear?" Nicholi chuckled and this time Siön Baptiste and Sevastian both looked worried.

Blah... Blah... Just get to the point. I was two seconds away from having a full-blown Samantha meltdown. Nobody liked it when Samantha Houston has a melt down it wasn't pretty.

"I took for granted I was here to review the terms of our contract regarding the protection of you and your family." I answered. "And to review the details of the murdered man in the pictures and anything else that revolves around this investigation."

Nicholi glared at Siön Baptiste. "Surely your brother told you our plans?" Something must have given away the surprise on Siön Baptiste's face because his father laughed again even more hideous than I had imagined possible.

Crap, I had a bad feeling about this.

Nicholi's laughter stopped abruptly. "Oh Sevastian, you have been a very naughty boy."

Siön Baptiste's expression was guarded, careful not to let his emotions show his true thoughts.

Nicholi whispered softly, "You will be a special addition to our family, my dear. Forget the murder, it is unimportant right now. We have you and that is all that matters."

"How can you just forget something like that?" My voice raised, Siön Baptiste eyes met mine.

"You will also forget in time. I know your past and the life you would have lived. I can tell you of your mother." His voice floated across the air.

"What the heck does my mother have to do with this case?" I asked, suddenly very aware I was in way too deep and needed an out really quick--before someone was killed. *That someone being me!*

"Yes, your mother, Samantha. I can tell all you desire to know." Nicholi's voice buzzed in my mind.

The tension in the room intensified into a thick haze. It was a power unseen, saturating us all as I carefully scrutinized the danger, taking a step back. I glanced toward the door and noticed Siön Baptiste shifting on his feet as if he sensed what I was feeling. Nobody else in the room seemed to be bothered, but I felt a heavy weight pressed my against my chest making it almost impossible to breathe. I panted, trying to get enough air.

Two men and a woman strolled through the door Nicholi had entered. *Now what?* They entered quickly and quietly. The man at the front had long billowing blonde hair. It hung well past his waist and had been pulled together in a ponytail halfway down his back. The hair was short on top, flowing down his shoulders and revealing chiseled features under wisps of blonde hair. He had a feral look in his eyes. The light from the lamps cascaded around him in all the right places, illuminating his glowing skin as he walked toward us. He had light gray eyes. A color I had never seen before on any living person. *Like a wolf.* He wore a pale green shirt that was tucked nicely into his pants revealing a fine cut waist. His shoulders were broad and his legs long. The gray pants swayed while he walked. You could see every muscle working under his skin. He was handsome and the evil that surrounded him and the other two filled the room as he came to a stop beside our happy little group.

The woman and other man stood to the side of Sevastian. The woman had long black hair and pale brown eyes. Her pale skin was vibrant against the black leather. She wore a one-piece leather set that looked painted on her body. Her shirt was sleeveless and covered with a leather jacket that came to her ankles. It covered the entire length of her body. She had black leather boots with heels, even with the heels she was still a good five inches shorter than me. Her bright red lipstick contrasted nicely against her pale skin. She was beautiful in an I-am-going-to-hurt-you way.

The man next to the woman was wore all white. Long silver hair flowed down his back. It looked metallic against his skin. His shirt was unbuttoned down to his pants revealing a pale smooth chest. His eyes flashed past me towards Nicholi. Yellow eyes glared from one person to another, searching, and finally settling on me.

The blonde man strutted towards me, and slid his hand down my face. I yanked back from his vile touch. He snickered turning to Nicholi. "Is this your little pet project?"

Siön Baptiste stepped between the newcomers and me. "Don't touch her, Alastair." He glared at the man. They were about the same height and build. It was their auras that were very different. This close the auras blended together causing a rainbow of colors. One aura was cool and strong the other warm and powerful.

I moved out from behind Siön Baptiste. I was tall but not that tall and I wanted to see the action. "I am a big girl and can take care of myself."

As if on cue, the woman who had been waiting patiently why the men spoke, strolled over to me. Her hips swayed while her jacket flowed around her body. She walked seductively, settling casually in front of me. Too close for comfort, but I stood my ground. She sniffed the air around my face and then my cheek. Nuzzling her nose down my neck, I could feel her hot breath tearing at my skin. I was shaking but I hid my fear deep in my mind, controlling my emotions. Every sane thought in my mind cried shoot her, but my wits told me to relax.

She purred in my ear as she spoke. "Darling, I can hear your heart beat and smell your fear and it tastes delicious." She slid her hand around my waist drawing me closer. I struggled to push her away but she was too strong. She could break my body in two, if she wanted.

"Stop, Cassarah, IMMEDIATELY!" Siön Baptiste commanded.

She stepped away from me and circled me like a predator going in for the kill. Her hand cascaded down my back and up my arm and finally rested on my stomach. "I could rip her heart out before you reached me," she mocked.

I moved my hand to my gun and as I did, she turned her back on me and looked at Siön Baptiste. *Her first mistake.* "My dear sweet Siön, I only want a bite. She smells of fear and power. Just a few nibbles. I promise not to spoil the child." She laughed.

Siön Baptiste took one step closer to her. "I will kill you," he said.

Sevastian moved to the side of Siön Baptiste. "You will do no such thing," he said quietly backing up his brother. The power clashed all around us, and I knew this was going to get ugly.

Siön Baptiste's face was void of emotion. "You dishonor my father and our guest with your displays." He took a deep, silent breath and stepped forward blocking my view.

I was getting myself into a mess. I wrapped my fingers around my gun and took it out slowly as not to draw attention to myself. I pointed it at Cassarah from behind Siön Baptiste. I wasn't sure who would attack first, but I would shoot the first person that moved.

Nicholi's laughter blew over us like hot molten lava. "My children, we shall not fight tonight. We have searched too long to fight now. Let us see if Miss Houston is going to take our offer before we bicker." He turned toward me. His eyes widened and he shot an angry glance at Siön Baptiste. "You did not check her for weapons before she entered?" he roared.

Guess my reputation for being a gun-carrying NRA freak preceded me.

I walked out from behind Siön Baptiste where everyone could see my gun. "Frankly, I am sick of this crap. I don't want your bloody job," I said.

Cassarah's eyes flared with anger. "How dare you. Do you know

who you are dealing with? We will rip your heart out for this threat."
She was pissed and it showed.

I shrugged my shoulders, and waved the gun in her direction. "Don't
think I won't kill a psychotic witch like you." Okay, maybe I took that
a little far, but she was crazy. Crazy just oozed from her pores.

"Oh yes, Samantha Houston, you fear our kind. You kill more
vampires than you save. How can we deal with a death dealer? We do
not need you." Just then she lunged towards me with inhuman speed. I
fired the gun before she reached me. She flew back from the impact to
her shoulder. I wasn't trying to kill her just slow her down a bit.

"Oh crap!" I hollered. Pissing off a vampire, not good.

She screamed, blood flying across the room. I didn't want to kill her,
just stun her a little, but as angry as she looked I might have to kill her.
She flew in the air knocking me down to the floor before I could get
another shot off. *Dang, she's fast.* She reached for my neck, grabbing
my hands and the gun. She opened her mouth wide enough that all I
saw were fangs. Oh yeah, she was out for blood, my blood. Her nails
shredded my blouse shredding my flesh. I screamed as the pain tore
through me. Her fangs grazed my neck nicking my skin, the blood
oozing from my wound fueling her attack. She was going to kill me
before anyone could reached us. I looked up and saw Siön Baptiste
looming over us. He grabbed her by the hair and neck and threw her
across the room. She hit the wall and fell to the ground. She was up in a
flash running back for more.

"STOP!" Nicholi's voice roared over the screaming. His hand waved
gently towards Cassarah and she stood motionless. He held her still
with his power.

Siön Baptiste put his hand out and I gladly took it. He helped me to
my feet then took my gun and tossed it across the room. "Hey!" I
growled. He didn't look happy. Did he expect me to come unarmed?
What was a girl to do?

"Thanks a lot," I chided.

"Did I not tell you I would protect you?" he scolded.

"A lot of good that did," I mumbled looking down at my bloodied
blouse. "This wasn't even mine!"

Staring at Cassarah I promised, "I'll kill you for this. Better enjoy
what time you have left because your arse is mine." I struggled to get
by Siön Baptiste, but he held me tightly.

Cassarah just stared. I could sense and see fear in her eyes.

"You did not tell me she was a death dealer." Nicholi's voiced
boomed over us all.

Sevastian shook his head. "We did not know."

"What is a death dealer?" Annoyed at the pain in my arm and chest. Siön Baptiste's face was stricken. "One who kills our kind."

I shrugged. "It was either me or them." I don't know how Cassarah knew I had killed vampires before. I kept it a secret even from my own mind. It wasn't something I was proud of, but it was necessary at the time.

Nicholi released his grip over Cassarah. "Enough! It is time we told you our business, Miss Houston. Everyone sit!" His last words an order not a request. Siön Baptiste took me by the arm and sat me down on the love seat next to the couch. Everyone else spread out throughout the room. Sevastian plopped down in the chair right in front of me across from the fireplace. He smiled, and I quickly turned away. Normally if so many unbelievably handsome men surrounded me, I would feel lucky but under the circumstances tonight, I was feeling a little apprehensive about the whole situation.

I usually ramble in stressful situations, but tonight I would sit quietly and listen because my life depended on it. I had to concentrate on the quickest way out and how I could kill whoever was in my way. I looked over past Nicholi to the couch on the far wall. The sword I had cut myself on earlier was closer to me than my gun, which was now behind the bar near the pool table. I had taken fencing in high school and had moved on to swordplay in a local fencing club. I was good and it had only taken me a year to be the number one swordsman or woman in our club. I had made sure to be trained by the best in hands on combat and weaponry.

My instructor was an ex-CIA agent, at least that was the rumor. He only took students who had potential and he'd thought I had a lot of killing power. *Lucky me!* I was the only woman he ever taught and still worked with him monthly. I counted how many steps it would take to get to the wall and how many seconds it would take to pull it off the case. I estimated five seconds to jump over the couch, roll, and grab, ten seconds if I walked around carefully. Every second counted and jumping, rolling and swinging sounded like the best option. I would bide my time until the moment was right.

Nicholi watched me, speaking quietly as if I was the only person in the room. "Your mother was an elegant woman with lavender eyes like yours. She loved you dearly."

"How do you know?" I asked.

"I knew her when she was with child. Her brother was a blood donor for us in New Orleans. He brought her to the Silver Fang when she was eight months pregnant. He donated, then left." His voice was soothing and I believed he was telling the truth.

He continued. "The night she entered the club is the night she was killed. They left the club and a vampire followed them to their apartment, greeting them inside. The vampire killed your uncle then turned on your mother who he raped and murdered." He was moving closer to me as he spoke.

Siön Baptiste watched the anguish on my face. "Father, is this really necessary?" he asked.

"How do you know all this?" I asked, ignoring everyone in the room but Nicholi.

"Father," Siön Baptiste pleaded.

He waved a hand at Siön Baptiste silencing him. "Your mother was turning into a vampire. She didn't realize what had happened to her. She called the cops and they sent her to the hospital. Her neck wound was bleeding profusely. Believing she would die, the doctors performed a c-section, removing you from her womb." I gasped but he continued. "She became violent and they tried to restrain her. The cops outside the door attempted to help the doctors and that was when in her fit she grabbed a cop's revolver, shooting a man in the stomach. They killed her because she killed a cop. She was considered rogue. You were put in foster care and the rest is history, so you might say. You were so young they sealed the records and gave you a new name." He stopped for a moment and hesitated. Siön Baptiste grabbed my hand and squeezed as if he knew the pain Nicholi's words had caused me. I could feel the tears fill my eyes, but I blinked hard to keep them back. I had to keep a clear head. I needed to get out of here when the time was right.

"You also fed that night my dear. When your mother was forced to drink of the vampire blood, she took his power and so did you. When they pulled you from the womb before your mother finished turning, they caused a partial turning in you. Somehow, the event affected your genetic makeup. You are part vampire only your soul waits to awaken the monster inside. Your powers will be strong if you choose to turn. If you were to be turned at this point due to your vampire DNA, you would become a powerful vampire able to live in the light. The vampire who unknowingly killed your mother left a genetic mutation in your cell. Normal humans have 46 chromosomes. You, my dear, have 47, which makes you closer to us than you would like to admit. You are already more powerful than a human and can sense things a normal human cannot detect. You have benefits that we do not. The blood lust does not control you or your desires."

While Nicholi talked, Alastair moved out of his seat and walked closer to us. He whispered, "The prophecy is true?"

The information swirled inside my head. This can't be. "It isn't possible." I whispered.

Nicholi looked at everyone and announced, "She will fulfill prophecy of old. If another vampire who can stand the light impregnates her, the race of vampires will be invincible. We will no longer fear silver and light. We could crush our enemies both night and day."

Everyone seemed a little to eager to use me. Siön Baptiste stood and grabbed my hand forcing me to my feet. "What are you saying Nicholi?" he asked.

"We will mate her with my sons producing a new vampire race." He was now smiling.

Fear flowed through my body like a lightning bolt. I had to get out of here NOW. Someone walked into the room as we all stood there hovering. The man simply said, "We have a problem."

Everyone was expressionless but they moved like they had a purpose. Siön Baptiste gave my hand a squeeze and moved me over to the wall. I was closer to my intended target; the sword was only about three seconds away now.

Alastair, Nicholi, Sevastian, the other man, and Cassarah all left the room. Siön Baptiste pulled me into him, leaning up against the wall. My stomach pulsed with the prospect of being so close and now so alone. I wasn't sure if I wanted to kiss him or kill him for getting me in this mess.

He gently moved the hair out of my face and bent closer. "You want to kiss me." He whispered taking my lips hungrily. His tongue swirled over mine. As quickly as he kissed me, he was gone. Leaving me eyes closed, trying to catch my breath. I swayed, unsteady on my feet the spicy scent of him washed over me. Then the realization that I was alone hit me. What the heck, he left me alone in this hole.

A slow throbbing power seeped into the room. I turned just as two vampires entered. They stared at me and then began to stalk forward, wicked smiles on their faces. One man lowered to the ground, a low rumbling resonating through the room. Their auras were bright red and their eyes shifted from black to auburn right in front of me. They were going to try and hurt me if not kill me.

"You bloodsuckers better take a step back. Nobody is going to bite me today, fellows." I waited for them to make their move.

One vampire cocked his head, and inhaled deeply. "She is the one." He said. They both stopped for a moment while I spoke. "Don't get any ideas, I'm off the market," Then as if in perfect unison they took a step closer.

Both vampires' fangs had elongated right before my eyes. They were salivating all down their chins. "Gross!" I pointed my stomach lurching as they began to laugh. I backed up, careful not to make any sudden moves. "This is your final warning, stay away from me." They inched closer. "STAY!" They stopped for a second, shrugged their shoulders and came closer. "HEEL!" My heart threatened to beat right out of my chest. They both growled. "SIT!" *I really hated vampires!*

Chapter 9

Either they were too stupid to listen or didn't understand English because both vampires ignored me and came at me. That was all the motivation I needed as I made a mad dash for the sword on the wall. Adrenaline pumped through my body as I leaped into the air and over the sofa, in a single leap, I flipped rolled to my feet and in one swift motion I snatched the sword off the wall. With my back to the assailants I turned the sword sideways, tucked snugly to the side of my body.

I took a chance and shoved with all my might. There was no resistance, as the sword slid through the vampire's midsection, like a warm knife through butter. The vampire's eyes widened in shock at my rapid movement. I yanked the sword out reversed, dropped my shoulder, swung the sword in one quick flash. I brought the sword back to me as I veered to the left landing on my feet. The second assailant fell to the ground his hand reaching up to his neck as blood flowed freely from the gapping wound. Both creatures began to sizzle and smoke as their bodies began to decay. I was leaving and nobody was going to get in my way.

"My gun," I whispered. I jogged to the corner, leaned down and grabbed my weapon. A shadow crossed my site as I knelt to pick up the gun. It moved so fast if I hadn't taken a second look I would have missed it stalking closer. As it moved nearer, I immediately flattened low to the ground. It flew over me, my hair moved in the wake of its flight. When it landed, I fired four rounds into its chest. The creature fell back twice and yet it still rushed forward. "Dag nabbit, die already!" I had just enough time to shove the gun into my skirt, and ready myself, sword in hand. I waved the sword in a motion that any normal human would fear but this monster laughed in my face. Twirling the sword in a circular action, I took a step back. He threw a chair and it crashed with a loud thud cracking and splintering with his strength. He walked toward me as I continued to retreat slowly. I hit something hard behind me, the pool table. I couldn't swallow past the lump in my throat. He stopped as if listening to an unheard command. "Come on you coward," I taunted.

He rushed me in a blur of fangs and blood and as he lunged, I placed my feet on his chest and grabbed his arms, using all my strength to flip him over my back. Once he landed, I turned and prepared for another onslaught. He flew into the air lunging at my neck. This time he had the edge, as his body slammed into me. Helplessly thrown across the pool table, adrenaline pushed back the pain I shot up using the end of the table as support. He came at me again and I maneuvered to the right of his attack bringing my sword across my body. He stopped in mid-motion as his torso flew in one direction and his legs fell to the ground. I walked away to the sound of hissing burning flesh. I whipped the sword off on the couch and took it with me.

There were two exits. I darted out the nearest door, only to notice rug instead of stone. As I turned to head back, something grabbed me and forced me roughly to the ground. The sword was pinned between my body and the beast that stared into my eyes.

"My brother wants you but I will have you." I recognized the voice. Sevastian had me trapped on the floor and the sword sliced painfully through my blouse and into my chest. I felt a sharp jab of pain on my stomach as I wiggled to get free. "Oh struggle, my little butterfly," he laughed. "You will surely kill yourself." He pulled me over so I was on top of him and quickly threw the sword down the hall. Then he rolled back onto me pinning his legs over mine. He traced his hand down my blood-soaked blouse before ripping it off me. He threw my gun next to the sword. I fought back, but he was too powerful. His eyes were molten lava, and he was covered in blood. My blood. "You don't know what your doing Sevastian, the blood lust has you. Let me go!" I choked.

He growled moving his face over my stomach, his tongue flicked, licking the cut between my breasts.

"Stop you don't want to do this." I screamed.

He looked up, eyes gone red. "Yes, I do." His tongue scorched a path over my wound as he fondled my breast, returning to the sliced skin. Fangs scraped the cut, causing blood to seep from the wound. His body tensed as he moaned with desire. I thrashed about trying to free my hands and legs, but he held me with the length of his body. The more I fought the more excited he became. If I didn't calm down I would cause him to lose total control. I forced myself to breathe and relax. "Sevastian," I whispered trying to get his attention. "You have to stop!" I cried, heart racing.

He ignored my pleas, slowly traced the cut to my neck. My body grew cold, my fingers dug into his arms. The fight slowly left me as wave after wave of magic inundated my senses.

"This won't hurt love." He whispered against my neck. "You might even enjoy it."

My hands loosened their hold as he kissed my neck gently nibbling at my pulse. I was drowning in the pleasure of his energy. My body began to quiver and spasm as I felt my fear turn to need. He was forcing his will on me, controlling my actions and mind. "No," I gulped bile burned the back of my throat. I couldn't think or move, held in his trance. I could only feel the warm buzz of my skin and the slick heat of desire slide up and down my body. A tear slid down my face as the numbing relief took over. His mouth took mine, forcing his tongue between my lips. He slowly began to grind his hips against mine.

A hot desire filled me and I knew it wasn't my own. This couldn't be happening. Helpless against his power my mind relented. His fangs scraped along my throat, I groaned, "please." The pressure built, my hands wondered up to his head as I pulled him closer. I wasn't begging him to stop I wanted him to bite me.

"Will you willingly have me?" he asked, voice raspy with desire.

I couldn't think. I wanted him more than I had ever wanted anyone and it felt so good. "Yes," I cried.

He moved his mouth to my neck while his hand moved to my skirt. Warm fingers brushed against my thigh as he slid my skirt up. His fingers brushed against my underwear and my legs spread as a warm wetness built with my growing excitement. He slowly caressed me with his fingers, moving them delicately back and forth, and then pushed my panties to the side and slid a finger inside of me. His tongue circled over my pulse. He thrust his finger deep as his fangs penetrated my throat. The pain was lost under the movement of his finger. My back arched with the pleasure his hand wrapped around my waist lifting me into him as he sunk his fangs deeper into my neck.

I was floating, his power spewed inside me, submerged within every cell. I felt the crushing movement of his fingers caressing me down low as a hot heat burned with each pull from his mouth. I shifted, slipping him further between my thighs, sliding under him as his smoldering magic brought me on the brink of orgasm. Hips jerked to meet his finger. With every thrust, I lifted to meet his eager hands as they dived deep within me. I shook from pleasure and pain as he drank my warm blood.

A low deep groan came from him as his power engulfed me, swallowing my soul. My body was boneless liquid in his unrelenting energy. Tucking his head into me he rotated his fingers faster, in and out of me wet, hot and twitching. My sight began to fade in and out, blurred by his passion and loss of blood. White lights flashed beneath my eyelids, as the heat between us melded our bodies together. If this was death, I welcomed it with open arms. My life flashed before me as

Tamara Gray

I felt myself slip slowly into an orgasmic death. He filled me again and again with his energy, wrapped us in mutual ecstasy. His heart beat with mine as if we were one. Slower, slower until the darkness became complete.

Chapter 10

Everything had gone dark and quiet, peaceful. I could still feel and smell Sevastian as if he were inside me. Was I dead? I saw a shadow in the darkness. I could feel warmth on my face. I put my hand up to swat at the warmth and hit a something hard yet soft. It hovered over me, as ran my fingers over it I found a nose. From the nose, my fingers moved to a cheek. Something wet and warm flowed from the face. Was it blood? My eyes adjusted, but I could still only hear my heartbeat slow and quiet ringing in my ears.

"My love, stay with me, don't... Now that I have found you, don't leave me," the voice pleaded.

I tried to speak and nothing came out. My eyes blurred, still not focusing on the shadow over me. I heard laughter ringing in my ears.

"Don't speak, I will take care of you."

"Yes, take care of me." I giggled.

My body buzzed to life, wrapped in the aftermath of pleasure. I felt so loved and warm; I wanted to stay wrapped in this feeling forever. "I want this forever," I whispered.

"No you do not, it is a reaction to the magic." I recognized the voice. It was Siön Baptiste he held me in his lap, so close. I looked up into his face. His tears fell and slid down my body. I reached out to touch him and asked "what happened?"

"You almost died." He sighed, wiping the hair from my eyes. "We must go. Are you strong enough?"

Before I could answer, he scooped me up into his arms. A man lay with his back on the floor smiling up at me. It wasn't until I turned around did I see Sevastian laughing at us, smiling as if he were drunk.

He yelled, "Do not leave me brother."

Sevastian's voice faded as Siön Baptiste carried me around the corner, and out of sight. I stared up at the man who held me so close. He watched me as if searching, trying to read me, but for what reason I didn't know. He waved a hand at the door in front of us and it burst open. We walked through as shards of wood and debris flew through the air. I heard screaming from behind us and Siön Baptiste picked up his pace. The limo was still parked in the driveway, he hit the roof and entered, and as soon as we were safely in the limo, it pulled out of the driveway and took off down the road.

I huddled against Siön Baptiste, snuggled warmly in his lap, strong arms firmly around me. "Rest, you will need your strength, my beau l'orage. We have done a very bad thing tonight," he spoke low, as he ran his hands through my hair.

Gazing into his eyes, I saw the light green globes flash with emotion. A few hairs fell forward covering his eye. I raised my hand reaching for the stray hair. He caught my hand pulled it to his mouth, and kissed my fingers lightly. I laughed. "What does beau l'orage mean?" I was drunk on power. Whatever Sevastian had done still affected me, but part of my brain started to clear.

Siön Baptiste smiled. "It means beautiful storm." He sighed. "You are my beautiful storm."

I giggled, warm energy still moved through my veins. Except for feeling exhausted, I felt high as a kite. "Why? Why do you call me that?" I laughed again, unable to control the blissful feeling inside.

His smile broadened, taking my breath away. I gasped at the sight of this vampire who stared at me with such tenderness. With the exception of being a vampire he was perfect, every woman's dream come true. I wanted to kiss him, but didn't have the energy to lift my head.

"When I met you, Samantha, you were a storm of fire and heat. You are reckless and beautiful like a thunderstorm." He paused. "You can be destructive but once you're done, a cool breeze floods over everything in your wake." He placed a kiss on my forehead as we huddled together.

I felt my body give way as he spoke quietly in French. "*Je t'aime, my beau l'orage,*" he whispered.

"What does that mean?" I asked.

"When the time is right, I will tell you. Now you must sleep." He waved his hand over my face and my eyes closed.

I slept, the soft whisper of his voice the last thing I remember.

Chapter 11

I tossed and turned, not remembering where I was. It seemed to be happening way too much lately. I rubbed my head, felt pain, and cried out.

Something stirred beside me and flew straight up. "Are you okay?"

This was really getting to be a bad habit. Waking up with a vampire in my bed once was bad enough, but the same man twice in a row? I rolled over and cried out again. It felt as if I was being twisted from the inside out.

My voice was shallow and dry as I spoke. "I can barely move." I tried to get up and a hand pushed me gently back to my pillow.

"You must rest, Samantha, you have lost a lot of blood."

"I'm chilly yet my skin feels like it's peeling off my body. It burns."

"You are in shock." As the words came out, he moved himself against me drawing me towards him. I felt the warmth of him all over easing the pain. I was suddenly aware that we were both very naked.

"Why is it I keep waking up to you naked in my bed?" I asked.

"Many women would be pleased. Are you not?" He laughed, my body responded with a resounding yes.

I ignored his comment and tried to move again. "I feel like I've been hit by a train. What is wrong with me?" A flashback of Sevastian over me flooded my mind, I cried out. I could still feel him within me, pulling and caressing my body. A shudder ran through me.

Siön Baptiste squeezed me closer to him and his touch warmed me to my core, calming the aftermath of what Sevastian had done. "What is going on?" I asked.

Kissing my forehead, he clung to my body as if holding me would keep me alive. "You almost died, Samantha. Another moment and Sevastian would have marked you for life. You would have been his and not mine," he purred against my hair.

I am not either of yours, I thought. I bit my lip to keep from speaking. I took a deep breath afraid to close my eyes for fear I would never open them again. I was as close to death, as I ever wanted to be.

I heard his purring before I saw him and my black cat, KoKo, jumped up onto the bed rubbing his head against Siön Baptiste then turning to me. I was surprised he didn't attack Siön Baptiste. KoKo was normally very jealous of men. He didn't even tolerate Trevor. I shrugged it off and let his purr soothe my nerves as I clung to Siön Baptiste. I wrapped my arms around his waist and wiggled closer into his heat.

After a few minutes of drifting peacefully in and out of light sleep, I decided to pry into what happened. "How did you get in my house? How did we get here?" I asked.

He pulled away, his hand moved a curl from my face. He watched me his gaze intense. The sheer beauty of his eyes mesmerized me. His face seemed flushed as if he had been running a marathon. I would almost say it was a hint of a blush. *Could vampires blush?*

"I can read minds if I choose to do so." He said it so calmly I almost believed it should seem normal.

Yep, read minds, why not?

"Can your father and brother read minds too?" I asked. I was now concerned that they knew where I lived and that scared me more than anything.

"They can read only those who open their minds to them. Sevastian can reach your mind, but if you do not give the information willingly, he will not have access. He cannot rape the mind but he can rape your body. He has powers controlling lust and sex." His voice had a hint of anger behind it.

"What are your powers?" I asked.

He smiled. "I can read minds without permission, and I have some talent in the lust department." He chuckled as he spoke quietly. His face was so close to mine, I could feel the warmth of his breath against my mouth. I inhaled sharply, his spicy scent intoxicating.

I shook my head trying to remember what happened. "Did Sevastian rape me last night?" It was a simple question but it stirred an emotion from Siön Baptiste I had never seen before, hatred.

He jumped out of bed. My eyes popped open, as he stood before me naked and growled, "My brother will die for what he has done." He started to pace the room. I tried to keep the smile from my face, but it isn't every day a tall dark and handsome vampire paces your room totally naked.

He grabbed his arms holding himself. "My brother will die and my father will kill me for what I have done. Tonight we will go get Trevor. We must keep you both safe." He watched my expression searching for my reaction. I hid my thoughts, with only a smile to show what I was thinking about. My eyes drifted from his face, to his chest, down his chiseled stomach, the fine patch of hair pointing to… I looked up quickly only to find him with a huge grin on his face. My tongue flicked over my bottom lip, and his body instantly responded to my perusal. It was hard to hide his growing excitement.

I slipped out from under the covers and attempted to get off the bed. As I moved, a wave of dizziness and nausea hit me and I toppled to the floor taking all the covers with me. I couldn't stop shaking, as I lay cold and naked in a heap of cotton and flesh.

Siön Baptiste sprinted to my side. He knelt, sweeping me up in his arms, and laid me on the bed. "Stay put, my sweet, you are still very weak." He waved his hand, "Sleep." I just looked at him. "Sleep." He waved his hand again.

"No, I'm sick of sleeping."

He looked down at his, moved it in a circle, then back at me. His smile deepened. "You resist me. Good!" He kissed me lightly on the head headed for the bathroom.

"Make yourself at home." I mumbled under my breath. "Jeesh, he acts like he owns the place." I heard the bath water running. "What have I gotten myself into this time?" The sexiest man I had ever met running around my house naked as if he owned the place. Twice now, in two nights we had slept together. Twice now, in two nights he had saved my life. Why did he even care? It was a question I would ask one of these days.

I heard him move around the bathroom. *He was humming again.* Well one thing for sure, he was the happiest vampire I had ever met. The bathroom door opened slightly and he peeked out. "I am going to take a bath, want to join me?" He smiled flashing his handsome grin.

I can't say that I wasn't tempted. "No, I think you can take care of yourself."

"I only intended to take care of your needs, my dear." He smirked. "Besides now you cannot say I never asked you, my love." The door shut and a second later all I could hear was splashing in the tub.

What the heck, it sounded like Moby Dick was beached in there. I chuckled at the thought. After seeing him naked, I realized he was definitely a Moby. With that disturbing but delightful thought, I tossed my head into my pillow and started to relax.

Chapter 12

Sevastian walked up to me his hand held out to me. He was dressed in jeans and a black shirt. His auburn hair flowed over his shoulders, bringing my attention to his face. He smiled. I backed up my heart nearly jumped out of my chest as my stomach turned. He saw the fear in my eye, and let his hand drop. His emerald green eyes churned with passion, but the memory of his attack had me turning and running. He lunged at me wrapping his arms around me. I couldn't break his grasp. He turned me around and took my hand in his, and placed over his rapidly beating heart. "Our hearts beat as one." I could hear the low thumping of a third heartbeat.

"We are connected," he sighed. "We will always be connected until you die."

"You attacked me." He released his grip only to offer me his hand.

"I did not know what I was doing. There was magic greater than mine at work." His hand held out, "Come with me, I promise you will not be harmed." I took his hand, my body trembling in fear. He led me down a hallway. I felt warmth and sunshine as we strode unexpectedly out into the most beautiful garden I had ever seen. The walls of the garden were stone with lilacs draped over everything. The aroma of lilacs filled the air, hovered all around and over my skin. A fountain in the middle of the garden flowed quietly, spraying us lightly. He sat me down by the flowing water.

"I am sorry for taking you, it was wrong." I could only stare nothing came out. "You must know by now I almost killed you." He turned away as if he felt guilty for harming me.

He looked back holding my hands in his, eyes glowing with emotion, and said, "I don't know what came over me. I could not stop; it was like nothing I have ever felt before in my life. Please forgive me." He paused as if to say something else and then stood before me watching my face. "Say yes, Samantha."

His energy flooded my body. "What... are... you doing?" I stuttered trying to catch my breath. My mind was flooded with sensations. I tore my eyes from his gaze as he hovered over me. "Say yes, Samantha and I will keep you safe."

How could I refuse? His eyes were earnest, and despite the fear churning in my gut, I felt some sense of peace in his presence. My mind screamed magic. My body didn't care.

He knelt and placed his lips over mine. I moved my hands to his chest and tried to pry free. His grip tightened nearly painfully as he slid his tongue across my lower lip, drawing it into his mouth. He tormented me, teased me with his skilled mouth and tongue. I groaned softly as he thrust his tongue into my mouth. I was torn between anger and desire.

Sevastian wrestled me to his lap as he leaned against the fountain. "I am sorry, Samantha." Tears were rolling down his face.

I shivered at the thought of the control he so easily wielded over me. "I hate you."

"Here me out Samantha, please."

"Fine talk, but know this you ever use your powers on me again, I'll kill you."

He nodded. "Nicholi made it clear if one of us did not turn you, he would kill us all. I thought it would save your life and ours. I knew Siön Baptiste would never force you." He paused. "And I knew my father would have no qualms about killing you if he could not use you. Do you understand why I had to bind you to me?" he asked.

"Thank God Siön Baptiste stopped you," I said.

"He did not stop me. He might think he had something to do with my release, but he really didn't. Otherwise, you'd be one of us already. You must drink our blood to turn completely. I have only enhanced your tie to our race," he confided, waiting for my response.

"What is this all about, Sevastian? I don't understand why your father wants me so badly."

He ran his hand through my hair, pressing me closer to him. "Your hair is like fine silk," he said, while twirling a curl around his finger.

It took steady control not to cringe at his touch.

He sighed. "You do not understand if we did not take you, other vampires or worse, werewolves will see you as a threat and destroy you. They will not care whether it is painful or pleasurable. Most prefer pain but I can make it pleasurable, Samantha. It's either now or later and your choice is only with whom."

"You're telling me I will be hunted by vampires to create this master race?" I asked my hands tightened around his shoulders. The idea sent waves of fear down my body.

"Yes, and not just vampires, my dear. The werewolves will be after you also. They do not want vampires to gain such power over them. They already hunt my brother and me relentlessly," he explained.

"Well, let them come, I will be ready."

"You are very entertaining." He grinned widely as if the thought of me fighting the werewolves excited him. "When I first saw you, I knew our paths were destined to entwine. It is a gift of mine to see lifelines and ours is entwined for eternity. I cannot argue with destiny, but I promise to give you a choice. If you choose to live then I will ensure your safety. However, my sweet, if you were a vampire, your life would be much more difficult to extinguish and my job would be easier." The stern look on his face only emphasized the fact I was in over my head.

"I really don't think this is funny. At least my life was somewhat normal before you and your brother slammed into me."

"Siön Baptiste is with you?" he asked.

"Yes, he brought me home," I answered.

He pulled my face up to his and kissed me gently. Then his eyes went literally green with envy. "I can feel him." He looked angry. "I will come for you," he said confidently.

Then he asked in my ear, "Who is Trevor?"

My body tensed as the realization of his name hit me like tiny nails under my skin. "No!" I screamed. He pulled away from me smirking. "Is this a dream?" I asked.

"Yes," he answered, still smiling.

I tossed my head back and forth. "How, are you here? I feel you, taste your kiss."

"And I taste you, my darling." He beamed as he placed his arms around my waist lifting me to him. I stood on wobbly legs, looking at this man towering over me, his silky hair brushing my face. "We are one," he said, brushing the hair away from my face as a warm breeze blew gently in the garden. Lilac petals fell around us and the smell of flowers surrounded us while the cool wind blew over our skin. The feel of our bodies entwined intoxicated us both as we held each other. He moved his mouth to my hair and whispered, "Do you care for him? Is he your lover?"

I reluctantly tore myself from his embrace. "Yes, I care. He is like a brother to me."

"Do you love my brother?"

"I don't know your brother--how can I love him?"

"I sense something between you. I will not give up that easily, my darling. I will fight for you. No one will stand in the way of our destiny." His eyes flashed widely. "I will find you," he promised.

The wind began to blow violently and the water and flowers flew hitting us like stinging bees. We were being separated as our bodies lifted into the air.

Chapter 13

"Samantha, Samantha." Someone caressed my head, forcing me to wake.

I slowly opened my eyes. Siön Baptiste was leaning over the bed trying to move me. I shot straight up like a bolt of lightning and screamed. Tears ran down my face, and I could still taste Sevastian, the smell of lilacs lingered in the room. I glanced around the room for any sign of him. If this was a dream, it felt all too real.

I started to shake my stomach pulsated painfully. His power lingered, sending exhilarating sensations around me.

"He will not have you." Siön Baptiste scowled. He grabbed my shoulders and shook me. "Shake it off. He will find you. You have opened yourself to him," he yelled. He got off the bed and ran to the bathroom. I could hear water running. He returned, sweeping me out of bed.

"Put me down now," I screamed.

Once we entered the bathroom, he slid me into the tub. I yelped as my body dove under the chilly water. I tried to get out but he held me firmly in place. "I'm freezing, let me out!" I croaked, hitting him as he tried to trap my hand. I managed to slap him in the arm but his other hand quickly captured me. He was so strong I couldn't break his hold.

"Calm down, Samantha, this is for your own good. Nicholi will find you if you connect with Sevastian. He will read his mind." I started kicking as my teeth began to chatter from the icy cold water.

"I'm going to get hypothermia if you don't let me out." I held back my tears as I pushed him, trying to pry my hands from his.

He held my body completely submerged as his eyes filled with anger. I couldn't tell if he was upset at Sevastian or me, but he was scaring me. I no longer felt safe. My body began to shiver uncontrollably. "I am so cold."

The emotion displayed earlier now disappeared and concern took its place. "I had to break the connection. Do you understand?" he asked.

I nodded, too cold to talk. I definitely couldn't taste Sevastian or feel him anymore. I could barely feel my body let alone anything else. Siön Baptiste's hands slid off mine and I slipped further into the tub. He turned the hot water on.

Siön Baptiste knelt by the tub. He had a towel wrapped around his waist and I was immediately aware of my own naked body. I could feel the blush move up my neck to my face. Siön Baptiste shifted his hand to my forehead removing the hair from my eyes. The cuts on my arms and stomach were burning in the water.

"I am sorry I was so rough," he whispered.

He was handsome even while he held me down in a tub of freezing cold water. His lips were fuller than Sevastian's and his eyes were gorgeous sage green oceans. I watched his eyes move from mine to my lips. He deliberately slid his tongue across his lower lip as his gaze fell to my breasts. I quickly covered them with my hands, leaving him a perfect view of my lower body. His eyes left a trail of heat as his glance traveled from my waist to my hips, resting on the soft hair between my legs. He licked his lips again, sliding his hand down my arms, cascading slowly to my stomach. He brushed his fingers lightly against my stomach, sending a burst of warm sensations between my legs. His hand was so warm despite the cool water.

"If everything is okay now, you can go and I will finish up in here." My voice was raspy as I looked away from his heated gaze.

I kept my eyes on the tile wall hoping that by the time I turned back he would be gone. Mortified at my nakedness and his brazen behavior. He stood beside the tub and his towel dropped to the floor with a soft swoosh of cotton. I don't know if it was curiosity or just plain stupidity, but I turned to see his fully erect member in my face. He slid into the tub with a splash. With one fluid motion, he maneuvered his body under mine. "Relax, Samantha, I won't bite. Well maybe just a little." He chuckled, forcing me to rest in his grip while his legs made it impossible to move. I sat in between them, feeling his engorged area against my buttocks.

"God, you're huge." I couldn't believe my ears. I felt him against my back thick and hard and now I made it known I was thinking about his special part.

He laughed softly in my ear. "You are so extraordinary, Samantha."

I struggled to get up but his grip tightened, holding me firmly against his now extremely erect member. His strong arms and legs made it impossible to move. He had effectively trapped me. His legs wrapped around mine, pulling me into him. Whatever cold I'd felt a minute ago had dissipated, and all that was left behind was the burning desire to feel Siön Baptiste inside my body. He pulled my hair back and over to one side leaving my neck bare. I jumped when his tongue slowly caressed my pulse, moving its way up to my ear.

"I am sorry," he whispered, sliding his tongue into my ear. My hands escaped from his grasp, pushing on the sides of the tub as my body reacted.

"Oh, don't do that, Siön," I groaned.

"Why not?" he innocently asked, pushing and nibbling on my ear, causing my body to clench below.

He placed his hands on my hips lifting me over his shaft. The tip of him pushed at my opening coaxing my body to open. I cried out the ache to have him inside almost too much. He slid his tip in while I tried to push down with all my might. I wanted him, all of him. He stopped and then raised me back off him, panting against my back. "Not yet, my sweet. We have time." He licked my back up to my neck, and kissed me gently.

I settled back against him, my breathing rapid as I fought for control. "I really am fine, you can let me go," I cried out as his fingers glided between my legs, prying them apart. He grazed my soft hair, moving lower. I caught his hand but he quickly positioned his over mine, tugging my fingers closer to my heated opening. He grabbed my other hand as I tried to break free.

"Relax, Samantha, I won't hurt you," he coaxed.

Nobody had ever been this brazen with me and gotten away with it, and now I felt compelled to explore this man. "Please…" I wasn't sure if I wanted him to stop or continue.

He maneuvered both our fingers down to my swollen slit, pushing his, and mine inside the wet tight opening. I groaned and squirmed as he moved our fingers in unison within me. He traced my lids, entering me again, causing my legs to pull together. He wrapped his legs around mine, dragging them further apart, opening me fully. He released my finger, but held me in place with his arm so I could feel him pulse within. I couldn't move. He was relentlessly thrusting inside me, immobilizing my body in pleasure. He nudged my neck closer, bringing my face to his with his free hand. His lips covered mine as his long fingers made love to me. Never had a man done anything like this with me. He swooped down eagerly, suckling and kissing me with his mouth. His tongue parted my lips, slipped inside my mouth as his fingers danced below, shoving inside ferociously. We moaned together as the pleasure rode our bodies. I could feel his heartbeat quicken against my back as he moved his tongue and fingers. His free hand took mine, forcing me to rub and tease my nipple with his direction. He was tantalizing me in three different locations, causing our bodies to blaze out of control. I thought for sure the tub would boil as our own bodies simmered to the point of pain. I wanted him so badly I could taste it. He released my hand and reached for the soap. Normally I would have been embarrassed but I was beyond those feelings. The fiery ache rushing through me caused irrational thinking as he claimed my mouth, rotating his fingers in small circles. The hand with the soap clutched my breast, washing it gently. I cried into his mouth as his tongue continued to explore deeply. His fingers quickened the pace as I tightened around them. The suds washed over my skin caused my nipples to ache with every slippery satin touch. He shoved his two fingers in harder, thrusting deep inside. I gasped as I came so suddenly; my legs moved together trapping his hand. The warmth that flooded my body was incredible. My stomach writhed as the orgasm shook my entire being. He released my mouth and kissed my forehead. I leaned against him, feeling his unreleased power grinding into me. He lifted his leg, moving the nozzle to the tub until it flowed with ice-cold water. We both laughed as the cold water cascaded over us, cooling our desires.

He proceeded to soap us both down, washing me all over. He took a great deal of time washing my breasts. "You must be spotless." He smiled.

When he had finished bathing me, he jumped out of the tub. He wrapped the towel over his hips and waist and stood holding his hand out to me. He had water dripping from his hair down his chest. He looked like a god with his black hair now damp around his face. Chest hair so soft and just enough down his stomach showing a clear path to his… Strong long legs dripped water all over my floor, all the while he smiled his hand held out waiting.

"You're always very helpful, aren't you?" I smiled, a blush rushed across my face.

I reached for his hand. He wrapped a towel carefully around me. "I can do it myself, you know."

"You fainted on me once. I will not take a chance of you falling and hitting that beautiful head of yours." He grinned.

He escorted me into the bedroom, both of us now dripping on the floor. "Dress! We have much to talk about and you standing there naked is too great a temptation. We need to go get Trevor, make sure you're armed. I will wait for you downstairs while you get ready. I left clothes on your dresser. They will fit." He seized a bag by the bed and left.

God he was handsome, sexy, talented and dangerous. *Get a grip, Samantha!*

Siön Baptiste explained that Trevor could possibly be in danger if Nicholi knew he could use him to agree to his plan.

Twenty minutes later, I was dressed and sitting on my bed looking at the outfit Siön Baptiste had chosen. I was contemplating whether I should actually give him the satisfaction of wearing it. I glanced down at the black leather pants with a matching leather tank top and long jacket. The leather tank was short exposing my stomach and my silver dangling belly ring. Two years of doing 150 sit-ups a day really paid off.

The long flowing jacket settled right below my knees. Everything but the jacket was skintight. I got up, walked across the room to my dresser, and took the key out of the bottom of my jewelry box. I unlocked the bottom drawer, grabbed my machete and sheath. Then strapped the sheath to my thigh and grabbed my gun holster. The hide was top quality, only the best for my weapons. The holster strap was hand-molded to fit my body, giving it a precise locking fit for my guns. The edge of the holster and belt were rounded, burnished, and then edge dressed. I laced it on and placed my guns in, right under my chest. My guns were Smith & Wesson Models 686, 357 Magnum enhanced twin eight shot revolvers with reload in stainless finishes. Basically easy to load and reload in a hurry. The ammo was silver, of course. The guns have adjustable rear sights and the barrel cut down to 3" with non-glare sight blade added. The work had been completed beautifully and professionally. I paid a pretty penny for both of them.

Finally ready, I strolled out of the room, the leather jacket flowed behind me as I descended the steps. Siön Baptiste stood at the bottom of the stairs, leaning casually against the wall, coat thrown over his shoulder, waiting for me with a grin on his face. His eyes never left mine as I descended down the steps. A warm blush crept up my chest and my cheeks. I watched as his smile broadened as I approached.

My own smile awakened in response. He was breathtakingly handsome in black leather. He looked magnificent. His hair lay in waves down his back and around his face. The outfit was almost identical to mine, right down to the leather tank top. His arms bulged with muscular definition, which would make most men look frail. His broad shoulders and muscular biceps flexed as he watched me. He was the perfect male specimen.

He held out his hand as I moved towards him. "You look stunning," he said.

I reached for it and then hesitated, pulling back. The look in his eyes screamed pain. He seemed hurt that I didn't take it but I had to keep my focus sharp and if I touched him, I couldn't concentrate. "Thank you."

"You are welcome." He turned abruptly and walked into the living room. The room was spacious with two brown leather couches, a recliner and an old-fashioned wood fireplace. A picture of my adoptive family hung over the mantle. Siön Baptiste sat in the recliner near the bay window, facing my front yard.

I sat on the couch across from him. He leaned forward in the chair, placed his elbows on his thighs and leaned into his hands. I couldn't keep my eyes off him. His lips were full and soft, the taste of his mouth still lingered in mine. His silver ring brought my gaze to his long masculine fingers. As I watched his hands, a flush crept across my face as I realized the ring was on the same finger that had pleased me all too well earlier. I quickly turned away from him, looking at the picture over the mantle.

I rubbed my forehead, in hopes the headache I was developing would go away soon. "So, you wanted to talk, here I am."

I waited but he sat silent. I glanced back and he was staring at me. "What is going on, Siön Baptiste?" He was lost deep in thought.

"He is coming here," he answered.

"Who is coming here? I asked, hastily.

"Sevastian is on his way."

I shook my head. "How do you know?"

"He told me." He stood up and walked over to the mantle. The leather covered his body completely and left nothing to the imagination. His muscles pressed against the fabric. He propped himself against the mantle, his arm rested comfortably, as he viewed the painting of my family. He ran his fingers through his hair; it was obviously a habit when he was in deep thought.

He took a deep breath, and faced me. "Sevastian will help us. He has agreed to do whatever it takes to ensure your safety." He watched my face very closely. "Does this upset you?" he asked.

"Of course it upsets me. Sevastian almost killed me and despite the fact he apologized, I don't trust him. He has done nothing but tread all over my rights. I can't have my choices taken away from me, and I won't stand for it. He even invaded my dreams, my thoughts. Need I say more?" Certainly, the thought of seeing him in person again sent chills up my spine, but it was more fear of the control he so easily wielded over me.

Siön Baptiste glided towards me. "I will make sure Sevastian doesn't hurt you. He made it clear that we must all meet." He stopped just in front of me, so close that I could smell leather and cologne.

My voice a little breathy as I asked, "Why do we need his help? I don't really like the fact that he is coming to my home."

He smiled. "Sevastian has his sources and he feels that we are in too deep. He comes against my father's will."

"Oh and that is supposed to comfort me. I don't trust him," I said.

Siön Baptiste's face fell into empty, mindful lines, only his eyes held heat like a fire. "Nothing will happen to you Samantha. I swear it."

I nearly jumped out of my skin when I heard the doorbell. We both just looked at each other. "What aren't you telling me?" His face was once again totally void of emotion as I slowly pushed myself up off the sofa. Siön Baptiste stood his ground, forcing my body to brush up against him. He turned and grabbed my arm. "I will get it," he whispered.

Pushing me behind him, he stepped past me, and glided gracefully to the door. I followed him with an apprehensive lump in my throat. The doorbell rang again. Siön Baptiste opened the front door and Sevastian stood casually, arm over his head leaning against the frame.

A smile curled his lips. "I thought I might have to break the door down. Have you been waiting long?" he asked, looking past Siön Baptiste, staring directly at me.

"Not nearly long enough," Siön Baptiste replied angrily, and waved at him to come in.

Sevastian ushered a rush of warm air into the house as he entered.

I took a step back. My breath caught in my throat as the man who'd invaded my dreams now stood before me. His eyes were emerald globes, watched me intently. His hair was long and sinfully auburn and his skin tanned flawlessly. He wore black pants that emphasized his long legs. I took a few more steps back as his heated energy filled the room. My heart raced in fear as I watched him. His face was perfectly chiseled with high cheekbones and a strong jaw. His lips were smooth and plump, perfectly kissable.

He saw the fear in my eyes and stood his ground directly in front of me. He turned, to the door. I peeked past him just as Trevor entered the house.

He was wearing a baseball cap and sunglasses. He was the same height as Siön Baptiste and as they stood side by side I had the distinct feeling I was oblivious to what was really going on. Something was different about Trevor. I stared, mesmerized by the sheer masculine splendor of him and how brightly his aura pulsed. Even with his baseball cap and sunglasses on, he seemed flawless. I was relieved to see him unharmed, but worried at the electrical charge floating in the air. Jeans hugged his long, muscular legs, while a black T-shirt showed every ounce of his chest. Black boots covered his feet and I felt the tears choke me while I ran to him. I wrapped my arms around him and he stood there motionless. No warmth, no movement. My gaze swept from his face to his well-defined chest, moving my hands over him. "Are you okay?" I searched him looking for any sign of harm. I wanted to feel his warmth and the special bond we shared but there was nothing.

I glanced at Siön Baptiste and then Sevastian. "What is going on?" I turned back to Trevor and a single tear slid down his cheek, rested on his chin. I wiped the tear grabbing his face. "Trevor, what is wrong?" I panicked, drawing him to me, and he stiffened in my embrace. Heat poured from him.

He slowly raised his hand to mine and pulled it to his neck. He ran his finger down his neck as he moved his head away from mine.

My heart leaped into my throat, what had escaped my notice earlier was only now so evident. There were four small puncture wounds on his neck. "I don't understand," I managed to cry out in anger.

I backed away from Trevor and shook my head. "No... NO! WHAT IS THIS?" Tears were now raced down my face, in a torrent of emotion. His aura, the heat, the energy. I faced Siön Baptiste, then swung my attention to meet Sevastian head on. "What the hell did you do?" I screamed.

Before he could react, I was on him. We tumbled to the floor, crashing through my living room. We hit the end table, sent the lamp flying through the air as I landed on him. He was pinned under me when I removed my machete from the sheath. He grabbed my hands as I swung the machete at his throat. By the time I reached his throat, he was holding both of my hands in a tight grip. He swiftly flipped us both, rolling on top of me. Pinning me with his body, he placed most of his weight on his arms, leaning above me. "I had no choice," he whispered.

I could see Siön Baptiste straining to hold Trevor back and I screamed again. "What did you do?" I cried, as I tried to fight his hold with all my might. He was too strong.

"I saved his life," he muttered, resting his mouth on my ear.

"I don't believe you!"

A soft curse escaped his lips as he laid his head on my neck. "I had no choice. He would have died. Nicholi is cruel." He moved his lips over my neck and over my face. His lips moved over my mouth as he spoke, "I saved him for you. Trust me Samantha." He kissed me but I refused to open to him. His tongue flicked against my mouth, prying my lips apart. The fire and power flared between us. The feeling of his mouth on mine was too intense.

Trevor's voice jolted me. "Get off of her, you son of a b....."

I stole a glance past Sevastian to see Siön Baptiste walk over and with one hand on his shoulder threw Sevastian off me. Sevastian was tossed in the air across the room, hit my couch and rolled to the floor.

He stood in one quick motion and stalked back to Siön Baptiste.

"You have no right, brother."

Trevor remained frozen as I scrambled to his side. His hands clenched in tight fists, he blocked my view. I removed both guns from my holster, swung around Trevor and aimed both barrels at Sevastian. "Don't you dare move."

Sevastian froze and I fought an uncontrollable urge to go to him. "I will shoot if you take one more step."

The look of surprise was mixed with what appeared to be respect. He took one forceful step. I squeezed the trigger in my left hand and sent a bullet speeding through the air. It all happened in slow motion, his shoulder jerked back as the bullet hit his arm. He didn't flinch or move, just stood watching me with those cool emerald eyes. Blood seeped through his black silk shirt, gliding down his body, pooling at his feet. He took another step and this time I pulled the trigger in the right hand, hitting him in the shoulder. The impact of the second bullet sent him back a step.

He wasn't going to stop. "Please don't come any closer." As I prepared to shoot him a third time, Siön Baptiste stepped in front of him, glaring at both Trevor and I.

"What is the meaning of this? Stop at once," he cried, disgusted at our behavior.

Trevor removed his sunglasses. His eyes were filled with fear. He grabbed my hands in his, removed the guns, and tossed them to the floor. "He saved my life, Samantha." His voice so low it was nearly inaudible. "They left me for dead and he saved me." He hugged me against him, clasping his arms around me. "He gave me a choice, Sam." He hesitated as if searching for the right words to say. "I chose to survive."

I buried my head into his chest and tears soaked his shirt. I cried out, punching Trevor repeatedly. "Why?" I asked. He had chosen an immortal life. Sevastian had turned the only family member I'd ever had into a monster.

Pushing away from Trevor his eyes hurt beyond belief, I stomped over to Sevastian. He stood there; chin lifted defiantly no visible emotion other than a twitch in the corner of his right eye. "You should have let him die," I hissed, spitting on him. Turning, I stormed to the front door.

Siön Baptiste blocked the path in front of me. "Don't leave Sam. He did it for you. If he hadn't saved Trevor, you would have blamed him for all eternity." He watched me carefully looking for a response.

I pushed past him and picked up my guns. I turned to look at the three men in my living room. "Who did this, Sevastian?"

Sevastian took a step forward then stopped. He rubbed his hand on his chin. "My master." He looked at Siön Baptiste and then at Trevor. He was about to say something else but before he could get another word I pointed my guns at them all.

"Don't even think about it. I will shoot the first person that moves. And this time I will aim," I growled, as I backed out of the room and into the hall. I bumped into the front door, reached behind me, opened it and slid outside into the cool evening breeze. I had to find Nicholi. I would kill him for what he did, and I only had a few hours until dawn. Despite tales of vampires being easier to kill during the day, which was true, it was finding them once the sun rose that was difficult. Once he went into hiding it would be nearly impossible to locate and kill him. I only had few hours to find Nicholi, so I ran.

Chapter 14

There were three cars parked in the driveway. I quickly opened the trunk of my car and grabbed the black bag filled with my work equipment. Ralph, Siön Baptiste's driver, waited patiently by the limousine. I stomped over to the limo and shot out two tires. I moved to my car and locked the door.

Ralph's shocked expression made me smile. "What the.."

He took a step towards me, and I waved my guns. "Don't   interfere Ralph its none of your business, and I'm not in the mood." I pointed the gun towards the third car. It was a black 66 mustang. *Nice!* "Get in Ralph." Ralph glanced back towards the house and then to me. "No."

"Get in the car RALPH!" I hollered.

He opened the door and slid in behind the wheel. I threw my bag in the back seat and sat in the passenger side of the car.

The keys were conveniently stashed in the visor. *How predictable.* "Do you know where Nicholi is?"

"No."

"Yes you do don't lie. Take me to Nicholi." I sighed aggravated at myself for trusting Siön Baptiste. "Believe me Ralph," I said between clenched teeth, "I've already shot someone tonight, and I'm not beyond shooting you." Ralph sat quietly, shaking his head, watching the house. "Listen Ralph, they aren't coming to help you. Get me to Nicholi!" I screamed, pushing the gun into his temple.

He nodded. "You won't shoot me, but I'll take you."

"Put the pedal to the metal, Ralphie." Holding the gun to his head, I started to laugh nearly hysterically. *I was going to need therapy after all this.*

He glared at me as if I'd sprouted horns, but he gunned the engine and our speed never dropped below 70 until we hit a gravel road an hour and half later.

"What are you planning on doing, Miss Houston?" Ralph asked.

"I plan on killing your boss." I grinned. "How far are we Ralph?" *I was actually looking forward to killing him, scary Samantha, really scary.*

"About a mile, Miss Houston. I don't think this is a good idea," he answered, visibly shaking from the ordeal.

I nodded. "You're right it isn't, but I don't give a flying flip what you think. Now, stop the car, Ralph."

"Miss Houston?"

"STOP THE DANG CAR!" I screamed the gun shoved to his temple.

He jerked the car to the side of the road. Grabbing my bag from the back seat, I scooted out of the car. I strolled casually to the front of the mustang, and placed my bag on the hood. Unzipped the bag removed a large knife and smiled sweetly at Ralph. He sat motionless with a worried look on his face.

"I won't hurt you, Ralphie, if you behave and if you stop calling me Miss Houston. I thought we would be friends by now," I chuckled. *Oh yeah, I was loosing it.*

Rounding the front of the car, I pierced the tire with my knife. I repeated the action to the back right tire. I seriously doubted he had two spares. Walking back to the driver's side, I leaned into the window, placed the knife against Ralph's neck. "Which way?" I whispered, blood boiling with adrenaline.

"That way." He sighed. "I'd better come with you or my master will kill me."

"If you follow me or call anyone, I will kill you. Just sit tight until I get back and then maybe we can find a way home."

"You know I can't do that, Samantha."

"Then you will get hurt, Ralph. Don't underestimate what I am capable of doing," I warned.

"You are going to sit tight, Ralph, if it's the last thing you do." If he only knew how screwed we both were, he would be running like mad. Opening my bag, I removed a shotgun and shoulder holster. I strapped the gun in the holster and stuck the ammo in my belt. I positioned the throwing stars securely in my jacket pockets. I grabbed the additional ammo for my Magnums and tossed the empty bag on the ground.

I took off, running down the dirt road. The moon shone brightly, but I could see with or without it tonight. I ran, moving swiftly and silently down the road. At the end of the road, there was a huge iron gate. It was open and a stone wall surrounded what looked like a mansion. I had been here before but never got a good look. It was gorgeous even in the shadowy cover of night.

Maybe coming at night was a mistake. Killing a master vampire after sunset wasn't going to be easy. I knelt down, moved quickly and quietly along the wall until I reached the left side of the estate. I leaped up my fingers latched onto the cold stone. Using all my upper body strength I pulled myself up onto the ledge. I scanned the yard below, empty. Easing myself backwards I slid down the other side. It was dark and the drop was about six feet. When I hit the ground, I tumbled and landed soundly with guns in hand. Straining to hear anything past my own heartbeat, I held my breath. The moonlight sent shadows and light shimmering dangerously over the yard. Too many places to hide--too many possible ways to be ambushed. I aimed my gun at monsters only imagined in my head. I knew somehow, there were creatures that stalked me in the night, which waited for my first mistake. I shook my head, wiped the sweat from my face, and silently cursed Siön Baptiste for getting me in this mess. *It's okay, Sam, take a deep breath.* A cool breeze moved a bush and instinctively my finger went stiff on the trigger of my gun. I held my breath, body rigid as I waited for any sign of hostile movement. After what seemed an eternity, when the area seemed clear, I started cautiously forward.

I stopped dead in my tracks as a fierce cry pierced my ears. It came from the woods behind me. The inhuman scream filled the night.

"What was that?" I asked my self softly.

My heart thumped wildly as the thought of what might be in those woods. "Keep moving," I coaxed myself then slowly crawled to the side of the house. The house was dark and empty as I peered into a window. Scooting around the outside wall of the house, I dove between bushes and trees. I got caught on one bush. "Shoot," I whispered. I could feel the thorn pierce my hand. I raised my hand to my mouth, yanked it out, spitting blood and thorn on the ground. The metallic taste of my own blood seeped onto my tongue. *The question was, could they smell it?*

I continued to sneak along the house until I reached a corner. I knelt low in the flowerbed, my knees covered in dirt, and peeked around the bend. There was a small light shining through the window of the back door. Crawling on all fours to the entrance, I heaved myself up beside the door. I slowly moved my hand over the doorknob. The knob moved under the twisting pressure while I carefully opened it. I winced as the door squeaked noisily. It seemed like forever before I began to breathe normally again. I tiptoed through the door into a small hallway. It was dark except for one lantern down the hall.

My attention was drawn to a movement in the corner of my eye. A man floated through the corridor and into the next room. Every cell in my body told me it was Nicholi. My heart thundered so loudly that I was sure he would hear it. I inhaled deeply, and moved toward the shadows he left in his wake.

The door he entered was still open. I immediately recognized the room. It was the great room from my first visit. There were no visible signs of the attack that occurred. I dashed across the room to the door that Nicholi had entered that fateful day.

Stopping to catch my breath, I peered around the corner to look for any signs of movement. The hallway beyond was dimly lit with lanterns that hung from long chains attached to the ceiling. I crept through the door with my back against the wall. Ducking low I peered into the darkness. Nothing! I moved further down the hallway. My hand guided my steps until I found a gap in the wall. *Stairs.* I could see a light at the bottom of the steps, but nothing else was visible. My breathing came in shallow gasps as I struggled to control the heart pumping fear now threatening to force me to run for my life. I was surprised I made it this far undetected, but Nicholi was too confident in his own powers to think anyone would attack him after sunset. I was either too angry or just too dumb to know any better I guess. His power covered me and I could tell I was getting closer. The magic had this aftermath; the stench of evil overpowered my senses.

I descended the steps gradually, watching for any sign of trouble. My gun was pointed ahead ready to fire at whatever moved. I almost fell when my feet hit the bottom step. Reaching out into the dark, my hands found a damp cold wall to guide my way. As I slid along the wall, I noticed a light coming from a long corridor to my right. I tiptoed silently, guns in hands. I stole a glance and then quickly moved back. I flattened myself against the wall fear engulfed my senses. I took a second look and in the far corner of the huge room, Nicholi waited, his back to me. He wore a long red silk robe and appeared to be anticipating someone or something. *Me?* The only piece of furniture in the room was a bed. I stared silently as he stood unmoving. *This was my chance.*

I rounded the corner with in one fluid motion. "Nicholi, how nice to see you again."

He laughed, a cold fearless sound that sent chills down my back. "My darling, you came back to me."

My hair stood on end as his hideous voice slithered across my skin. I needed to get the upper hand and fast. "Nicholi you scum, you made your first mistake." I growled.

"Oh, my dear, you are wrong. I do not make mistakes. I knew exactly what I was doing." He faced me and smiled a wicked satisfied grin.

"I am going to kill you for what you did to Trevor."

"You will not have a chance my dear. If you do not yield to my desire, you and your cop friend will die." He smirked.

"I will never do anything for you." I could feel his power move the air around the room swimming over me. No matter how strong he was multiple bullet wounds to the head would kill him.

His head cocked to the side in a sick twisted angle. "You cannot kill me." He waved his hand and my body lifted and with a flick of his wrist, I plunged into the wall behind me. My head and back smashed in the hard surface, the pain of the impact jarred my body so hard I saw stars. I managed to roll to my feet, stumbled and regained control just quick enough to get off a shot before he threw me again. The bullet hit his arm and his jaw dropped and with a menacing scream he floated toward me. I wasn't going to die, not here, not tonight.

I gathered all my strength and ran towards the bed, leaping into the air. I jumped rolled across the large mattress landed on the opposite side and turned in time to shoot. Three more rounds penetrated his body as he pounced. The third shot threw him back a few steps. His eyes burned demonic amber as he came at me again, floating a foot off the floor effortlessly.

I covered my ears, his voice whispered like a multitude of men in my mind. "My dear, we turned your friend to persuade you to help us." He hissed.

I pointed my gun at his head. "I will never serve you."

He laughed a piercing, painful sound. "If we cannot have you, no one will."

I shrugged. "My last boyfriend said that before I littered his body with bullets." I paused. "Don't think I won't kill your sons if they had anything to do with this."

He smiled. "They are ignorant my dear. As their mothers were when I took them. They are all tools for my empire. Their mothers were a means to an end, as will you be." He laughed.

He was moving toward me slowly, his eyes captured mine in his powerful gaze. "My dear, we will not rape you as we did their mothers. We at least will give you a choice."

The anger exploded within me as I asked, "What are you saying?" I couldn't believe what I was hearing.

"Siön Baptiste and Sevastian are not brothers. They were experiments from women the elders had taken for the purpose of creating a master race of vampires. We, even then, were striving for a supernatural power beyond the werewolves and other enemies." He paused and then cackled, sending vibrations through my body. "Oh, but you truly do not know. Tsk.... Tsk... You my dear were also an experiment." He waved his hand and a flood of emotions fell upon me. *Bastard!*

He smiled. "No, my dear, you are the bastard."

He read my mind?

He continued ignoring my tears and overpowering desire to harm him. "However we lost track of you when your mother was killed. Siön

Baptiste and Sevastian are mine to use as I please and you will be too."
He held his long pale fingers out to me. His power flew over my body,
causing me to gasp.

"What makes you think I won't tell them what you have done? You
lied to them their entire lives. They believe you are their father," I
screamed, the anger and rage causing me to shake uncontrollably.

"Oh my dear," he laughed. "You are so naive. Once you are mine,
you will do as I say. My slave to do my bidding," he hissed, hatred
filled his eyes. "I killed Siön Baptiste's mother for running and I will
kill you no matter what the cost if you disobey me." My body lifted
from the ground levitated helplessly before him. There was no way out
of his grasp as a numbing pleasure moved inside of me. Bile rose in the
back of my throat that burned hot as I fought back a scream of horror.
He raised me against him while his hands remained at his side. His
eyes swallowed my mind, testing my resolve.

"Can you resist me when so many have not?" he whispered.

I dropped my gaze from his, but felt an unseen force lift my chin to
him. The deep blue eyes now ate away at my soul as I cried out in
agony. There had been thousands of souls lost to this creature. I choked
down the vomit at the thought of him destroying so many over the span
of centuries.

"Give yourself to me." He coaxed. "Do not fight. I am wise in the
knowledge of pleasure and can give you an eternity of exquisite
ecstasy." He paused, "or pain."

His mouth moved over mine, stealing my breath. The evil that
surrounded him made me gag, as the warm sensation of his body so
close drew me to him. His kiss deepened as my body exploded in a
fiery blaze of desire. I trembled as he took all sense of revenge from my
mind, and replaced it with the lightning heat of his energy.

He was drinking my essence, draining my life-force through a kiss. I
was dying. My mind was pulled away as his power sifted through me.
"Samantha, fight him!" A voice echoed in my mind. I was so startled
by the masculine voice that it brought me immediately back to earth,
the cloud of pleasure Nicholi caused dispersing in its aftermath.

Part of me wanted him and the other part wanted to rip his heart out
and eat it for dinner. I lifted my hands, and placed my gun against his
chest. My finger pulled on the trigger. The shots rang out loudly in the
chamber, as my gun fired twice. We both flew backward, landing on
the floor. He rose as if some invisible force or cord lifted him. Floating
in the air above the floor, his aura strangled me with its strength. "You
can only resist for so long, my sweet."

"Don't call me your sweet. Only one vampire in the world can get away with that and live," I growled aiming both guns at his head as he moved around the huge poster bed. I knelt against the bed tears ran down my face. I could feel his power wash over my body influencing me to do his will. I slammed my elbow into the frame of the bed. Pain ran up and through my arm. The ache settled my mind aiding in my concentration. "You don't know me very well, Nicholi. I don't like taking orders."

His eyes flew open. "Nobody resists me." He screeched.

"Well guess what, I just did." I fired the guns before he could react, aiming at his head. Shooting from one hand and then the other, again and again until Nicholi's head exploded, scattering pieces of skull and brain all over the room and me. Sobbing I wiped my forehead, and plucked the chunks of flesh from my hair and face. The beast before me fell to the ground ablaze with flames quickly disintegrating to dust.

Slumping to the ground, I sighed, laying my weary head in the bloodstain sheets.

Out of the corner of my eye I saw a shadow move inside the room. It was still dark and my eyes were covered with blood, making it hard to see. I could only sense the movement. Whoever stalked closer now moved leisurely into the light. I wiped my eyes on my shirt, and they began to gradually come into focus. It was Alastair with his long billowing blonde hair. It was well past his waist and had been pulled together in a ponytail halfway down his back. The hair was shorter on top near his forehead emphasizing the smile on his statuesque face. His eyes flashed amber fire as he smiled, laughing aloud.

A chill ran down my spine as he inched closer, warily keeping an eye on my weapons. "Oh my sweet girl, you have just made my job much easier."

Fear flooded my body sending a charge of adrenaline through every cell. The rush balanced me as I stood to face Alastair. My body ached from the fight with Nicholi and I struggled to calm my shaky hands. I pointed the guns at him.

"*Run, my sweet, run.*" I looked around to see where the voice was coming from but then quickly realized it was speaking in my mind warning me of the danger. "*RUN!*" The same voice I'd heard warned me earlier. It was Siön Baptiste.

Alastair cocked his head sideways as if he'd heard Siön Baptiste in my head and then moved closer smirking as he edged his way towards me.

I waved my gun at him. "Stay where you are or I will blow your head off."

He snickered. "I can see your threat is genuine. But I will not let such a precious gift be wasted." He glanced away just long enough to allow me to leap onto the bed and roll off the other side. I moved faster than he expected. The look on his face was adoration as I flew by him. I glanced back at him as I took off in a sprint across the room. He didn't pursue me just stood and watched standing over the now decayed body of Nicholi.

"I made you, Samantha. I took your mother." He sneered. "I am your father."

I wanted to laugh aloud. *I am your father. Sounded like a line from a movie I once saw.*

"I did truly love her, Samantha. I loved her so much. When I found out she had been with Nicholi, I killed her. Now you have almost completed my revenge. Only Siön Baptiste and Sevastian remain. I will have their heads on a platter even if it means a pact with the werewolves." His sinister cackle hammered into my body.

His words halted me in my tracks and as I stopped, someone leaped onto my back. I felt nails sink deep into my flesh tearing skin and muscle. The attacker screamed as I was hurled to the floor hitting the stone with a crushing blow. I couldn't catch my breath as I twisted trying to get the monster off me. Managing to turn on my back, I aimed my guns at the assailant. Then our eyes met, it was Cassarah. She clutched my hands and pushed them roughly above my head. She was too strong and I couldn't get away from her death grip. Straddling me, she ripped the guns from my hand. I pushed her up with my hips but nothing worked. I was held immobile trapped beneath her.

She bent down whispering. "You didn't think it would be that easy now, did you?" She watched my expression and laughed. "Oh, Alastair, she is precious. She thought we would let her live."

Alastair strolled over to us and glared at me. "She will live. She will serve me for all eternity." He paused. "Bring her with us."

My hands were numb from the pressure of Cassarah's grip. I needed to reach my weapons. "I will kill you b...." I promised, but my words were stopped by the pressure of her grip.

"Not before I kill you, my dear." She picked me up by the hair, releasing my hands. Moving quickly I took the shotgun from my holster. As my right hand reached the barrel, she smacked me across the face with such force I flew through the air hit the wall behind me, and sunk down onto the cool floor. She seemed to be moving in slow motion as she stalked over to me. I wondered if she could kill me with one blow as my mind blurred. Blood dripped into my eyes and I felt my body give way to the beckoning darkness.

Chapter 15

Sevastian was gliding toward me like in so many of the other dreams. This time his eyes were filled with pain and sorrow. He wore white, emphasizing his tanned skin and long auburn hair. He seemed angelic against the setting sun in the background. He was striking as he led me through a gate into a garden. The same stone wall and lilacs filled the air. We strolled to the fountain and he drew me close.

"Is this real?" I put my hand on his face touching his soft skin. "It feels real," I whispered.

He shook his head. "You must wake up now, Samantha. You must break free from your captors. They mean you harm. Do you understand?" he asked.

"I don't want to wake up." I felt so warm and safe in his arms. I felt my mother's presence in this place and wanted to stay.

He put his hands on my shoulders and shook me. "You must wake up." His eyes flashed silky green swirling fire. He could not hide the fear in his eyes.

I nodded. "Tell me what happened to Trevor first."

He shook me again. "We do not have time." He scolded, releasing his grip.

I shrugged my shoulders. "Fine, then I won't go."

"You are insufferably stubborn, Samantha. Someday it will get you killed."

"It might get me killed but it will also get me what I want. Tell me."

"Nicholi ordered his death. He saw your friendship for your cop friend as a threat to his plan. I arrived at the hospital after the concern I felt in you for him. I knew where he was because you opened your mind to me. I knew he was the only family you had left and would never forgive Siön Baptiste or myself if he died."

I remembered the question Sevastian asked in my dream. "Do you love him?" It all made sense now.

He continued. "When I reached the hospital I witnessed Cassarah leaving with him in her arms. I moved in as quickly as I could for she had already drained him to the point of death." His eyes implored me to believe and forgive him. "I took him from her. He was dying and I asked him if he wanted to live as the walking dead or meet his maker. He chose." He seized me, pulling me to him. "He wished to be with you. It was his choice." I put my head on his chest listening to the thud of his heartbeat. "Do you believe me, Samantha?" he whispered in my ear.

"Yes." Just then the recognition of what I'd done hit me. Tears poured down my face soaking Sevastian's white silk blouse. "I'm sorry I shot you. I am sorry for everything."

He softly tugged my chin to him forcing my gaze upon his face. The lilacs fell behind us sent a breeze of petals and warm air rushing around us. I could only look into his eyes.

"I will heal." He paused noticing the sudden concern washing over my face. "You did not kill my father tonight." He stopped cursing silently. "He was not my father only my master." Lips in thin line he continued. "I know what he revealed to you tonight as fact. He explained himself when I approached him about his true intentions. That is why I saved Trevor and came to you in your dream. My…," he paused. "That beast lied to Siön Baptiste and me. He deserved a worse fate than death." He growled. "My only regret is that I did not kill him myself."

I searched those striking eyes and face wondering what type of mess I was getting myself into. I couldn't hate this man or Siön Baptiste. They had done nothing but save my life. My heart throbbed and pain shot through my body. I hunched over holding my chest. "What the…." I cried again as a sharp pain pulsed through me.

He released his grip, shoved me away from him with great force. I almost fell but caught myself on the fountain. "You must wake! Wake now!" he screamed, eyes wide with fear. "Wake, Samantha," he hissed and backed away, covering his eyes.

Chapter 16

My head felt like it was ready to explode. There was a hot flame behind each eyelid. I opened my eyes slowly and found myself at a stone ceiling. I attempted to move my hands, but they were stuck. My sight cleared, revealing a soft silk material tightly wrapped around each wrist and then to a bed. Someone started to laugh from across the room. My mind began to register the whole grisly scene as it unfolded. My arms were securely fastened above my head to large cherry posts attached to a giant ornately decorated headboard. Both arms were stiff and achy. *Where am I?* My gaze moved from the bedpost to my feet and I gasped at the sight. Alastair sat in a chair, feet propped up on the bed watching me. The silk ties on my ankles and wrist held strong as I thrashed about trying to free myself.

"My dear, don't struggle. You will hurt yourself." He chucked low within his chest.

Every time I moved, pain shot through my midsection. The sheets were soaked with my blood. He had cut me. "You son of a b......," I groaned.

He stood, "My dear," He wiped the hair out of my eyes.

"You are such a wicked girl, so much like your mother." His gray eyes filled with anger. "You are a slut just like she was." He slapped me hard enough to draw blood.

"Open your mind," his voice stiff with hatred. I was trapped physically and mentally.

"No." I cried.

I looked briefly around the room, noticing red silken drapes that hung loosely from the ceiling. Through the drapes, I could see a dresser and a door. It was too dark to see anything clearly but candles lit the room enough to see my jacket and guns on a Victorian style chair near the bed. My jacket and weapons were within reach if only I could get untied. There was a knife at the end of the bed littered with blood, my blood no doubt.

Alastair followed my eyes. "Ah, you want your freedom?"

I growled. "No wonder my mom left you." I wasn't even sure what happened between them, but if he was angry enough maybe he'd make a mistake. "Everyone knows she was only with you out of pity."

He lifted his hand to smack me again, and then lowered it. Leaning over the bed he whispered in my ear. "I see what you are trying to do, but it won't work. Despite your mother's unfaithfulness, we loved each other. Because of that love I will let you live."

"I will not serve you Alastair, no matter who you claim to be. Father or not, I serve no man."

"You will serve me, and you will learn to love me in time."

"Never." I bit back angrily down.

"Never say never my dear." His power flared to life just as I made a mental note of my surroundings. "Give in and this will be quick, prolong and you will suffer." I knew it was dangerous to open to his powers but I had no other option. I prayed he would not be able to read my intentions.

Closing my eyes, I hoped it would end quickly. I didn't struggle against his hold over me but gave in. I relaxed under his magic and he groaned in response. "Yes, give yourself to me freely," he whispered.

My bonds fell away. I scooted down the bed grabbed the blood soaked knife and reached for him.

He groaned opening his eyes only to see my now raised hand over his head.

With one smooth motion, I opened his neck digging the knife into his artery and pushing it until it reached the resistance of his spine. I slid off the bed while he choked and coughed on his own fluids. I was covered in blood. My reflection was hideous as I glanced in the mirror over the dresser. Grabbing my clothes, I started for the door. Sliding my pants over the painful cuts and bruises on my legs, I let out a sigh. I was tired, beaten and overall this had been the worst twenty-four hours of my life. Taking my shotgun, I opened the door cautiously. I could hear the strangling coughs and blood splatter as the monster on the bed turned, hand outstretched, dying. My heart was cold as ice, ignoring his cries as I moved into the hallway, shutting the door behind me. He was a monster and I felt no remorse. Peering down the hallway, I watched for any other vampires. The hallway was empty so I took off running, throwing my clothes on while I fled from the man who claimed to be my father. I would not mourn the loss of his life, but revel in the satisfaction killing him brought me. I felt myself changing into something heartless, cold and calculating and I liked it. The hallway was draped in soft white silk. The material gently caressed my sore tender body and a cool breeze hit me in the face. *Wind, Window?* Yanking back the drapes, I found an open door and window just beyond. The room was empty except for two coffins.

I wondered if Cassarah was lying peacefully in her coffin while Alastair died in his bed. I took one step toward the coffins determined to kill whatever was inside. A crashing noise from down the hall woke me from my trance. I took one last glance at the coffins, and decided to forgo my revenge for the moment, and ran toward the window. *I will kill them all. Hunting them down would be fun even if it takes the rest of my life.*

The window overlooked a spacious lawn surrounded by dark forest. Looking carefully around the grounds, I tried to see any possible danger. *What time was it?* I concentrated for a moment and knew dawn was right around the corner. I climbed out onto the ledge, surveyed the yard. Leaning against the side of the house, I put my jacket on and tied my boots. With gun in hand, I leaped eight feet to the ground, rolled silently onto soft lush grass.

I dropped my gun as I fell. I rotated to look for it when I heard a low rolling growl come from beyond the corner of the house. Two massive demonic dogs jogged into sight and stopped. Each had long strands of drool hung from their mouths, sharp teeth exposed readied for attack. They were all black except for their red glowing eyes. I reached slowly into my pockets and fingered the throwing stars. The dogs pounced, all snarl and teeth. I ripped my hands out of the pockets and whipped the stars in the direction of the attackers hoping to slow their attack enough to grab my gun. With two yelps and thuds, the dogs fell to the ground. Crouched low to the cold earth, I waited for another attack. I held my breath for what felt like eternity, as I sat motionless.

Move, Samantha, move! The voice in my head was my own. I willed my body off the ground and dashed full speed for the woods. Once I entered the cover of the forest, my speed increased, and I was suddenly running faster than I ever had in my life. I knew if I didn't get away from these woods and that house I wouldn't survive the rising of the next sun. I heard a blood-curdling howl from behind me. The scream resonated in my head. It was closing in faster than any human and much faster than a dog. Growls and screams continued while branches snapped and broke beneath the weight of the creature. The trees were tall and the brush thick as I maneuvered around each obstacle, slowing my pace. I wasn't about to stand around and wait to confront what followed me. I had a feeling it wouldn't be stop by guns alone. I kept moving picking up my already dangerous pace through the woods as light from the moon guided my every step.

A branch hit me across the face, the pain shot through me, and yet I still ran. I forced my mind and body to continue despite my aching muscles. Jumping over a log, I tripped and fell to the ground with a painful thud. I was immobile, the wind knocked out of me, as I laid on the ground completely still, gasping for air. My body was weary and bruised. The noises in the dark filled the forest. An owl screeched as it searched for its prey, while a deer ran from what was hunted me. Usually I would enjoy my stay in the forest but not tonight. My body couldn't move weighed down by sheer exhaustion until a ruthless shriek penetrated the cool night air, too close for comfort. My ear pressed to the ground, I could hear thumping as the large animal headed in my direction. *Thump! Thump! Thump!* It came closer. Quivering in fear, I forced myself to get up, struggling as pain shot through my head. Leaning against a tree, I gasped as a wave of nausea almost dropped me to the ground. Fresh blood covered my hand and I knew it was my own.

A loud crash of trees and brush forced me to take off running despite the pain. If I stopped now I was dead. It wasn't until the first light of dawn reached the forest floor that I slowed my pace. Sometime in the middle of the night I'd lost the creature that followed me ruthlessly for hours. Either that or it had stopped hunting me. Feeling safety of distance, I stopped, knelt by a brook and washed my hands and face of all the remaining bits and pieces of Alistair's blood and my own.

I still felt this urgent need to continue to run from the creatures I'd left behind. Those devilish howls were far from human and they followed me through the night, prodding me on. It was as if they were toyed with me, herding me in the direction they wanted me to take. I was just happy to be alive. I wanted to live. For the first time in my life, something spurred me on to live. I needed to see Trevor again and more than anything the two men who'd so thoroughly invaded my life. I wasn't sure why my heart ached at the thought of never seeing them again. I jumped over the brook and started running. The woods were thick and the sun barely broke through the dense shrubbery. Stumbling over a tree, I fell, rolled over and over while branches whacked my body. I raised my hands to my face protecting my eyes from the wayward branches. I rolled further as my speed of descent quickened, dropping down a steep embankment with a bang. I did everything possible to slow my rapid descent. Hitting the bottom of the hill, I rolled right out into a road. I froze as throbbing pain shot through my legs and arms. Lying completely still, I tried to focus my mind. The road signified civilization and internally I leaped for joy.

I heard a rumble heading in my direction. I pried my head off the road in time to see a truck rounding a corner coming straight for me. I leaped out of the way, as the truck flew past me.

"Close call," I whispered, trying to catch my breath.

The truck slowed and came to a stop. I gingerly strolled up to the passenger side, peering in at the driver. The man leaned over, opening the door. He was in his late 50's with graying hair and beard.

"Need a ride, young lady?" His smile was warm and friendly.

It only took me a minute to decide this man was harmless and I nodded and swung myself into the cab. "Well, you look like you've gotten yourself into some trouble," he chuckled.

I looked over at him, suddenly realizing my appearance. My gun had fallen from my hands when I rolled to the road and I was very aware of this man's knowing gaze.

"You can wipe the concern off your face, young lady. I mean you no harm. Your business is your own. Where can I take you?" he smiled.

I shrugged my shoulders as a numbing feeling crawled through my mind as I settled in the cab. "Where are we?" I asked, wincing in pain.

He pulled back onto the road and we were on our way. "Well, ma'am, this is Louisiana, where do you think we were?"

I was thankful my captors hadn't taken me too far and hopefully I could get home before nightfall. I had no desire to meet up with whatever was in these woods again. "How far are we from New Orleans?" I asked.

He chuckled softly. "We are over three hours from New Orleans, Miss. I take it you need a ride to New Orleans?" He kept his eyes on the road, thoughtfully rubbing his hands against his chin.

"Yes."

He gripped the wheel, his knuckles turning white from the pressure. "We are on the Arkansas border. The farthest I can take you is the Poverty Point area."

Inclining forward, placing my head in my hands, I watched the road ahead. "Thanks, that's fine." The woods seemed to go on forever. I was still over three hours from home, but I was alive. Staring at the older man driving, I wondered why he would care enough to stop and help a stranger. I was grateful for his help, and wherever he took me would be better than last night.

An hour later, he exited off Highway 20, taking a side road. My head hurt and my vision was blurry. I probably had a concussion. I tilted my head gently against the window. The road was void of all traffic and life. Five minutes later, he drove into the parking lot of a small beat up motel. It was rundown but the vacancy sign was blinking. *Better than the woods.*

He left the truck running, jumped out and walked to the motel office. "I'll be right back," he hollered to me. It seemed like an eternity but twenty minutes later, he came back. "Ma'am, you can stay here for the night or until someone can pick you up. My friend Mike will take good care of you." He smiled.

I grabbed his arm. He was wearing a white t-shirt and jeans. His southern drawl was strong but soothing. The gray hair and beard gave him the look of a loving grandfather. It's funny I had been with him for almost two hours and just now noticed the kindness in his eyes.

I squeezed his arm tenderly. "Thank you. I have no way of paying your friend." I sighed, wishing I had my revenge and wondering if it would be worth all this trouble.

I moved away from his truck giving him room to leave.

"No worries ma'am just get somewhere safe." He waved as he pulled out of the parking lot. "Mike will have clothes inside for you." Still waving, he pulled out onto the road and out of sight.

I needed to sleep and my weary body was ached as I headed toward the office. The road was empty nothing within miles of this motel. The sign was gaudy neon red that read Motel X. The rooms were all on one level. There was a pool filled with murky green water. Alligators had made their home in the pool, and some other creepy crawlies. The place looked beat up but hey, who could complain, it was a place to sleep and take a warm shower.

I stepped through the door into a spacious reception area. The air condition was ran quietly in the window and the room was cool. It felt great. I strolled up to the desk and leaned against the counter. I hit the bell on the counter three or four times.

Yep, impatient and annoyed even when exhausted, that's me. I smiled wickedly.

"Holy crap! Jim was right, you do need help." A young kid stepped out from around the corner, and slid behind the counter.

His accent was thick and barely understandable. He was tall with long blonde hair held back in a ponytail. He was cute for a kid.

He threw a set of keys on the counter. "Here, the best room I got. It might not look it on the outside, but the rooms are clean and big." He looked at me curiously. "Do you need a doctor, ma'am?"

I cursed quietly under my breath. I knew I felt bad but I must really look like something had run over me. The older man had seemed concerned and now the young kid showed an openly alarmed expression. "No, I'm fine. Do your phones work?" I asked.

"Yes, ma'am, you can call long distance, too." He looked around the room and then whispered. "Keep your door locked. Something strange is going on here lately. Rumors and such about vampires and werewolves fighting." He paused. "My pa did good business here until the last couple of months."

I frowned at the kid. "I will, thanks." I felt my stomach growl. "Do you have anything to eat?"

"Sorry, we only have vending machines." He pointed at the three machines in the corner of the reception area. "Ma'am, what size are you?"

"Size?" My eyebrow raised as the kid smiled.

"Yeah clothing, what size are you? Jim told me to give you some clothes."

"I'm a 9/10 depending on the material." I would never be a size six but at 5'10", I didn't really care. The kid opened a cabinet and retrieved a black duffle bag, and threw it on the counter.

"People leave stuff here all the time. New stuff," he whispered. "I'm leaving about 5:30 p.m. tonight. So lock your door and when you're done with the room, put the key in the drop box out front."

I took the key and the bag and headed to the vending machines. I bought four candy bars, Twinkies, and three cold sodas. I shoved it all into the side pocket of the duffle bag.

I walked out the door-waving goodbye. "Thanks, kid."

Leaving I could hear the kid calling out to me. "Remember, I leave at 5:30 tonight… Lock your door." His voice trailed off as I searched for my room.

I couldn't help but cringe at the sight of the motel. It was a hole in the ground. I cursed the kid when I finally reached my room. *Why the end of the motel?* Sore and exhausted, I unlocked the door and fumbled against the wall until I found the light switch. As the room illuminated to life, my mouth dropped in shock. The room was clean. No, the room was splendid. I had just finished calling him every name in the book under my breath, and now I was ready to hug and kiss the kid.

Lush carpet with a king size heart-shaped bed. It was spacious, clean and cool. There was a kitchen at one end of the room and a bed at the other with a sitting area in between. I turned towards the door. It had to be noon, and only six more hours until dark. I needed to get some sleep while I could relax. Plus somehow I had to get home, and I dreaded the call to my newfound buddies.

Shutting the door I locked it, leaning my head against the frame. Taking a deep breath, I turned to survey my new surroundings a little closer. The kitchen, sitting room, and bed were all in one space but the space was roomy. I put the bag on the bed and peeled my jacket off.

I tossed the jacket on the chair near the nightstand and sat down on the edge of the bed. Weariness crept through me and my stomach growled loudly. "Need sustenance," I told myself out loud in the best imitation cave man voice I could muster. Grabbing a candy bar and soda out of the bag, I devoured them within seconds.

I decided it would be better for me to be armed so I slid off the bed and snatched my jacket emptying both pockets. I had six throwing stars left, one gun, handful of silver bullets, and a folded piece of paper.

"How did the paper get in my pocket?" I opened it remembering Siön Baptiste had given me the jacket. I read the note.

Call me on my cell if you need me. (Anytime) 555-313-5252
Yours,
Siön Baptiste

Chapter 17

I stood over the phone and read the note again. Why was I so nervous to call him? Maybe because I shot his brother or maybe it was the way my body reacted to his. Just the thought made me blush. He was so arrogant at times and he infuriated me, but my heart was beating so hard I thought it might leap right out of my chest. I picked up the phone and the dial tone screamed into my ear. I slowly dialed and with each button I pushed, I became increasingly nervous. *Get a grip, Sam! It's only a vamp.* I never got this nervous about anything. The phone began to ring and after the third ring, I almost hung up. I wasn't sure if I really wanted the help of this man or maybe I was too nervous to ask. As I was about to hang up, a familiar voice came over the phone.

I recognized the Old World accent. "Hello."

I paused. "Siön Baptiste?"

I heard a sigh. "Samantha, are you alright?" His voice was steady, emotionless. "Where are you?"

I was surprised he didn't start yelling or screaming. His voice remained calm with only a hint of concern. Did this mean he wasn't upset that I shot his brother or killed Nicholi? "I am near Poverty Point at Motel X." I trembled as I spoke. I could feel the tears welling in my eyes.

As if he read my thoughts, he responded. "My sweet, everything will be okay. I can be there in two hours," he whispered.

I had this overwhelming desire to jump through the phone and kiss him. I wanted to scream that I missed his arrogant self. I wanted to scream I was sorry for killing his father and shooting his brother. This man who in such a short time had become so important to me only worried about my well-being. *Why?*

"Hurry," was all I managed to say.

"I will. My sweet, stay safe." He paused. "I... lo... I will hurry," he quickly added.

We both clung to the phone. I could hear him breathing softly on the other end.

"See you soon, my sweet." His voice was raspy as he spoke.

I hung up and wiped the tears from my face. I should've told him everything, but it could wait. I wondered if Trevor was okay and what Sevastian was doing.

Thinking hurt my head so I decided to take a bath. I wanted to remove all traces of Alastair's attack. I took off my outfit laid all the clothes on the chair. I lugged the bag and gun into the bathroom with me. My body was sore and a bath would be nice.

Fumbling through the bag I found a pair of jeans, t-shirt, socks, black panties and bra. All the clothing had tags. *New?* I started the water and faced my bruised image in the mirror. Eyes bloodshot with a few scratches on my neck and face were the only visible reminders of last night. I looked like a train hit me. A train that hopefully was dead or dying as I thought of him. Easing myself into the tub, I cried out silently as my battered body ached painfully. I had a black eye, a bruised hip, and the scratches and cuts were festering. I felt sore and feverish as soon as I hit the water. The battle scars would heal, but would Siön Baptiste and Sevastian ever forgive me for killing Nicholi? Would Trevor ever live a normal life? I washed my hair with the shampoo from the motel. God, I couldn't think anymore. I took the soap scrubbed myself, rinsed and then rested on the tub afterwards.

If I could only close my eyes for just a minute, I would feel so much better. My eyes drifted closed. "Just a few minutes." I mumbled.

I shot up out of the tub. Sitting forward I rubbed my arms, chilled from the now freezing water. The cold settled deep in my muscles. Something woke me up from my nap, but what? How did the water get so cold? I just fell asleep for a little while, hadn't I? My body was icy, cold to the bone.

"How long did I sleep?" I whispered to myself. I slowly stood. Lifting my body painfully out of the water and grabbed a towel. I was shivering as I wrapped one towel around my head and the other up under my arms. I jumped out of my skin when I heard a knock at the door.

I shuffled my weary body to the door, as the knocking became pounding. The door was flinching from its frame threatening to burst off its hinges. "Who is it?" I yelled.

Chapter 18

"Samantha, are you alright?" The accent rolled over me and I knew it was Siön Baptiste.

My hands fumbled with the lock and once I was done the door flew open nearly pushing me to the floor.

Siön Baptiste's tall elegance emerged through the doorway. His masculine frame and height filled the small space. He stared widely around the room. Strolling past me in a flash, he entered the bathroom and stood for a moment, then stalked to the closet and looked inside.

What did he think he was looking for? He took a deep breath walked past me to the door, slammed it shut and locked it. He moved like a predator, pacing back and forth. I retreated to the bed away from the wild energy he was giving off. The nervous flutter of my heart was a combination of him being in the same room and my worry he was angry I shot his brother; I sat down on the bed with a sigh. *Well, here it goes. I deserve it.* I fully expected him to yell at me and waited patiently for his retribution. For once I'd keep my mouth shut, let him vent.

When he visibly calmed, he glanced at me. His eyes widened as he glided towards me. His gaze moved slowly over my entire body. He wore the same outfit he had on last night. Leather pants and vest along with his jacket flowing behind him. He was wild with emotion and he looked sexy. I couldn't keep my eyes off his perfectly male face and those sage green eyes. I immediately became very aware of my lack of clothes and a blush crept across my body.

Heat washed over me as he knelt in front of me, eyes never wavered from mine. His fingers swept over my cheek and down my neck stopping at the bruise on my shoulder. His eyes filled with something I had seen once before, hatred. Would he hate me because of what I'd done? My heart jumped at the disgust in his eyes.

I looked away from his gaze. The emotion in his eyes was too deep it grabbed and touched the deepest part of my soul. He pulled my chin toward his face forcing me to look at his perfect symmetrical features. "He hurt you?" he asked tenderly, nothing but concern in his eyes.

It wasn't what I expected him to say. I nodded, choking back the tears, melting under his caring touch. Fire danced across my skin as his fingers caressed me. The cold chill now gone, replaced with a boiling heat. He moved closer and the realization I wasn't dressed fueled the flame inside.

"Is he dead? The one who did this?" His eyes watched my every move. Something in his expression sent a shiver down my spine. My stomach somersaulted, causing me to shudder all over. I think he thought I was cold, but it was much more than that. He soothingly put his jacket over my shoulders and sat on the bed beside me. He hugged my head to his chest rubbing his hands over my back. His warmth surrounded me, I felt so safe in his arms. "I am sorry, my sweet. If I hadn't barged in on your life, none of this would have happened," he sighed, drawing me closer.

I looked up into his face and his eyes held unshed tears. "I killed Nicholi and Alastair. But Sevastian said I didn't kill your father. Is he still alive?" I shuddered at the thought.

"No, you misunderstood. He was not our father, he never was. I know your heart and mind I am not angry Samantha. I will explain later." He paused. "I have been... nosy... Reading your thoughts, I found what I needed to know about my fa..." He stopped for a moment his anger evident. "Nicholi deserved death and if you had not killed him, I would have." He rubbed his hand down my back and around the towel. "I am sorry you did not trust me, Samantha." He sighed. "Did Alastair... did he rape you?" His voice was raspy and he turned his head towards the window.

I pushed my aching head into his shoulder and cried. I couldn't stop crying. What had happened last night made me feel weak and vulnerable. A wave of nausea crashed over me as I sobbed into Siön Baptiste's warm leather vest. The thought that Alastair might have been my father sickened me. I couldn't stop crying. Once the tears started flowing, they wouldn't cease.

Siön Baptiste removed the towel from my head and ran his fingers through my hair. "Shhhhh... my love, it is over, you are safe." He held and rocked me, and comforted me. While I still cried, he picked me up in his arms removed the covers from the bed, delicately placed me within its folds. Silently he loosened the towel, tossed it to the floor, and covered my chilly body with the sheet.

"I'm cold." I shivered, needing the closeness of his body next to mine.

"I know, sweetie." His hand brushed my forehead as he placed his jacket over the chair. Every movement he made was so effortlessly sensual, drawing my attention to his body. Then he removed his vest exposing his ample chest and fabulously muscled stomach. My mouth opened at the sight. He slipped into the heart shaped bed and shuffled over against me. The warmth of his breath on my neck sent a fevered chill over me. He gently tugged me closer. He wasn't always an arrogant or a condescending jerk; he could be kind and warm. It was as if something between us had changed forever and the vampire I'd once hated was becoming someone I cared for deeply. I wouldn't dwell on how much that bothered me, but concentrated on how good it felt.

Safely wrapped in his arms I began to relax, exhaustion claiming me as its victim I drifted peacefully off to sleep. I was securely snug in Siön Baptiste's arms.

I woke to the smell of coffee. I couldn't tell what time it was but my body wasn't aching nearly as bad as it had.

Siön Baptiste moved around the room, chatting to himself in French. He had showered and his spicy scent was intoxicating. His voice soothed all my fears and made me feel as if every word he spoke embraced my soul. Immediately my body reacted to his presence. He trapped me in his voice held my body hostage with desire. I doubted he knew the power he held over me.

"What are we going to do now?" I asked, pulling the sheet up to my face hiding my nakedness. Siön Baptiste stopped, his head cocked. I yanked the covers further up around me and then peeked out from under them.

"No need to hide from me, love." He stood completely still, no longer pacing the room. He raised his hand and then dropped it, paused as if to add more to the statement and then his face went void of all motions. "I do not think you are aware of how much I care for you, Samantha."

He used my real name again, which sounded like trouble to me. "What do you mean?" I asked, scared of his answer.

"You are not honest with your own feelings, so how do you expect to understand mine?" he asked, shrugging his shoulders.

"Are you angry at me?" I paused, quickly adding, "For shooting Sevastian?"

He threw his hands up in the air showing his frustration, but still kept his back to me. "Of course not. How could I ever be angry with you?" He hesitated and turned to face me. His eyes now glowed dangerously with unbridled passion. "I want you. I have desired you from the day we first met. You are beautiful." He took a step forward. "I do not know what you have done to me Samantha, but you have managed to steal my heart."

I almost choked on his words. How could this man want me after all I had said and done? "Why?" I whispered softly.

He took a second step closer his gaze seared my soul. A dark hungry look flashed across his features and simply faded. "You are unlike anyone I have ever met. Despite your unbridled behavior, you treat me like a man, not a monster. Samantha, you remained immune to my powers and have fallen for me as a man, not a powerful vampire."

"Just when I thought you were losing the cocky act. Fallen?" I wasn't sure I liked where this was all going.

Lifting an eyebrow, he smiled. "You will never admit your feelings to me or yourself. However I am willing to accept being a part of your life any way you please," he whispered.

"Why did you help me? I was hired to save you and all you have done is save me." I paused, took in the breathtaking man who stood before me. Long lean legs leading to a perfect butt along with other strong admirable parts of his body all gleamed. His chest stirred leisurely while he breathed, accenting his all too flawless abs. Those strong arms carried me out of harm more than once. Again, I asked, "Why?"

He turned his back to me as if he had seen a ghost. I cautiously slid out of bed. My head was so hazy I almost fell but swiftly steadied myself. I kept my eyes on Siön Baptiste. I felt nauseated but used the side of the bed to help pull me up. I took the sheet with me as I cautiously headed to his beckoning body. I tried with all my might not to collapse. Why did I feel suddenly weak when just a moment ago I'd felt so refreshed?

"Why, Siön Baptiste?" I whispered his name, rolling it over in my mind. Yanking the last section of sheet with me, I went to him. He flinched as I moved my fingers over his back. The feel of his skin and strength below it would be forever burned in my memory. He let out a soft murmur as his body shuddered under my touch. I pressed my mouth to the middle of his back and he groaned as his body tightened. Parting my lips, I licked the smooth skin tasting his salty flesh. He smelled spicy, sensual. My head swam in his presence. I pulled away, gazing at the length of him, and imagined myself pressed, my breast rested against him, nipples taunt and tight. I could feel my own body react to the thought. The sheet was neatly tucked around me as I snuggled closer. He moaned as my nipples tantalizingly scraped his back, yet he still stood his ground. "Answer me, why do you care so much?"

"Samantha, you must stop teasing me. I will not be able to control my hunger if you continue." His voice was hoarse with need.

Using his body as a crutch I leaned against him. A tear slid down my face falling to his waist. He slowly turned to face me. "Do you really need to ask why?" His voice was throaty. The soft leather of his pants caressed my legs, I could feel him through the sheets, and I knew he was fully erect. He pulled me closer and with one hand, he ripped the sheet from my body and threw it onto the bed. My nakedness brushed against his body. We both shuddered, as our desire enflamed our minds and hearts. He bent down and gently kissed the trail my tear left, while he moved my hand away from his chest. The movement brought our bodies together and the passion rose to urgent need. I had never felt this alive in the arms of any man. The intimacy of my breasts pressed firmly against him sent waves of pleasure through me that I'd never thought I could feel.

As he had done so many times before, he lifted me into his arms and carried me to the bed. He slid into the bed over me, pressed the full length of him into my body. I could feel the tightening and release of wet hot joy from between my legs begging him to partake. "Siön Baptiste." I cried out, my heart ached and my body begged for his touch.

He removed his pants, throwing them across the room. He stirred against me, kissing tentatively as I eagerly released myself to him, accepting his tongue as it entwined with mine. As he probed my mouth, his hard shaft pushed into my hips. Pain engulfed me as the need to have him swelled within me, rose past reason. This was not magic or power--it was pure lust and life. His hand fell to my waist, sliding down to my hips while he continued to probe my mouth relentlessly. I gasped as he maneuvered himself between my legs, pushing me apart. His fingers teased my soft curls as he skimmed nearer to my hot wet opening. He teased with his fingers circling my entrance over and over until I begged him to enter. "God, please." My breath ragged with wanting him. I grabbed his hair, screaming as he thrust his fingers deep. My body once cold, now felt like molten lava ready to explode in pleasure. I couldn't stop shaking as my hips met his fingers, guiding him deeper. I slid my hand down his chest, following the path of dark hair until it found its target. Placing my fingers around his erect penis, I caressed it slowly as his hips moved simultaneously with the action.

"My little storm, you are so beautiful," he growled as he moved down my neck to my breasts. His tongue flicked my nipple, circling and sending waves of stimulating sensations down to my toes. My back arched as I clutched his hair, releasing his shaft. His fingers moved further into me as I constricted, squeezing him as an orgasm took over my body. Writhing in pleasure from every touch and caress, I cried, burying my face in his hair.

"My darling, I am not sure I can control my hunger."

The heat from his breath moved over my breast. His tongue flicked my nipple delicately while I screamed, grasping the covers, ripping them from the bed. My breast ached with need for his touch as he continued to lick tenderly. Pain mixed with pleasure poured over me as he nibbled gently, teeth scraped my skin, sending flames deep inside. He kissed every cut and bruise tongue circled each wound. Every nibble triggered me to squeeze his fingers, tensing tighter until pleasurable explosions slammed my body. He pressed his lips against the curve of my upper thigh, following a path to the inside. Here he hesitated briefly, and then licked me in long luxurious strokes. He covered the folds between my legs with his mouth, sucking and teasing with his tongue, pushing and probing with his fingers. His free hand glided up my leg, under my hips, pushing me into him as I screamed in pleasure. The feeling swept over my body, every cell stirred in luxurious bliss. The orgasm pushed me over the edge as I seized Siön Baptiste's arm, digging my nails into him. He only drew me nearer, eating me while I pulsated.

"You taste as wonderful as you look," he purred in delight as he licked the wet juice, savoring every last drop. "I have searched an eternity for someone like you, Samantha." His voice rolled in my mind, sending me plummeting into an abyss of satisfaction.

He glanced up from between my legs, obviously pleased with my enjoyment and lifted himself over my body, pressed his shaft into my now swollen readied area. The tip of his penis pushed against my opening. Guiding his hips gradually forward, he slid within me. The size of him filled and stretched my body completely as I captured his mouth. Tongues tangled moving in unison to each of his thrusts. His long legs ground into me as his strong arms held me close. My body clenched around him, pulsing with the heat of his long shaft. His need floated over me and I saw the erotic images of his desires in my thoughts. His hair was spilled softly against my face as we made love. With every penetrating thrust, I cried out. He inserted his shaft in me wholly. The cry of pleasure and pain escaped my mouth, and he swallowed my breath with his kiss. The size of his hard shaft overflowed against my walls, spread to the limit. He pulled out softly only to slam into me harder, more fervently. His thrusts came more rapid as his eyes, swirled with need, locking on me. Butterflies swam in my stomach, clenching my lower body. He held me in his arms, cradling my head, as I savored the sensation of him totally embedded to my core. The strength of his power filled me and we became one. The room glowed as our auras mingled together, our hearts beat in concert. I felt his pleasure as he inserted and removed himself over and over. A warm tantalizing sensation moved up and down his legs causing me to scream above the beat of our hearts. He could feel me tighten around his throbbing shaft and he cried out again.

"I can... feel you...," I gasped, as his energy pulsed in my body.

"And I you, my sweet," he groaned, as he continued to pump me repeatedly. My body tensed as a mind-blowing orgasm vibrated through my body. He stopped moving as my sheath closed around him, squeezing his shaft. A shudder ran through his body as he stared in my eyes. "Our souls are connected." His breathing was rapid as he spoke.

"Don't stop," I begged grabbing his firm ass, pushing him deeper until his tip reached the heart of my womanhood.

His hips thrust forward in a hypnotic rhythm. "My sweet, I never want to stop." He bent down kissed me, white lightning spread through my veins. "You are the most beautiful woman I have ever seen."

The scent of his hair and our lovemaking drove me over the edge. I slashed my nails over his back digging into his flesh. Our bodies tightened in anticipation as he began to quicken his pace, ready to release his seed. With one last push of his shaft, he emptied his hot burning liquid. I constricted around him as he continued to discharge into my womb while our bodies writhed in ecstasy.

"Beau l'orage." His accent was low and sensual launching a new wave of heat and pleasure to assault my body.

I was lost in his gaze, totally fallen under the spell of sensuality and hunger. He stared with swirling lustful eyes; warm breath caressed my face, warming me to the bone. He leaned into me; his shaft still deeply embedded in my sheath and whispered, "I love you. That is why." His head fell onto my breasts. The aroma of his hair drifted over me as he wrapped his arms around my body. We stayed lost in the moment for several minutes before he slowly removed himself from my body. Moving his hips in a slow circular motion he sent a new wave of pleasure cascading all around me.

"Oh, don't do that. You're killing me." I could barely speak, my breath was coming in shallow gasps.

"Do what?" He chuckled against my breast, the vibrations sending another wave of spine tingling electricity through me. He shifted his hips, and pressed against me. "My goodness again?" He was already hard and ready for more.

Making love to Siön Baptiste was too addictive. The need to bask in his light, power and love made me almost forget he was a vampire. Siön Baptiste held me in his arms as we drifted blissfully off to sleep. His last words before I slept were, "I love you, Samantha Houston."

Chapter 19

I woke to Siön Baptiste draped around me mumbling softly in French. I hardly knew anything about him and yet felt so drawn to him. How old was he? Was French his native tongue? I suddenly wanted to know everything about him and his life. A million questions floated around in my head. His words while we made love still made my heart flutter. "I love you. That is why." *He loved me.* I smiled, just content to be held in his arms.

I watched while he nuzzled up to my waist. He'd hogged the bed and covers while we slept. He was the most arrogant, wonderful man I had ever met. The attraction between us was dangerously close to nuclear. I stared for several minutes, watched him breathe peacefully. His hair tickled my stomach while his warm breath caressed my skin, immediately creating a burning desire to have him. I wanted this man like no other and it terrified me. Straining to see the alarm clock on the end table, I tried not to wake him. It was 3:30 in the morning. We had only been sleeping for a few hours.

The last couple of days were a blur. From the moment, Siön Baptiste walked into my life it had been turned upside down. I flipped back to see if he was still asleep and realized he was wide-awake, staring at me with a sexy grin on his face. His eyes were dark with desire as he kissed my stomach, gently licking it in a slow sensual motion. My body reacted instantly, tensing, smoldering with need. I wanted him as much as he needed me. We had a similar past wrought with pain and anguish and in just two short days built a strong connection that was getting stronger by the minute. He smiled, sliding his hands up my waist, stalking closer. He sashayed his mouth over my waist onto my breast, brushing his tongue tenderly over my taut nipple. I held the bed while my body jerked under his touch. He left my breast only to move to my neck. Hugging his arms around me, he kissed my neck. I could feel the pressure of his fangs moving along my skin. His naked body felt so natural against mine. I wrapped my legs around his hips as he maneuvered his shaft over my opening. I tasted his desire burning within him.

"Something is wrong," I managed to whisper. "I can feel your desire. I know you want to feed. How is that possible?" I asked.

"Too many questions this early in the morning, beau l'orage." He chuckled, smiling against my throat. "Is knowing how I feel a bad thing?" The onslaught of caresses didn't stop and the power between us triggered a groan of desire as he entered my body. "I can feel your need, my love. I can taste it." I stopped thinking rationally and felt him let go of himself as he sank his teeth into my neck. White heat lightning coursed through my veins as he thrust inside. He was happy; something in my head told me he wanted to drink my sweet-tasting blood forever.

I longed for him to take me, all of me. With one smooth motion, he rolled onto his back dragging me with him still totally entrenched. I cried out as the movement pushed me further onto his hips, raising me over him.

Siön Baptiste panicked, as his pleasure consumed him. He was afraid to take too much blood. He released his hold on my neck. I could taste my own blood on his tongue.

"What's going on?" I asked again.

He couldn't speak. He was basking in the sweet delight of my blood. My heart quickened at the sight of him underneath me, embedded deep inside. I lifted myself over him, slipped up and down on his slick shaft. His hands guided my hip, slammed me into him. He was rock hard and long and pain never felt so good. His eyes swirled deep and dark. He held me with his arms, caressing my back. His hunger was still there and created a hunger of my own. I desired to taste his blood. I leaned into him, our naked bodies entwined, and kissed his neck. I felt his pulse quicken as my tongue stroked him. Something was opening inside of me, a craving I had never felt before. I wanted to taste him, feel his warm blood slide down my throat. I felt his craving and it filled me as he propelled his shaft forward more rapidly.

His voice was husky and low. "Do not take my blood," he ordered. "You do not know what you are doing."

I could barely hear his voice over the sound of our hearts beating together and our thrashing bodies. My teeth teased a pulse over his neck. I bit down on him and he grabbed my hair, holding me to him. "Don't Samantha." I knew he wanted me to taste him. I felt his need. I bit harder and broke through the layer of skin that separated me from wondrous pleasure. The ravenous thirst devoured me as I consumed his life force, swallowing it greedily. He cried out, his legs and body encouraged my assault. With every movement he made, I dug my teeth deeper, swallowing more of his sweetness. My body was on fire, explosion after explosion of sheer ecstasy pulsated inside me.

"Stop, Samantha!" he cried, his seed exploding, filling me with warm fluid. He pushed me away as I tried to keep my position on his neck. "Stop!" he screamed and rolled me over, landing firmly on top. I immediately released my hold. The pressure of his body caused me to shake uncontrollably. My loss of control excited him and I knew it.

"What have you done?" His eyes filled with tears, as I laughed, drunk on his power.

"I want more." My voice was quivering.

He held me down, pushed my arms to my side. "What have you done?"

I laughed again. "Why do you keep repeating yourself?" I couldn't stop giggling. I was intoxicated on his blood.

An intense energy crept through me. "More," I begged.

Everything got quiet. I saw Siön Baptiste's mouth moving and heard no sound. He was shaking me and it hurt. My whole body shuddered from the agony I was now feeling. He kissed me but I felt nothing. He continued opening my lips, sliding his tongue into my mouth and slow warmth streamed over my body. I could hear his heartbeat and feel the tears running down my face. He released my mouth, his eyes filled with alarm. I raised my arm up to his face and he kissed my palm.

The door flew open, crashing to the floor. Three men walked in, holding shotguns. One man aimed his gun at us and shot. Siön Baptiste fell off me, landing on the bed beside me. Blood poured from the huge wound in his chest. He grabbed my hand, and held on as the men came to my side. I covered my face with my free hand expecting to die. The man who'd shot Siön Baptiste put his arms around my body and picked me up. Another man stood above Siön Baptiste, weapon aimed at his heart.

I tried to hold onto Siön Baptiste's hand but the man who held me was too strong. I was tired and weak, unable to fight back. I sensed Siön Baptiste's weakness as my own. He was dying. "NO!" I screamed.

He released my hand, tears streaming down his face. *"I love you. I always will."* His lips never moved, but I could hear him in my head. We had formed a connection, a bond and I was aware of his pain. The man who held me walked out of the room and the second man followed. The third man stayed behind. The person holding me jumped into the back of a van. As they shut the door, I heard another gunshot.

"Let me go," I cried out, trying to free myself from his iron grip. I hit the man in the chest but he didn't flinch. Everything grew cold and dark as Siön Baptiste slipped away.

My captor had long brown hair with ice blue eyes. He was a large man well over six foot and burly. His arms were strong and with every slap to his chest, he held me tighter. I started to shiver, my body blazed with pain. I jerked away from the man, but it wasn't my strength that released me but a power flooding over the dark van.

The man slanted forward, knocked on the front van wall. A bald headed man opened a small window and asked. "What's up, Ty?"

The man who held me whispered, "She's sick."

The bald man hollered, "What the hell, I thought you said you got her before she turned."

I peered around the van trying to find a weapon. There was nothing but a mattress. A voice made me jump.

"Ma'am, promise me you will behave and I will release you." My kidnapper smiled sweetly down at me.

I nodded and he set me on the mattress. I was still shivering and as soon as he released me, my body began to shake violently. My muscles clenched and twisted in pain. I was in so much pain, it even hurt to cry. "No!" I cried out as my fist hit the man in the stomach. *That actually felt good!*

He doubled over and I scooted away from him. He started to laugh. "Oh you're a wild one, alright." He scooted to the front of the van, opened the small window. "Daniel, we need to go," he ordered.

When the van started moving, I threw myself at the door kicking it with my feet. "Let me out. What did you do to Siön Baptiste?" I screamed.

The man launched towards me in a blur of speed. "I am sorry I have to do this." Needle in hand, he held my arm. I struggled to push him back, but he seized my waist swinging me around. My back tucked into his chest as his hands held me in place. He then wrapped his legs around mine while his jeans rubbed against my naked body. "I am really sorry."

A painful stinging sensation shot threw my arm. The pain moved up my arm and through my whole body followed by the sweet relief of darkness. I relaxed in the man's arms.

Chapter 20

Sevastian walked toward me, dressed in black from head to toe.

Before he had a chance to say anything I asked, "Is this a dream?"

He nodded, holding out his hand. His eyes were filled with tears as he stopped in front of me. He put his hands on my shoulders, and slowly pulled me into his warm welcoming arms. Whispering in my ear, he said, "Samantha, I am sorry. Siön Baptiste…" He stopped. "I sense your pain. Our bond is not as strong but I still feel him in you." Then he moved my face to his. "You have joined us." He was searching for a reaction, for an emotion and I had none left to give.

"What happened?" I asked.

"You're in danger."

"I don't care. Do you know where Siön Baptiste is? They shot him. THEY SHOT HIM," I screamed, angry at my inability to help him.

"Use your power, your anger against them." He tried to smile but the fear in his eyes was too great.

"What power?"

He pulled my head to his chest. "You drank Siön Baptiste's blood. You are one. The cycle of change begins. It will be painful. You need a lot of sleep and blood."

I tried to see his face but he held me tightly. "What cycle? What are you talking about?" The tears streamed along my face.

"You will become a Vampire." He sighed. "You are as the prophecy predicts. The third heart I heard in our line. A third beats now."

"What are you talking about? Can't anyone talk normal to me? Riddles nothing but riddles, Sevastian." I could smell lilacs and turned my head against his chest to see we were in the all-familiar garden. The smell was intoxicating, relaxing me, and giving me a false hope of safety. "What third heart?" My head spun as I tried to figure out what was happening to me.

"Your child," he said.

Chapter 21

I woke up to the smell of lilacs. The last few days was quickly turning out to be one never ending nightmare. I convinced myself as soon as I opened my eyes, things would be back to normal and everything would be fine. Opening one eye and then another, I tried to adjust my blurred vision. Only flecks of light and color phased in and out making me dizzy. I closed my eyes trying to regain balance and heard voices. Why did I hear voices? Whose voices?

"Ty, she is changing, it's too late," a man whispered.

"No, it's not too late until I tell you it is. We are not going to kill a woman just to please your clan, Adeem."

"You are weak! Remember our agreement and your family," Adeem warned.

The voices quieted down as I shifted my aching body. I cried out as my eyes and memory cleared. "Siön Baptiste!"

"I told you to tie her down," Adeem's voice bellowed through the room.

Ty ran over and knelt by the bed. He held my hands down with one of his. "Calm down." His voice soothed my aching body.

"What's going on?" I coughed. "I think I'm going to be sick." He released my hands and snatched a trash can, helping me to lean over the bed. I threw up, my body heaved violently with every gut-wrenching spasm.

My muscles burned, aching with intense agony. It felt as if I was being broken in two. I curled back into the bed while Ty pulled the covers over me. I glared at both men. Reality set in. Siön Baptiste was dead, and it was their fault. I was filled with hatred and anger. Then the pain diminished, replaced by only thoughts of revenge.

Ty watched me eagerly, trying to read my expression and then turned to Adeem. "She will not die by my hands or yours."

Both men faced each other. They were equally frightening in size and hostility. Ty had to be 6'4" and Adeem only an inch shorter. Ty had long brown hair with ice blue eyes while Adeem was bald. They were both built like body builders and wore blue jeans and white t-shirts. Ty had a petite nose and his chin was square. He was a looker and those ice blue eyes were enough to drive a woman nuts. Except me, I only wanted to kill him. *Cut his bloody heart out. I hated him!*

He glanced in my direction as if he read my mind and I covered my face avoiding his gaze. "I can feel your hate, little one. It is I who saved you," he stated, confidently.

I peeked back over the covers and noticed Adeem leaning into Ty, whispering. I strained to hear but only heard mumbling.

Adeem nodded his head. "Agreed, but it must be tonight."

Ty shook his head. "She is in no condition to drift tonight."

"She must or she will turn and it will be too late." Adeem's voice and anger rose in those black beady little eyes of his.

Ty grabbed the man by the shoulder shaking him. "By Al Kinide Clan, she will be ours."

Adeem seemed satisfied with Ty's last statement and left the room. Ty moved towards me, eyes gleaming with satisfaction.

I scooted up against the headboard. "Oh no, you don't, big boy, stay where you are," I squeaked.

He ignored me, strolling closer. He stopped right over me. "Don't what?" He grinned.

He actually had a great smile. He didn't look so menacing, and it only made him more handsome. Then the flashback of Siön Baptiste's hand in mine being ripped from me as he scooped me into his arms seared my memory. Rage and hatred inundated me and I felt something inside my body that had never been there before, power.

He cocked his head to one side, his long hair flowing over his shoulder and laughed. "You aren't going to make this easy, are you?"

My head cleared as I stared into his ice blue eyes. "Make what easier? What do you want with me?" I blurted out, face flushed with the hate boiling under my skin.

He sat beside me on the bed, his long legs draped over the side, leaning against the cherry headboard. He folded his hands in his lap, staring intently. "Well, were should I start." He sighed. "The vampires are trying to create a master race as you already know, I am sure. My clan, as well as several others, fear that the vampires will destroy us if you should aid them in their quest. My goal tonight is to infect you with lycanthrope to counter the vampire blood coursing through your veins. If it works, you will be connected to us. If it doesn't, you will die by either my clan or another--your choice."

He was brutally honest; I had to give him that. "I won't allow it." I smirked, as the blood and power rushed through me. His pulse beat temptingly in my ear causing me to wonder how it would feel in my mouth. His aura was as fresh as his eyes, washing over me like a cool drink of water. I could sense his power and he, unlike Adeem, had fire and ice beneath his aura.

He clenched my wrist. "We can do this the hard way or easy way." He paused. "I really don't want to do this to you, Samantha. I have no choice." He shrugged his shoulders and released me.

I shook my head. "You always have a choice. If you choose to do this, I will kill you and your entire clan. I promise you that much." I snickered, my laughter not of joy but sheer insanity as I contemplated the last few days.

"Well, are you going to relax and make this easy on both of us?" he asked.

"Do I have a choice?" I sneered, feeling a rush of power flow over my body, causing me to sway. "What was that?" I asked.

He smiled, those eyes flashing widely. "It's just a hint of my power, something I can offer you."

I felt a second wave this time, pushing me into the bed, stroking my body. A hot rush of wind brushed my skin. I shuddered at the coolness, wrapping my power within his. A grunt escaped my mouth as his power plummeted inside me. My body lifted in response as he sat perfectly still.

"I knew the moment I first saw you in New Orleans you were the one for me, but the damn vampire got to you first."

"That was you that night standing across the street. It was you." The reality of these two creatures fighting over who would own me was too much to handle. Just how long had they been watching me? Was Siön Baptiste in on the whole charade?

His eyes were suddenly dark globes as he bent down towards me. "This can be pleasurable or painful, it is your decision."

"You are all starting to sound like broke records to me. What do vampires and werewolves go to the same cheesy line class in monster school or what?"

He hovered over me as I stared helplessly in awe. He whispered again but my heart was beating too loudly for me to understand. My arms and legs wiggled in pleasure as a second wave of spine tingling energy hit me. Reaching out to stop him, my hand met his arm and the power shot inside me, electric surging between my legs. My hand was stuck to his skin as I thrashed in ecstasy. I felt my own power pushing against his. I tested the wave of heat, merging his rift with mine. Tugging on his power, I experimented with the extent of my strength. I thrust his energy back from me and he flew through the air, hitting the wall across from the bed. When my eyes cleared, I could see waves of light flowing through the room. Both of our powers merged again, searching the air for weakness. Sensing his anger as he stood, I laughed, facing him fearlessly. He was not going to touch me again.

I was thankful I had clothes on, as the sudden blush crept over me as the thought of him seeing me naked entered my mind. I tucked my t-shirt into my jeans. "I am a slave to no one," I hissed, catching sight of the door from my peripheral vision, backing slowly away from Ty.

He let out a hideous laugh, half-human, and half monster. "I will give you one more chance. Pleasure or pain?" Pausing, he tilted his head, waiting patiently for my reply. "What will it be?" he growled. He took a step towards me, and removed his shirt. His chest was smooth and tan. His muscles moved in places I could only sense. He was magnificent, a flawless male specimen. Turning around he placed his back to me, and chuckled low in his throat. "I will give you a head start, Samantha Houston," he rumbled.

I watched him as he removed his jeans, revealing a smooth tight ass that would make any woman flush. I stood motionless as his power pricked at my skin. I had this urge to run into his arms, to feel his naked body against mine, but I froze in time unable to move or breathe.

Only his voice woke me out of my trance. "You only have ten minutes. I cannot guarantee your safety once the sun has set." He shrugged his shoulders as he continued to keep his back to me.

I backed up until I hit the door. His body began to vibrate and hum. Skin and power began to pulsate through his aura. His skin bubbled, he fell to the ground screaming as he began to extend and contort. I took a step closer then stopped, as the horror unfolded before me. His bones and muscles popped and bent, stabbing the air around us. He howled as his legs bowed and unfolded. Claws formed where hands and feet had been. A thick gel seeped from his skin as he slithered across the floor. His head flew back and what once had been a handsome face was now a distorted bloody monster. I screamed as he howled. He turned to face me, one eye blue and the other a black slit, glowing with an inhuman animal shine. His jaw cracked, wiggling free from his skull, elongating into a huge monstrous snout. In place of teeth, there were now fangs, dripping with blood and slime. The smell made me gag and the power overwhelmed me, causing me to gasp for air.

He laughed and growled all in one breath as a demonic voice streamed from his once handsome face. "Run, Samantha... RUN!" he howled, falling on the floor, his body was now well over 8 feet tall. His eyes turned an amber color as his ears lengthened, pointing back against his head. Fur slowly pierced through his skin and the demonic voice screamed again. "RUN," he gurgled.

I stared in unbelief at the creature before me. Its full 8-foot frame hovered barely able to fit inside the room. The werewolf turned to look at me, sniffed the air with its unnatural snout. Lips peeled back, revealing a line of sharp needle like teeth. It growled, snarled baring teeth as it slowly stalked towards me. Every step crashed as the heavy beast moved. Its arms were longer than most mens' as it swung a table, smashing it across the room. The beast crouched, ready to attack and I ran, opening the door, never looking back. The door slammed behind me as I took off, down the darkened corridor. I ran into furniture, banged into the wall but still I ran. I heard another howl from behind me, the pain in chest tearing at me as my fear threatened to devour my senses. A light at the end of the corridor guided me. It was a small window. I was surprised how clearly I was thinking. The horror of what gave chase coursed through my veins, sending a power, my power, pulsating through me. I remembered the window seemed small enough to keep the monster behind me contained as I sprinted towards my target. I flew through the air as I ran with unearthly speed, diving, smashing through the panes. *Could I fly?* My question was answered when my stomach churned and I began to fall. I wasn't flying, I was falling. *How high was that window?* The earth rapidly came into view as I twisted my body, tumbling along my back, landing on my feet. *No human moves this fast. Was I really a vampire?*

I heard a cry from the window above me. "Get up, Sam," I whispered to myself.

I stood frozen, praying for my body to work. *Don't let this be the end, not now, don't let that monster kill me.* I got up, running as the unearthly sound above pushed me on.

"Run," a voice in my head screamed. I ran like never before, everything blurred but a small tunnel of light before me. I heard a boom behind me, only turning enough to see the beast soundly landing in the yard. I saw the werewolf in my mind sniff the air, its snout lifting to the sky. With a long howl it lowered its head cocking it to the side as if it sensed me and then ran after me. The tunnel before me shone brightly as if the sun lit my path. I could sense the cool night air and the nocturnal creatures fleeing from the monster hunting me. I tripped over a root, falling and hitting my head on a tree. My head settled into the grass while my ears rested on the ground.

A galloping noise vibrated through the grass. "Thump… Thump… Thump… Thump…" Faster and faster, it came towards me. The noise thumped as loud as my heart thundering in my ears. I knew it was the werewolf. I saw it sprint with inhuman speed, headed directly for me.

The thumping slowed as it saw its quarry lying in front of a tree. The werewolf slowly crept towards its meal. *Get up Sam and run or you're dog food.* I rose, wiping the blood from my eyes. It sniffed the air, inhaled the fresh blood, which allowed it to follow the scent of its prey.

I ran through a stream, the moonlight sparkled brightly on the water and rocks. A loud splash further down the stream followed mine as the monster continued its hunt. It was going to try to outrun me, cut me off. My power cleared my head and calmed my beating heart. I rounded a tree and ran back towards the beast, retracing my steps hoping to divert it off my scent. I jumped as the creature screamed nearer than before. A light ahead guided me as I ran full force hoping to find shelter. The light flashed closer as my speed increased. I leaped over a creek, over logs and under brush, moving like the wind.

I stopped before entering the clearing. It must not have beaten me to the field. I crouched low to the ground and quieted my breathing as I watched carefully for any signs of its presence. Another high-pitched scream came from behind, and I didn't wait around to find out how close. I bolted out into the open field. The moon illuminated a farm with a fence and horses grazing in a field. Following along side the fence, I ran for my life. A startled horse bolted, running beside me as if it sensed the werewolf in pursuit. My feet barely touched the ground as I cut past the horse, and sped down the path through the field. I flew over the fence in one clean move, landing without losing stride.

Siön Baptiste's blood pulsed through me, spurring my speed. I no longer feared the power within. I welcomed it with open arms, embraced my past and future. I was free; my soul soared above as I sprinted in the dark. I lost time, a vision of a man badly beaten, slumped in a room clouded my mind. He was chained, bloodied and beyond recognition. I felt him call out to me, pushed me to survive. *"Siön Baptiste!"* I screamed, hatred for the creature behind fueling my power.

I ran faster, turned down a narrow trail, and headed for the glow of an inviting home ahead. The fence, horse, trees and sky blurred. I could see an old man sitting down for supper. I sniffed the air, smelled the meat he now ate. My only thought was to survive to save Siön Baptiste.

Chapter 22

The farmhouse slowed my run as I crashed into the door. Screaming, I begged, "Let me in. Help me!" I turned, peering around the spacious field and yard, no creature to be found. I sensed he was coming closer. The door opened slowly and an older man smiled kindly at me. I watched the yard nervously, waiting for the werewolf to jump us both but he held back. *Why?*

"May I help you?" the old man whispered.

"I need shelter, something is chasing me."

He looked behind me, his face full of concern. "Come in quickly." He ushered me in, standing back against the wall, watching the yard. I quickly stepped into the house as he slammed the door shut and locked it, lowering a wooden beam across it. "Strange things happen in these woods at night. Why are you out here all alone?" he asked.

I hesitated. "I had a flat tire a few miles back."

He shrugged his shoulders. "I see." He walked ahead of me down a hallway. Animal heads hung from the wall the entire length of the dark hall. *He was a hunter so he had to have guns.*

He waved me to follow him and we both walked into a spacious kitchen. He sat down at an old pine table, gesturing for me to join him. "Here, have some dinner." The kitchen was decorated with solid pine cabinets. I was surprised at how modern it was for a farmhouse. It was both spacious and clean.

"I'm really not that hungry." I looked around the room for any sign of a weapon and quickly added, "but thank you."

"Well suit yourself young lady, but I've worked hard and I'm hungry." He smiled friendly enough, but the suspicion in his voice didn't go unnoticed.

"Do you hunt?" I asked.

"Yes, I hunt."

I fought back the growl of impatience. I needed a gun or weapon and we were running out of time. I fidgeted nervously and began to pace.

His eyebrows shot up. "Are you in some kind of trouble?"

I could feel the creature as it hunt us. I couldn't wait any longer. "Do you have a gun?" I blurted out not caring if he thought I was crazy.

"I'm a hunter. Of course, I have guns." He paused, looking at me. "Why do you need a gun? What is going on out there, young lady?"

His eyebrows drew together and he became very serious. "Did you lead them here?" he accused.

I didn't like the way he looked at me. "What?" I asked, but knew the answer.

He stood, threw his chair against the wall and cursed. He walked over to a large pantry tossed open the doors with a bang and entered. He came out carrying several guns. He threw them on the table. "Do you know how to handle a weapon?" He cursed under his breath. "I heard the screams and howls. I should have known." He walked back into the pantry. I stood, watching him as he returned with boxes of ammo and more weapons. "Dammit!" he shouted. "You should have kept running." He threw open the ammo and loaded his shotgun. He tossed me two guns. I caught them with ease, twirling them in circles.

"Good, you can fight. We might die tonight but we'll die fighting. Take as many down with you as possible." He laughed, pointing to the guns I now held. "They are damn nice guns. I had them made special since the wolves came to town. Folks laughed at me when I told them these things weren't your normal wolves. They were monsters, deadly creatures that stalked our community. The mayor thought it was rabid dogs." He spat, face red with anger. "Most left without a fight, I stayed" He sighed. "Thanks to my stubbornness they killed my wife and daughter and the law did nothing." He pulled the chair up, sitting quietly. He continued to load the weapons as he spoke. "Damn wolves killed my whole family, even my dog." He paused. "Why are they after you?"

I strolled over to the table and sat down. I felt no emotion, no pity, just hatred for the beast that stalked the farmhouse, moving slowly towards us as we spoke. I could sense the fear the beast had for the man. The old man looked at me and I at him as we both heard the monster scream. It was calling for back-up.

I positioned the guns on the table. "They want me dead because I am a vampire." I heard my voice but was shocked at the words. *I was a vampire, I knew it and felt the power and liked it.* I ran my tongue over my lengthened canines. They were razor sharp.

The man appeared stunned but pleased. "I don't know what you are, dear, but if it means you can kill the wolves then that is enough for me." He opened one of the boxes he brought from his closet and dragged out two leg straps. They held cartridges. "The guns I gave you are twin Modified Berettas converted to full auto with a drop-in unit. Each set of drop-in cartridges are filled with silver bullets." He smiled. "You can mow down a herd of cattle with those guns." His hand lifted, waved the guns his way. I slid them along the table and he took them both. He swiftly detached the cartridge and reloaded. "Quick, easy reload will help you. There are four cartridges in each leg strap. Strap them on over your jeans so you can access them quickly."

I watched the old man from across the table. He was weary and tired, but the fire behind his eyes told me he would help in this battle. I could feel more monsters coming towards us and knew we didn't have much time. I would take out as many as I could before I died. "I am sorry I got you involved, old man."

He shrugged his shoulders. "I've been waiting a long time for a little pay back. Now is as good a time as any." He paused, letting out a deep breath. "My name is Carl." He put out his hand.

I got up out of my chair and walked over to him, offering my hand. "You have a firm handshake, Carl, and my name is Samantha." We both smiled. He motioned to the leg straps and I placed them over my jeans. I secured one on my right leg and the other on my left. They felt odd at first but I reached down to grab a cartridge and it slipped out effortlessly. Easy reach, easy kill. He handed me the guns and I strapped them into the waist of my jeans.

He finished loading a shotgun and took my hands in his. "Let's kick some butt, Samantha." He smiled and the wrinkles on his face softened. He was a handsome older man in his sixties but took good care of himself. Tanned skin and a muscular build told me he worked hard on his farm. He would fight well against these monsters.

Something caught my eye over Carl's back. There was a bay window directly behind the man. I squeezed his hand gently, and reached for my gun. I slid my hands gradually over my guns while I watched the glow of eyes move in the darkness. They felt natural in my hands. Light and loaded, what more could a girl ask for. I drew them from my jeans holding them at my sides. The creature backed up and disappeared into the darkness.

Carl breathed in. "How big are they?"

I didn't answer honing my newfound powers in on the target. Then realized we were outnumbered. I whispered. "We need to get upstairs." As I reached for him, the glass shattered and the creature outside crashed and rolled into the kitchen.

Carl yipped and ran past the creature. "Holy cow." He screamed. "God help us!"

Glass flew over the floor and all around us. I shot before the werewolf could move and it fell back onto the floor. It was smaller than Ty and I knew it wouldn't be the last. Carl and I ran like the wind as I yanked him out of the kitchen. He motioned to a door and we sprinted into his living room, ascending steps that entered his second floor. The lights suddenly went off.

"Smart buggers aren't they?" I whispered.

The man spoke quietly eyes blinking. "I have never seen anyone move that fast."

Ignoring the old man, I peered into the dark hallway, searching for any sign of danger. My sight was perfect in the dark. "Do you have an attic?" I asked. We heard a crash in the living room and another werewolf entered the house.

"Up to the third floor," he said.

A howl came from below and I could sense the creature creep towards us. We reached the third floor entrance and Carl quickly opened it.

"Up here." He pushed me and shut the door behind us. I fumbled along the wall with guns drawn while he found a wood plank and shoved it into a slot across the door. I saw a second and third plank. Seizing them, I inserted them both in the remaining slots. We heard the creature coming up the steps. I felt the power within me beg to pour freely from my body. It flowed under the door and smacked into the creature, sending it plummeting down the stairs, screaming and clawing at the energy that hit it.

"What happened?" Carl turned toward me. "What did you do? I felt something warm flow through me."

"Don't worry about it, keep moving." We ascended the steps and entered the attic. He placed three planks across the door in the attic and bolted it shut. I searched for another opening and found a small window. Carl walked over to the corner of the attic and flipped a switch. He then moved to the far wall and opened a box. A dim light came to life in the middle of the room.

"For years, I prepared for this night. When they would once again come after me. I have a generator in the basement. We have light for six hours."

"We need to block the door. They will get through eventually." I remembered the beast tearing through a wall earlier and knew they would rip the door right off its hinges. There was a bed, two dressers, desk, metal cabinet and a refrigerator. I walked over to the cabinet and began to slide it across the floor.

The man stared at me mouth wide open. "That cabinet weighs 300-500 pounds."

"Help me Carl," I whispered. He got on one side and me on the other and we moved the cabinet against the door. I walked to the dresser pushing it towards the entrance.

He held his hand out to me. "Wait!" He opened the cabinet and removed two vests, ammo and a leather bag. "Now." We pushed the dresser into the cabinet.

I wasn't going to take a chance. Dragging the mattresses off the bed, I took the headboard, and placed it against the window. I moved the second dresser firmly against the headboard, shutting off the window. The old man lugged a toolbox from the corner of the room, removed the wooden planks off the bed frame, and took them over to the door. He slipped the plank between the cabinet and entrance hammering it to the wall. "Never can be too careful." He smiled.

He plopped down on the mattress, placed all his weapons, bag and two vests on the floor. "Here, put this on. If they manage to get in, it will protect your vital organs." He handed me the bag and the vest. I opened the bag and inside was a pair of leather pants, leather tank top and jacket. Carl turned while I stripped and put everything on. The leather pants were a little big on me, but the vest and jacket fit perfectly. I put on the bulletproof vest, which was snug over the leather tank top. I then strapped the leg straps to my calves for easy reach.

I sat down, leather creaking, beside him and sent my power out into the night. Searching with my energy for the werewolves. I could feel that there were eight of them hunting us. They were devising a plan of attack. These creatures were mean and smart, a bad combination. One creature pressed its power into mine, sending tremors down my body, forcing me to break the connection.

Carl snatched my arm as I trembled. "It will be okay, Samantha." He was trying to comfort me, but it wasn't fear that I felt but hatred.

I turned to the old man, guilt consuming me. What had I done? I'd endangered this man who had already been through so much. Carl reminded me of my stepfather, strong and kind.

"What happened to you, dear? There is something different about you." He picked up the other vest and put it on.

"I was kidnapped by these creatures. They want me to become one of them."

He looked surprised. "Why would they want you?"

"A couple of days ago I was introduced to a vampire whose father knew my mother. She died when I was born. Except he really wasn't this man's father but was using him to find me." I paused. "He claimed I had vampire blood in me and that I was part of a prophecy. Nicholi, the vampire who wanted me, was planning on creating a master vampire race that could live in the light." I glanced at the old man and his expression still held concern. "He wanted me to mate with his sons to bear him an army of vampires." I thought of the night with Siön Baptiste and my stomach churned. Heat and desire washed over me and I could still taste his blood.

I told the old man everything. I told him about the kidnapping and how they shot Siön Baptiste while we were in each other's arms.

When I finished my whole story, the man had tears in his eyes. "Bastards, they are all bastards." Tears ran down his face as he captured my hand, squeezing it tightly. "My dear, you've been through so much and you're so damn strong. You remind me of my daughter." He sighed, crying silently. "They tore my daughter to pieces. I could do nothing. They raped and killed my entire family." He faced me, shaking my shoulders gently. "Promise me if you survive tonight, you will kill them all. Promise me." He cursed quietly. "You have power, use it for good." He whispered, "Don't let them do this to another family."

I hugged him. "I promise. I promise you will not die tonight and I will use my power for good." I paused. "I will have my revenge and yours." I stood up, holding the Berettas in my hands. "They will all fucking die." All the emotions poured over me and I fell to the ground, guns in hands.

The old man asked, "Are you alright?"

It was the change. Siön Baptiste's blood mixed with mine, overtaking my humanity. How I knew, I wasn't sure but I knew. "Yes--stay back." I felt a desire overwhelm me. I wanted to kill. I needed to kill. Energy glided through my cells into my blood. Somehow, I knew the change was complete. My head snapped back as a flash of light and memories poured into my mind, Siön Baptiste's memories and all before him. It was like an awakening, my mother, my father, the history of vampires passed down from generation to generation in bits and pieces. I knew why I was here and what I had to do. Destroy the evil and unite the pure. I had a purpose and a clear memory from someone else entered me, changing me. I was still Samantha Houston but older, wiser, stronger. Whatever I was before drinking his blood was nothing compared to what I would become.

Chapter 23

I cried out in pain as my mind began to fold under the impressions left behind by Siön Baptiste. I fell into darkness.

I awoke as I floated through a large set of doors; my feet never hit the ground. Twelve men sat in chairs before me. One of those men I recognized as Nicholi. They all glared at me.

"You are the chosen one, Samantha." Their voices slapped my body. "You will free the human race from death and destruction." The voices spoke but their mouths did not move. "You will bear a master race of vampires." They echoed in my head, causing me to fall to my knees. Power flooded the room as they spoke. "The werewolves have grown strong, but there are others you should fear more." I felt a cold air wash over me and looked down at my naked body. "If you do not stop the Drackontz, all will be lost." I couldn't move, held by their power. "The Drackontz will come for you and destroy all those you love. They will destroy vampires and werewolves, making humans and monsters alike feed and serve them as animals. The world as you know it will cease to exist." All the vampires were dressed in red. The red caught my eye and I wondered if they tasted as good as they looked. I shook the thought from my head as I watched them.

I put my hands up shrugging. "Why me? How can I stop them? What are the Drackontz?"

"They are demons who created the vampires and werewolves. They have none of our weaknesses and all of our strengths. They have been sleeping for the last millennium waiting for you. They will awaken, Samantha, to destroy you. Your time is short. You must unite enemies and bear a son. A son will be born to destroy the Drackontz, saving the world. Vampires and werewolves will fight for you but you must unite them. If they do not battle together, all will perish. Only destroy those you must for the time is at hand when the world as you know it will cease to exist. The bottomless pit will open, bringing with it Drackontz to rule the world."

"What do you want?"

"Your mother sacrificed, so will you." All the men chanted in unison holding a cup as they walked towards me. "Drink of our blood, power and memories." They circled me, their power enhancing my desire for blood. I had no fear, only the need to drink. I reached for Nicholi's cup first. I drank readily and the blood seeped into me, spreading his strength through me. I drank from all twelve cups, all filled with warm blood. I fell to the ground as their memories engaged my mind.

The vampires stood in the same room, surrounding my mother. I could smell her, taste her, and feel her. They forced her to drink their blood, forced themselves upon her.

Like a dark shadow, Alastair moved, stealing my mother. He flew with inhuman speed, anger and hatred seethed across his distorted face. He blamed her, not the men who took her. He hated her and me. He was not my father, but the twelve vampires who now beseeched me to help them through my dream.

I fell to the ground, shaking as the nightmare unfolded. "NO!" I screamed. "NO!"

"We had to sacrifice one for the multitude. As will you." The voices echoed.

My mother had marvelous long flowing black hair. I had her eyes, a radiant amethyst. I felt her love flood over me as she came towards me. The men parted as she approached.

She held out her hand, touching my face. "My child, I willingly gave my soul for you. The world needs you to save them. It was a sacrifice I had to make." I held her hand, crying as calm washed over me. I felt power engulf me as I fell to the ground. The world was spinning, growing dark. I was safe in my mother's arms.

Chapter 24

Carl was shaking me as I opened my eyes. We both had been crying and tears ran down our faces. I could still smell my mother's scent. "Sam, it's okay." Carl's voice soothed me.

A banging sound on the second floor cleared my mind. Carl stood, taking my hands, yanking me off the floor. "They are coming."

An evil presence was all around us and I couldn't help but feel my own power, pulsing within, aching to explode in a fury of anger. I readied my guns as Carl grabbed the black bag and shotguns. He shoved ammo into his vest as he pumped his shotgun, aiming it at the door. We heard the door at the bottom of the steps blast open. The dresser and door shook as the werewolves pounded at the opening in front of us. I closed my eyes, steadying my shaking hands. *You can do this, Samantha.* I told myself.

"It's not going to hold," Carl yelled. "If you get out of here, I have a car in the barn and the keys are in the ignition," he whispered.

Opening my eyes, I concentrated on sending my power through the wall and door, searching. "There are four werewolves on the second floor," I whispered, pushing my energy to its limits sending it further. "There are four more outside, circling the house." The banging grew louder. "I can't feel any near the barn." The walls shook violently as I narrowed my eyes looking beyond the room. "The roof is clear. If we could get on the roof, we can get to the barn."

"Darling, its three stories up, how do you suppose we get down-- jump?" He looked at me, eyes wide. "Damn girl, this old man won't make it."

I smiled. "We'll make it." As I turned toward the window, I felt the surge of power fill the room. "Ty," I whispered. The monsters beat at the door. It rattled, splintering against the pressure. I raised my guns. "He's here, get behind me," I yelled over the inhuman screams.

He shook his head. "Like hell, girl. I'm fine."

I shoved him behind me, backing up towards the window. I threw the dresser and bedpost across the floor with one smooth motion. "Get out on the roof," I yelled.

"No way will I leave you."

As he spoke, the dresser and cabinet burst open. Two werewolves entered the attic, low to the ground, ready to attack. I shot the first creature giving it no time to react, hitting it in the head. The second was shot in the chest but still standing. The smallest of the monsters howled as I aimed my guns at its heart and filled him with bullets. A third werewolf entered, rushing us. Carl's shotgun in unison with my guns repeatedly hit the creature. It fell as its head exploded all over the room. I broke the window with my hand and slid out. Turning back I seized Carl, pulling him head first through the window. As he came through the opening, he lost his footing.

He screamed, "Get me out, it has my leg." A werewolf snatched his ankle ripping the skin from his flesh. He yelled as I shot the werewolf directly in the face. Grimacing as I helped him lean against the siding, he grabbed my arm. "Thank you."

"Thank me later," I said. Aiming my guns back into the room, I fired as Ty attacked. He was larger and stronger than the other three werewolves and made it past my shots, latching on to my arm, tearing away the sleeve of my jacket, leaving a long painful scratch down my arm. Its claw hit my face, knocking my head against the side of the house. I almost fell off the roof as I stumbled back, firing at the creature. I waited for it to crash through the wall, but the werewolf was gone. There was no sign of Ty anywhere.

"He scratched me. The son of a bitch scratched me" Carl cried out.

I put my hand over his mouth. "Shhhhh. It got me, too." I pointed to the ground. I knew they were circling the house waiting for us to descend. Carl was badly wounded and I was banged up pretty bad, but we had no time to waste. Carl could barely move as we carefully maneuvered around the roof searching for a way to the barn. I heard a scream as a werewolf broke through the second story window. It pulled itself onto the third story roof just above us.

"It's coming for us." It moved like lighting in a blur of fangs and fur. I crouched, shooting several times, hitting the creature in the leg and chest. Screeching, it fell from the roof, hitting the ground with a thump. Prodding Carl to move, we rounded the side of the house. There was a power line leading directly from the house to the barn. *Hell YEAH!* If we could manage to slide down the line and make it to the barn, we might have a chance. Carl limped, whimpering in pain. I pointed to the line. "We can make it, old man." I took off my vest and tossed it over the line. "Can you hold on?"

"Girl, I might be hurt but I'm not dead." He took his vest off. "You first."

I held onto the vest as it glided over the line scooting towards the barn. I slid safely onto the barn roof turning to see Carl still on the house roof.

"Come on, old man," I whispered to myself. "Come on!"

He was standing completely still, gun in hand. He had turned away from me, facing the corner of the house. I could see an unnatural shadow stalking across the roof toward him from the opposite side. In front, a second werewolf pursued him. They were cornering him in and he couldn't see them hunting him from below and behind.

The werewolf in front of him slowed its pace, standing up on its hind legs. He held the shotgun up shooting the massive target before him, but as he shot, the second werewolf attacked.

"CARL!!" I screamed, startling him. He shot but it missed and both werewolves quickly descended upon him. I took aim at the second werewolf, shooting it squarely in the back. It hesitated but continued to attack. I shot again as Carl slipped in the blood of his injury, falling, sliding off the roof. He landed on the second floor roof, just as a third werewolf appeared around the corner, crawling toward him. I fired again, this time missing. Carl had dropped his weapon and the monster took advantage, lunging and latching onto Carl's throat. It tore into the flesh, severing his neck.

The beast held on as Carl looked over at me. "Run." His voice was choking on his own blood as he raised his hand towards me. "Run!" he screamed.

The werewolf ripped through his neck and Carl's body fell to the ground. Hot tears ran down my face. I aimed my guns at the beast, shot, blowing its head and Carl's to the ground. The two werewolves on the third floor jumped down, stalking across the moonlit yard, heading to the barn. Only two left. I tried to shoot, but the guns were empty. They stalked closer as I ducked down and with inhuman speed replaced the empty cartridge with full ammo. Snapping the ammo in with a click, I got eight shots off shooting the two werewolves both in the chest. They fell, crying out in pain. I fired again until their screams quieted. I remembered Carl's words. *The keys were in the car in the barn.*

Everything had taken place so quickly and now I was alone. Despair crept into my mind as I perched on the edge of the barn roof overseeing the bloody landscape below. Dead or dying werewolves surrounded Carl's body. The fog swirled lazily across the trees, billowing down to the yard, covering them in a blanket of gloomy mist. Rolling my shoulders, trying to release the tension and fear, I huddled against myself, wrapping my arms tightly around my legs. I couldn't believe what just happened. I felt a mind-numbing chill run up and down my spine. My body was trembling uncontrollably, caused by a mix of terror and adrenaline. Concentrating on survival was the only way to dispel the pending feeling of doom that now inundated my senses. The only hope of escape was inside the barn and somehow I had to build up the nerve to make my next move. I scanned the area one last time and reluctantly stood. Taking a deep breath, I leaped into the fog, floating effortlessly through the cool night air. The mist chilled my skin while the long leather jacket I wore flared out around me. Flipping in mid-air, I landed safely with a small thud. Nostrils flared as the stench of the dying creatures mixed with freshly cut grass. The smell of blood and danger mingled in the cool evening breeze causing my stomach to churn with hunger. I shook my head, trying to clear my thoughts and forget the flashbacks of the attack. Now what lay before me was silence, filled only with the pounding of my heart.

Squatted low to the ground, I peered cautiously into the night. The moon illuminated the gloomy world, causing silver light to dance over everything in its path. Aiming my guns into the darkness, I propelled my power searching for what my eyes could not see. My energy flowed effortlessly, but could only find dead or dying creatures. Dawn was approaching and the moon was descending rapidly. I might actually survive this hellish night.

A bolt of fear jolted through me as a long sharp cry pierced the silence. My power probed the creature nearest me. I stiffened, waiting for a possible attack. Sending my energy deep inside the creature, it turned to meet my gaze, red eyes glowing angrily as he sniffed the air, feeling my presence. The werewolf let out a blood-curdling scream, trying to escape my grasp.

"Die," I whispered, wrapping my power around its beating heart, squeezing with the unseen force. I watched from afar, as my energy captured its heart, exploding it into a million pieces. The monster's deafening screams and claws slashed at me, breaking my trance even as I felt its life slip away. The smell of rotting inhuman flesh and muffled whimpers was the only evidence left of the fight that had occurred moments before. I stood, my emotions buried somewhere deep within. The numbness moved across my whole body as the rush of power tingled over every muscle and cell. Smirking wickedly over my triumph and the fact I was still alive and the sun was about to rise, I turned to face the barn doors, shoving them open. I cringed as they swung inward, creaking and banging into the wall.

"Shoot!" I cursed, knowing that the noise probably woke the dead.

As I entered, a wave of stagnant, warm air floated over my face, stealing my breath away. The moon's light cast ominous shadows around the barn, but I did not need the light to see my intended target. "God bless you, old man." I whispered, thankful the car was parked exactly where he'd said it would be. Staring into the dimly lit building, I waited patiently for any sign of the creatures that hunted me. *Nothing!*

I bolted for the car, wrenching on the door handle. *Locked!*

My hands were shaking as I raced to the passenger side. It was locked also. *Just my bloody luck.* "Who leaves their car keys in the car when it's locked?" I grumbled to myself, getting angrier by the minute. From what I could see, the car looked to be in good condition and the keys were exactly as the old man said, in the ignition. I screamed internally as I kicked the door of the car.

I was going to get messy. That thought made me chuckle softly as I looked down at the cuts and bruises inflicted by the werewolves. I quickly removed my leather jacket while moving back to the driver side, wrapping my arm and gun in its velvety protection. I struck the weapon against the glass shattering the window, sending shards of glass onto the front seat and barn floor.

Tossing the gun and jacket into the car, I bent down to unlock the door. That was when the hair on my neck bristled standing on end. Clenching my fists, I swerved around to meet the beast, sensing the evil clawing at my mind. The creature's power engulfed me, sending fear pulsing through my veins. Waving my hands, I frantically tried shoving the wicked energy away, to no avail. I backed slowly up against the car and reached in grabbing my gun, never taking my eyes off its amber demonic stare. Gun in hand, I moved away from the car as the beast stalked closer.

Losing my footing, I stumbled back as the monster took another step forward, mirroring my every move. The werewolf was hideous, eyes glowing red with demonic power and hate. Its body elongated, standing on hind legs that had once been human. Blood dripped from its massive fangs pooling in the hay at its feet. Its claws had chunks of skin and flesh clinging to its long razor-sharp nails, some of the flesh, my own. The smell of death forced me to retreat until I was cornered between the beast and the vehicle. I was trapped, nowhere to go, frozen in horror.

Move, Samantha! MOVE! My mind screamed in terror as I contemplated my options. The thumping of my heart roared in my ears, drowning out the growls of the beast before me. As I inhaled the warm musty air, pain shot through my lungs. I slowed my heartbeat, attempting to catch my breath while the adrenaline raged unchecked inside my body. The creature effectively blocked the barn doors with his enormous frame. *Samantha, stay in control.*

"Ty, you don't have to do this," I pleaded, hoping it could understand what I was saying. "You have a choice."

The creature only watched, oblivious to my pleas. In a whirl of inhuman speed, I darted past the car, heading for my only escape, a ladder leading to the second floor of the barn. The ladder seemed to be moving away from me, rather than closer, as I sprinted towards it. If I could get to the second floor, I would have a clean shot at the beast. Turning, I sent a couple rounds in his direction. It avoided the bullets with ease. Reaching the first step, I leaped up, grasping the rung, holding on for dear life. Swinging myself into action, I started to climb.

The monster crashed through the barn following its prey. Crouching directly below my escape route, the werewolf lunged into the air. It made it up two steps when it reached for my leg. A warm power tore through me as its claws began to shred my flesh. I screamed as bones snapped, tearing tendons and muscles beneath the onslaught of its fury. My leg dangled as it continued to rip into my soft tissue, exposing crushed bones beneath. It jerked me downward and as it did, I dropped my gun, screaming from the pain. Blinding white light and dizziness overwhelmed me as I fell back landing on the ground with a thud. Slowly pulling my body up I tried to crawl away from the monster. I could only move from the waist up. The rest of my body was immobile with throbbing pain. My arms steadied my weight as I slid across the floor. Straw stuck to my wound, causing me to cry out in agony.

The werewolf jumped, landing with a loud thud. For the longest time it remained motionless in front of me, watching my painful progress. I screamed as it put its lengthened claws around my neck, lifting me into the air. I dangled helplessly as it held me inches from its distorted face. Excruciating pain shot through my body as it shook me mercilessly.

It was going to snap me in two.

The creature's lips curled back, baring its needle sharp fangs. The blood on its breath made me gag while my eyes blinked in disbelief at the repulsive monster. It leaned over my neck, taking me into its mouth. I felt warm liquid flood down my neck and chest as it crushed and shredded my muscles, growling with pleasure. With every beat of my heart, the warmth spread over my body.

My sight blurred as I fumbled for my second gun. My fingers shook as I aimed the weapon at the demon's deformed head. My body shivered uncontrollably as I could feel my life slip slowly away.

I managed to gargle what would be my last word, "DIE!"

I fired the gun over and over until it clicked empty. It released me as the werewolf fell, while my torn limp body slammed to the floor. I had to get to the car. With every ounce of strength, I dragged my body towards the vehicle. The smell of my own blood blending with the straw made me retch with nausea.

The memories of the last few days crashed over me as I realized the end was near. I was dying, alone and cold. I'd never feared death but dying by the hands of this monster just didn't feel right. Little did I know that the story of my life was just beginning.

My eyes hazed over, bringing on the welcoming darkness. Soon my cries of pain diminished to shallow whimpers as the smell of lilacs filled my nostrils. *Lilacs? I don't remember....*

Chapter 25

No more dreams. No more pain. I had an overwhelming desire to be held in my mother's arms. I walked quietly through the garden were I had first met Sevastian. The lilacs fell around me, as an overwhelming peace flooded my soul. My mother appeared through the mist and headed straight for me, arms outstretched. The sky was filled with dark rolling clouds rushed fall in with the alluring cool breeze. She wrapped me in her warm arms and held me tightly. She pulled me away, looking into my eyes and a familiar masculine scent flooded my senses. It was no longer my mother who held me but Sevastian. His long hair blew in the wind, caressing my face.

His eyes filled with unshed tears as he caressed my arms. "Show me where you are, Samantha? Let me into your mind," he whispered.

A warm glow appeared to spark in his eyes as he leaned in to kiss me. His lips pressed against mine, and his heat flooded my body. His tongue parted my lips while his hands held me against him. I shuddered under the taste of his tongue moving softly in my mouth.

He pushed me away, moved his hands to my face. He steadied me with his legs. "Open your mind." He held me while his magic curled through me. It was as if his hand was sliding in and out of my body, squeezing and touching the places between my legs. I tightened as I felt a release of my own energy and we held each other, melding our powers as one. It felt so good and yet it scared me enough to push him backwards. His eyes swirled with desire as my legs dropped out from under me.

I willingly opened my mind to his thoughts. He knelt beside me, taking my face in his hands. "Hold on, we are on our way."

Chapter 26

I wasn't sure if I was in a dream or awake. Faces invaded my dreams and I only recognized some of the people or monsters that knelt by my bed. I drifted in and out, from dream to dream, nightmare to pleasure. *Was I dead?*

I woke slowly, sheltered against a warm body. I tried to roll over away from the body and found myself held by someone with strong arms. I was pinned beneath a naked torso. I had no idea who was curled against me but he was definitely naked and very male. My eyes opened, adjusting slowly to the darkness that surrounded me. I tried to turn my head to look at who held onto me so tightly. I was, in fact, trapped in his arms. The arm around my waist was long and muscular. I could feel his energy curving over and in my body. I let my own energy seep into the room and through his power and quickly drew back. I could tell instantly it was Ty. I tried to shove him away only to be pulled tighter against his body. I felt no pain from the wounds he had given me but fear gripped me. Memories of the monster's attack fueled my rage and power. I cried out and as I opened my mouth, his covered mine, his tongue invaded my body. All sense of time ceased to exist, just his body and mouth over mine was all that mattered. He tasted of power and strength. My mind blurred as an awakening of sensations overwhelmed me. I could feel my arms reach for him as my tongue probed deeper. I was no longer just warm but on fire as my stomach clenched with each stroke of his tongue against mine. I tugged him closer as a tremor shook me.

I hated this man but he ignited a flame of desire for his touch, begging to let loose the monster within. He released his hold. He slid his mouth down my neck and over my breast, suckling it softly. The feel of his tongue on my nipple tugging and pulling gently was too much for me. I cried out, squirming under his tantalizing caresses. He swallowed my nipple, rolled it between his lips. Moving my hands to his head, I ran my fingers through his silky hair. He moaned softly as his lips left a trail of fire that lead to my stomach. His tongue circled in a soft, wet, sensual motion. Lifting his body, he kneeled beside me, tasting my velvety skin, rubbing his hands over my aching breast.

"You taste so good." Ty's voice was low and husky. "I want you, Samantha," he whispered. "I need you. I want to taste every part of your body." His skin was hot and every part of my body he touched ignited uncontrollable shaking. His words melted my very core, moved me against him.

He slid his hands to the insides of my thighs, forced my legs apart. He moved his palms to my hips, lifting me to his face. He pleasured me in long smooth motions. I gasped at the response of my body as I ground myself into his eager tongue. The magic held me, mesmerized me. I had no power to control my own actions. I was caught in his web of power. My heart thundered in my chest and his heartbeat matched mine. I wanted to feel his warm strong blood slide down my throat, taste his power. I tried to talk and a breathless cry escaped my mouth but no words. I was powerless while his strokes caused my body to break in pleasure. His tongue explored me repeatedly, pushed inside of me, licked every inch of my being. He took a hand, moved it inside my thigh. His finger entered me in thrust after thrust, causing such bliss, triggering every sexual nerve to explode in orgasmic response. Reaching for him, I grasped his arms, holding on as the pleasure rode me. Waves of satisfaction pulsated through me as orgasm after orgasm wracked my body. The sensations were so great my eyes dimmed causing me to fall into a blissful dark sleep.

I woke this time to Ty kissing my neck. I moved away from him and he followed my movement. Every twist and turn I made he countered with his long lean body pressed against mine. I felt cold air as he released his hold, sensing my wariness. I wanted to cling to his warmth, but refused, rolling over to keep one eye on the predator. He lay staring at my body, his head propped up on his hand with ice blue eyes revealing his desire. His hair fell softly over his shoulder and I couldn't peel my eyes from his muscular naked body next to mine. I blushed and he laughed. His laughter energized me down low. He was so handsome but he was a monster.

He almost killed me. Who knows maybe I was dead and this was hell.

He smiled. "I am a monster, Samantha. I warned you. Pain or pleasure and you chose pain." He chuckled and this time it made me angry.

My body had a mind of its own as it responded to his voice. It shook with need as I tried to control my actions.

"How could you kill that man? He was innocent." Tears ran down my face. "I will kill you." Clenching my fists, I hit the bed. What I really wanted to do was punch him in the face.

He frowned. "I forbid them to kill him. I only wanted you. Those who went against my orders are being punished." He mumbled under his breath, "I don't ever want an innocent murdered." Anger flashed across his face. "I did not want this, Samantha." He sighed.

I sat up and slapped him across the face. I stood angrily, yanking the sheets with me. It was then that I realized we were back in the same room where he'd changed into his beast in front of me. "I hate you, you son of a bitch. You killed that man and his family," I screamed, angry with myself for letting this beast get near me.

He stood, strutting casually towards me. His tanned skin shimmered in the dark and even then, I noticed he was well endowed. I backed away from him as his hips drew my gaze back to the lower half of his body. I was mesmerized at his size. He smiled, catching my reaction. I timidly licked my lips, not realizing I was staring at his mouth. It was so soft and his tongue felt great inside of me. I wanted him all inside of me yet I hated him more than life. I fell to the ground as my legs tightened, causing me to gasp.

"Stay away," I whispered.

He continued forward and knelt beside me. He ran his hands down my bare arms leaving a trail of burning nerves in his wake. I trembled as he pulled me to him. "Will you ever forgive me? I wanted this to go so differently but they got to you first." He shuddered as he held me. "I wanted to woo you, not ravage and hurt you."

"You son of a b….." I punched him in the stomach, but he still held me tightly. "You killed a man, you kidnapped me and attacked me. You expect me to ever forgive you?"

He held me closely, our skin melting as the heat rose between us. "No, I don't. I only pray that one day you will be able to look at me without hatred in your eyes. I never wanted this, Samantha. It was either turn you or terminate your life. I couldn't let your death be on my hands." He released me and I suddenly felt cold and alone. "We are connected now, Samantha. We need each other. You will die without my touch."

The chill that came over my body told me it was true. "We must be mated for your survival and mine." He held his hand out to me. "You can survive for a while, but without my touch, we will both die. We must drift soon or we shall both perish. We are destined to be pack mates." He towered above me, hand held out and I saw pain in his eyes. He regretted what he had done or just regretted the fact I hated him for doing it to me.

I sent my power over his body and his head flew back as his shaft became hard with pleasure. His hand dropped to his side, clenched in a fist as I explored him. I wanted to know the truth. I could feel myself inside him. He was sweating and the sound of his pulse beat deliciously in my ear as I caressed him. My energy floated repeatedly over him. I crawled inside his head. I stood next to him, reaching out to him. His mind was strong. He was a courageous warrior, saving more lives than taking. He had not wanted to take me, but the threat on my life had pushed him.

He begged, whispering inside my head, "don't."

I probed deeper, putting my arms around him, drawing him close. Feelings of lust and desire inundated me and I knew from his mind and body he wanted me. The truth hit me and I stumbled back from him, looking at his eyes in horror.

"How can you love me?" I could barely speak, my breath coming in gasps. "Stay away!" I screamed, my power forced through the room, knocking over the table by the bed. The wind subsided and my breathing calmed as I watched him suspiciously.

He turned his back to me and took two steps toward the bed, holding onto the bedpost to steady himself. "I have never been touched that way. What did you do?" His voice was low and raspy.

All of this felt so natural, wielding a power I'd only just received. The elders had given me the knowledge of thousands of years of vampire history and power by drinking their blood. I smiled, giving into it, letting it wash over my mind and take over my whole being. I couldn't explain what had happened, I just knew I was different now, complete.

I read his mind and thoughts and I wondered how this monster could be so civilized? He had nearly killed me and yet he cared so deeply for human life. He had fought off fellow werewolves for hours trying to preserve my life. Killing his own kind and trying to save the old man. I saw his thoughts and read his mind. Why had I not sensed this before? My hatred for him overwhelmed any sense of reality. Siön Baptiste was actually alive because of him. He'd battled the others for his freedom, Adeem's clan refusing to release him. I drove into his mind again and he held onto the bedpost with both hands, trying to keep from falling. I drove deeper than before, trying to find an answer.

Adeem's clan was strong and their numbers were massive. They held Ty's sister captive, threatening, killing pack members, and forcing Ty to do their will. Ty was strong but could not stand against Adeem and his kind. They outnumbered him. I pushed further. Adeem had killed Ty's mother and father, and turned him at age seven. Ty hated the man, waiting patiently for revenge. Ty fell to the ground as I drove myself further into his mind. I found my answer and he collapsed to the floor.

I looked over at the man buckled in a heap on the ground. He did not intend to create a master race of werewolves. He never planned to use me like the vampires. He wanted to save me from the vampires, and only when Adeem interfered did he promise to turn me. I fell into a heap, my head hitting the floor. I felt very tired, but relieved that the man before me wasn't the monster I had thought he was.

He crawled over to me, collapsing beside me. "Forgive me."

"Forgiven, but get me the hell out of here. You help me get Siön Baptiste out of here, too," I answered calmly.

"You must rest first. Gain your strength." He stood, recovered from my invasion of his mind, swept me into his arms and placed me carefully in the bed. The sun was coming up as he crawled in beside me. His body spooned mine as he moved closer. "You must heal from the wounds completely. You have my blood coursing through your body and still haven't reached your full potential." He laughed. "You are going to be a force to reckon with, Samantha Houston." His voice trailed off as his heat permeated the room, forcing me into a deep comfortable sleep.

Chapter 27

I was hungry when I woke. A hunger I had never felt before. I sensed the sun slipping away and night draw nearer. From the elders memories I knew my power would be at its strongest in only a few short hours.

Ty curled his body around me. His heart clamored temptingly in my ear. Moving to his neck, I sniffed his skin. His blood was warm and strong and I could almost taste it in my mouth. I licked my lips as the pulse beckoned, drawing me closer. Just two days ago, the thought of blood would have sickened me. Now an overwhelming urge beckoned me to partake.

"I can feel your hunger," he whispered. "You may feed on me."

The words sent a chill through my body as I moved closer. I couldn't control myself, something snapped. I wanted the sweet taste of his blood and energy. Licking his neck, I sent my power surging through him. He arched his back as I entered his mind, touching him, sending pleasure through us both. My hand moved to his groin, feeling him hard and long in my hands. I bit into his flesh, broke the skin and drank. Blood seeped into my mouth as our minds rolled in the power. My own magic touched his body with energy, he thrust his hips into the air in response. Pushing his hard shaft into my hand repeatedly, I swallowed his power. He tightened under my touch and with a burst--he swayed as the orgasm moved his body. I had the ability to control his pleasure as I drank from him, feeding my own hunger. His blood tasted metallic and sweet, filling me with power as I pressed my hips against him. I released his neck, falling back in an explosion of ecstasy. His breathing was ragged, as he lay covered in his own semen. With our powers entwined we could pleasure each other. It was like a drug as we both shuddered from the after effects.

What did I do to myself? What had I become? I felt shame and fear rush through me at the power I now wielded wantonly. I read his desire, his thoughts, easily as he wanted me to take more blood from him but I knew it would be too much blood loss. I felt his longing to be inside me. The thought made me shiver as I moved away from him. I closed my eyes, slowed my rapid heartbeat and pushed my power within, forcing myself to sleep and heal.

I woke as the sun's last rays faded behind the trees and the night sky took over. How long had I been here? I rolled over, and tossed my hands where Ty had been earlier, he was gone. My hand reached further across the now empty bed, seeking his body but it was nowhere to be found. The room was empty, and I felt empty with the lack of his presence. I sat up, pushed my legs over the side of the bed. A flashback of the creature tearing my skin caused me to fall back, crying out in pain. The terror of the beast crashed all around me and I stood shaking in a cold sweat. *How did I survive those wounds?* I lifted my leg, no wound, nothing. I was healed. I felt great other than a splitting headache and some chills. I wanted to be close to Ty. I sent my power searching for the relief of having him near me. He was nowhere to be found.

I walked to the velvet chair by the bed. It had been moved in front of the bed and in the chair lay clothes and the two Berettas. Folded neatly in the chair was a pair of black jeans and a black t-shirt along with my boots and leg straps. One leather strap had been torn but the ammo sat beside the torn leather. I dressed hastily, watching the door, waiting for someone to come in. Tying my boots, I laced the leather straps securely to my legs. I tied the broken strap to the belt loop in my jeans. I could still use the ammo.

I caught a glimpse of myself in the mirror over the dresser. My hair was dangling in curls around my face but the cuts and bruises were gone. My neck showed no visible signs of the attack. The only remnant that remained was a slight aching beneath the surface of my unmarred skin. I ripped a leather strap from the broken leg harness and pulled my long hair back to the nape of my neck. I fixed it securely in a ponytail, falling well below the middle of my back. At least it would be out of my way.

The door opened and I swung around, nearly shooting Ty in the head. He held his hands up. "Whoa, I give up." He flashed a wickedly handsome smile as he strutted to me.

He had jeans and a t-shirt on and his hips swayed seductively, pulling my mind back to what had occurred between us earlier. I could feel the heat wash over me as I looked from his body to the darkened sky through the window. I felt comfort in his presence and the pain diminished immediately. He stopped, stared at me, his gaze swept from my face to my toes. His body tightened and hardened, giving his thoughts and desires away. I had to figure out a way to stop peering into his mind because when I saw his thoughts, my body reacted almost embarrassingly.

A hand on my arm brought me back to reality. Ty was standing in front of me looking down, his face worried. A tingling vibration ran through his fingers, sliding across my skin. I pulled back at the sensation of his power, as it crawled over me. His hair was wet and fell down around his face. I moved my hand up and wiped the strands from his eyes. His eyes widened as my touch brought a gasp from his mouth. His lips were full and sensuous. I moved my gaze to his neck where I had fed from him earlier and the bite mark had already begun to heal. His neck was a bulging mass of muscles and the t-shirt he wore emphasized his flawless chest. He was utterly masculine in every breath he took and every move he made.

He broke the silence first. "They are coming for you?" It was a question.

In the distance, I could feel Sevastian. "Yes, they are."

He smiled and when his lips parted, I couldn't help but watch his tongue as he spoke--that soft, flexible muscle that pleasured me. I took a sharp breath in while he talked.

"Your friend is alive. You will find him in the basement. The keys are on the dresser."

He paused, ran his knuckles down my face, leaving a trail of heat in its wake. He moved his finger in circles over my lips. His eyes were dark with desire as he moved his hand down to my chin, pulling my lips to his. He stopped only an inch away while his free arm pressed my hips into his erect manhood. "I will meet up with you again, Samantha Houston. And when I come for you, be ready for me. We will drift or we will both die."

I didn't have time to say anything and his mouth covered mine, kissing me softly. Ty's power crashed over me, the attraction between us burned out of control, like a fire streaking rapidly through the forest. I could taste him--smell the masculinity of his skin. My mind told me to pull away and end this now before something bad happened, but my body pushed into his long lean frame. He held me, kissing me softly and then loosened his hold, staring down at me full of longing.

I knew what drifting meant. We had to join our bodies and minds. I peered into his thoughts and knew this would bind us together for eternity. Before I had a chance to argue, he turned and walked from the room. He was gone and with him the power that made my heart beat, my body ache, and my skin crawl. I wanted him as badly as he wanted me. I needed his touch so much I could still feel his presence. It was his blood, the lycanthrope infection, coursing through me that caused our connection. Equally as strong was my desire for Siön Baptiste and I knew deep down neither man would relinquish their hold on me anytime soon. I knew one of them perished, it would be the end of me, but how could I give up so much in such a short time?

I had to research and find out how to rid myself of this dilemma. I could feel both monsters within fighting for supremacy over my mind and body. I was at war with myself in every way.

The keys were on the dresser. I put them in the pocket of my jeans and shoved the two Berettas into the waistband. I was getting the hell out of here and Siön Baptiste was coming with me.

Chapter 28

I tiptoed to the door, leaned my head against the hard wood gathering my thoughts. *Samantha, you can do this.* After facing the werewolves last night, I knew I could face them again. A war had started and my war was with anyone who got in the way of me escaping. I would take no prisoners. With my left hand, I grabbed the door handle and my right hand held a Beretta. I had been down this hall last night. Now I sensed my freedom and it steered me cautiously forward despite my fear.

I didn't bang into furniture, not tonight, I could see better in the dark than I could last night. I could sense the floor, walls and furniture as if I was one with everything. I jumped as shots rang through the air. The shots came from outside the house and seemed to move in my direction. Stopping, I flattened against the wall. An evil power floated down the hallway from the dark. A massive shadow moved menacingly along the wall. Inhuman glowing eyes peered through the darkness, pinning me with fear where I stood. I could sense the wickedness in the beast. A werewolf larger than Ty began sprinting towards me. It tossed furniture, sending fragments crashing around as its large frame barely fit in the corridor. I crouched low to the ground, facing it head on. I snatched the second Beretta with my left hand and aimed both weapons at the beast coming at me. A rain of fire fell upon the creature and it disintegrated before I got a shot off. Standing behind the now screaming burning flesh was Trevor. He looked like an angel as he held the flame-thrower, eyes glowing angrily.

I tried to run to him but the fear of the creature still burning in front of me kept me frozen in place.

It wasn't until his voice penetrated the crackling of flesh that I snapped out of my trance. "Samantha? Sam, come home." Before he could finish, I was sprinting full speed, wrapping my arms and legs around him.

He pried my hands from his neck, placing me next to him. "God, Sam, I thought you were dead." He hugged me again, stealing my breath away as he crushed me to his chest.

I held the guns looking suspiciously around the corner as another man stepped out from the shadows. I aimed the gun at him as Trevor held me in his arms. Still aiming the gun at the man, I released my hold on

Trevor as he backed up, letting me fall to the ground, facing the man.

Amusement flashed across the man's face and then laughter. "Has it been that long, Samantha, that you do not recognize me?" The voice was familiar but the shadows and light hid his face from mine. I sent my power rushing towards him, searching for his identity. Both Trevor and the man stepped back as the power flooded the tight space, making it hard to breathe.

"Crap, Sam, what was that?" Trevor gasped, his breathing rapid.

"Samantha, we must go, no time for a happy reunion." He walked towards me, moonlight from the hole in the house hitting his face.

"Sevastian," I whispered. Tears were running down my face as I fell to the ground, withdrawing my power. Both men stood over me as I wept. Everything that had happened over the last few evenings and now the sight of this man brought a torrent of tears. I sobbed as I crawled to him, leaning my head against his legs. He knelt before me, covering his arms around me. I felt silly crying. I didn't want to cry but every soothing word he uttered sent a new wave of tears from me. I was suddenly so tired.

He gently pulled my chin to meet his emerald green gaze. "We must go. We are not safe yet. My vampires are outnumbered tonight, my dear." With one smooth motion, he lifted me into his arms, cradling me against his chest. He whispered something in French, reminding me of something or someone.

We started down the hall, away from the window and the nightmare from last night. He quickly descended a set of steps lit by candles. I had never seen past the hallway or bedroom. Trevor walked in front of us, flame-thrower bursting with fire around every corner. He looked so sure of himself. I could sense his great vampire power filling the air around us. I held onto the guns as I leaned my head against Sevastian.

The familiar scent of leather and lilacs soothed my nerves, but also reminded of Siön Baptiste. "Wait." Both men stopped. I looked up at Sevastian, his eyes sparkling in the dim candlelit room. "Siön Baptiste is in the basement. I have a key."

His eyes widened as if he saw a ghost. "Can you walk?" he asked.

I nodded and he set me down, steadying me with his arm around my waist. I placed the Berettas in the waist of my jeans and grabbed the keys from my pocket. We could hear screams and howls from outside as shots hit their target.

Sevastian looked past me to the darkness. "Shadow, retrieve my brother."

I peered into the darkness, my eyes still blurred from tears. A man appeared from the wall. He was as black as the shadows. His name fit him well.

"Yes, master." He had a thick accent, barely understandable.

They spoke quietly and then the man stalked towards me, taking the keys from my hands, disappearing into the shadows. His eyes were silver and his black hair was well past his waist, tied in a braid. He was completely naked but I would not have noticed except the power that surrounded the man was bright like the sun. Yet he was barely visible in the dark.

I followed him and as I stepped past Sevastian, he took my hand. "I'm going with him."

"No, we will not lose you again." Sevastian's voice encircled me warmly.

What does he mean by we?

"Can you walk?" Sevastian asked, caressing the pulse in my wrist.

"Yes, let's go." Pointing my guns ahead into the dark corridor.

I stood next to Trevor. His honey brown eyes watched me carefully. He wore leather pants with a leather vest and jacket. He seemed so much stronger. My eyes quickly adjusted as we entered a second hallway. I saw the creature before they could react, sending a substantial number of bullets into the werewolf's deformed face. It fell, screeching and clawing at its head. As Trevor walked past he fired the flames at the monster. We carefully walked by the scorched creature. The hallway ended as we reached a door. Sevastian strolled ahead opening the door. It led directly outside into the very same yard I had run through last night.

There was a black van parked in the middle of the yard, vampires draped around the van, shooting into the woods. Trevor grabbed my hand and started running. We reached the van and jumped in. Turning to face the werewolves heading directly towards us, we all fired into the night. The van took off as vampires stayed, shooting into the mass of fangs and fur flying at them.

We were thrown around as the van sped down the road. I was tossed into Sevastian and he captured me tightly in his arms. Trevor and Sevastian exchanged glances and something unsaid passed between them. Trevor climbed to the front of the van as Sevastian wrapped me in his heat.

"You have been through an ordeal, my sweet. We were worried we might never see you or my brother again." He whispered, kissing my forehead gently.

I didn't care what was going on. I was happy we were leaving. I prayed for Siön Baptiste's rescue, hoping against all odds that the strange Shadow would save him. I let go of my power, letting it flow through the van and back to the house. I was searching for Siön Baptiste. I saw a dark room with a shadow moving along the wall. He held Siön Baptiste in his arms as he crawled into the dark disappearing into the woods. Siön Baptiste's eyes opened, looking up at the sky. His face was bloody, jaw distorted from torture. However, his eyes were still that perfect shade of green. He saw me looking at him and for a moment his power surrounded mine, pulling me towards him. He was hungry. He needed to feed soon or he would die. Shadow shoved his power against mine, sending me back to the van.

Sevastian looked down at me, his eyes wide. He shook his head. "Samantha? What was that?" He looked at Trevor who had crawled into the back of the van.

Trevor glared at Sevastian and then at me. "What was that? I could feel a warm sensation over my whole body."

They both seemed confused. Their breathing was erratic as if they had been running a marathon. I remembered the effect of my power over Ty and how easily it had caused him such sexual pleasure. I peered curiously at the men, wondering if it had the same effect on them. I smiled at the thought and quickly pushed away the desire to find out.

"Siön Baptiste is safe but he needs to feed," I said.

"We know," Sevastian whispered. "We will be safe in two hours time. Sleep now, you will need your strength." He slid his hand down my face and the weariness overwhelmed me. I couldn't keep my eyes open. He pulled my head into his chest and the scent of him encircled me. I felt safer than I had in a long time.

Chapter 29

I woke to Sevastian rubbing my hand. The van was still moving down the road, but I could feel it slow as we entered New Orleans parkway.

Sevastian glanced over at Trevor. "We only have an hour till dawn, my friend. We must find shelter soon."

I turned to Trevor. He was a vampire. His eyes gave his fear away. Sun would kill him unlike Sevastian and myself who could survive. "My house."

Trevor moved to the front of the van and talked to the driver. We drove into my driveway with only fifteen minutes until dawn. Trevor and the driver shot out of the vehicle, never looking back. They headed into my house, drew all the blinds shut and retreated to the basement. I could see movement as we walked toward the house. I stopped and watched the sunrise. Sevastian held my arm as he took my guns. I didn't let go of them the entire trip. He pried them out from each hand, and placed them in the holster. The sun rose and I wondered if Siön Baptiste was still alive. The smell of lilacs drifted towards me. Sevastian released his grip of my arms and I headed to my back yard. The sky was orange, pink and blue as the sun slowly came to life. I walked quietly towards the cemetery. My father never let me play in the cemetery. He never let me come back to walk amongst the lilacs and weeping willows. "Too dangerous," he scolded.

I was determined to see what fell beyond my grasp for years. A large stone wall surrounded the cemetery and the gate was chained shut. I leaped over the wall, which stood over ten feet in height. I was getting use to my superhuman powers. They seemed so natural. I landed and a second thud soon followed. Sevastian followed me in silence. The long path seemed familiar. The trail led through a gate into a garden. A wall surrounded the garden, with lilacs reaching over the top into the sky. A fountain in the middle of the garden awakened my dreams. Sevastian walked beside me looking at what was before us. I stared up at his face.

His gaze fell to mine. "I thought this was a figment of your imagination. It wasn't you entering my dreams but me entering yours." He ran his long fingers against the stone of the fountain.

"I don't remember this place as a child, yet it was so perfectly replicated in my dream." I shook my head, shrugging my shoulders. "I don't understand." That was when I felt him. Someone was coming toward us. Sevastian felt him too. He hissed towards the wall.

Alastair leaped over the wall landing with ease. He looked around then walked past us towards the gate. He didn't see us. He walked through me to a woman standing in the corner of the garden. He kissed her, pulling her against him. They groaned as they tore the clothes from their bodies, lying in the bed of lilacs and grass. They made love, whispering sweet nothings. When they were finished, Alastair stood and brought the woman to her feet. He kissed her goodbye and simply vanished. The woman walked away, disappearing into the shadows.

The smell of lilacs filled my nostrils as I fell to the ground. The energy in the air was stifling; I could only kneel as I gasped for breath. Sevastian tilted his head, watching the wall. "A ghost. Maybe a relative? But why Alastair?" Sevastian held his hand out to me and I took it.

I was just happy Sevastian saw what I had seen. I didn't want to believe I might be losing my mind. I knew why Alastair was in the garden, but chose not to say and kept my mind blank. I gladly accepted Sevastian's help as I stood. His warmth spread over my entire body, as he pressed me against his body. I was so hungry. My stomach was burning with the desire to feed.

"You will feed, my sweet. Be patient. You must control the urge or it will control you." He sighed, releasing me. We were silent the whole trip back to the house.

The living room was dark, but I could still see the blood soaked into the carpet from when I'd shot Sevastian. He saw the horror on my face and wrapped his arms around me.

"You did what you had to do," he whispered, and then let me go.

Someone was in the room with us and I sensed their energy. I turned, grabbed the guns from Sevastian, and aimed them at the darkened corner.

Shadow stepped from the dark, Siön Baptiste in his arms. "He is dying." He held Siön Baptiste towards me.

Fear gripped my heart as Sevastian appeared before Shadow and took Siön Baptiste into his arms. "He must feed." He looked so weak.

Shadow dripped a deep black fluid onto the carpet. "I will feed him, my lord."

Sevastian looked at his companion and shook his head. "No, you must rest. You have lost too much blood." He turned towards me. "I am sorry, my sweet, but he must feed on someone who has his blood in theirs." His mouth twitched slightly as his last comment came out in a hoarse whisper.

When I had fed off Ty, he'd had multiple orgasms. It was a power vampires had over senses. They made their prey want them to death. I wanted Siön Baptiste to take my blood. I had no fear, just desire to feel him in me, on me, drinking me. Tears welled as the thought of his words the night we'd made love. "I love you; that is why." Those words troubled me. He had so willingly saved my life yet now I wasn't sure if I was prepared to save his. I was scared of giving my heart away, of feeling too much for Siön Baptiste.

"We must hurry, my sweet." Sevastian frowned.

I pointed up the stairs to my room. "The bedroom."

Sevastian walked in front of me carrying Siön Baptiste up the stairs. He laid him on my bed and whispered softly in his ear. Siön Baptiste stirred, opening his eyes. Sevastian wiped the hair and blood from his face. Siön Baptiste observed me from across the room. I felt his power flowing toward me, pressing against me, probing. I had never felt his power before but now that I had changed, I knew what he was doing. He was trying to read my mind. I shut the door on my mind and his power engulfed my body, sending vibrations over my skin. He tried to sit up and winced.

Sevastian pushed him back down onto the bed. "She will come to you." He stood walking past me and grabbed my arm. "Do not let him take too much blood. You will need to feed in your weakened state. When he is sated, call me." His eyes flashed dangerously as he exited the room, and closed the door behind him.

I stared at Siön Baptiste for a long time as he lay helpless on the bed. The bruises and cuts had already begun to heal. *Damn them all to hell, they would pay for this.* He'd been beaten relentlessly and near death when we found him. I sent my power over him, prying for information. He didn't have enough strength to fend my probing away and groaned as my own desire for food swept over him. Leaning down, I gently kissed his forehead, my lips smoldering from the touch of his skin. He seized my arms, and dragged me down onto him. Smelling fresh blood from his wounds, I fought my own desire to feed. I tucked my ponytail behind my back, and exposed my neck to him.

"I do not think I have enough strength to make this pleasurable, my sweet," he cautioned. "If you do not want me to take blood, I will feed off another."

His life was fading. I cried aloud, "Just do it. NOW."

There was a moment of razor-sharp pain as Siön Baptiste sunk his fangs into my neck. For what seemed an eternity I could only feel a throbbing pain that stung my neck and swept over my entire body. Then slowly a mind-numbing sensation began to creep slowly over me.

His life force strengthened, sending pleasurable vibrations over us as he continued to feed. As he sucked the rich nourishing blood, his power grew and I could feel my body boil and skin curl as wave after wave of pleasure rode me. Siön Baptiste wrapped his arms around me and one after another, he brought my body to orgasm, holding me against him as I writhed in his arms. I couldn't think or speak, just scream in pleasure. I dug my nails into his arms as another wave of orgasms hit me. We both screamed as I sliced him, and he swallowed me. He drew back, blood poured from his mouth. I licked the blood from his lips as he kissed me, moving his tongue over mine.

He released his hold and pushed me above him. In place of his once dull lifeless eyes, there was now a shimmering sparkle of desire. His face, once bruised, now lay perfect beneath me.

Smiling he drew me closer, holding my head to his chest. The sensual beat of his heart beckoned me. I kissed his chest through his bloody shirt and with one smooth motion ripped it from his body. I didn't need to be reminded of the cruelty he'd experienced.

I ran my fingers over his soft chest and the holes where he had been shot had completely closed. Only a few traces of blood remained, showing any lingering evidence of his injuries. Slowly I circled my tongue across his chest, and licked any visible blood away. Two days ago, my actions would have revolted me but now the beast inside spurred me on.

He groaned, "Samantha" as my tongue caressed his skin.

I slid my tongue over his nipple, tugged on it gently, bringing it between my teeth. He cried out, snatching my shoulder, heaving me closer. My hunger for blood overcame me as I sank my now sharpened teeth into his nipple. Screaming, he racked his nails down my arm as I swallowed his warm sweet blood. It flowed along my throat, sending warmth all the way through my body. My power flew over him, surrounding us both in bliss.

I enjoyed using my power, the feeling of it flowing so freely through me. I concentrated my energy on his hips and groin. As if my mouth hovered over his long hard shaft, the power embraced him. He called out again as I continued to drain him. Our world swam in dizzying colors from pleasure that threatened to devour us both. We quivered relentlessly as our energy, still entwined, caressed and fondled one another. I yelled and he echoed my cries as we floated on wave after wave of ecstasy.

I fell blissfully onto the bed, my hunger sated. Siön Baptiste folded his arms around me, tugged me gently under his shoulder. "I thought I'd lost you," he said, voice husky with desire.

My tears fell, hitting him in the shoulder. "I didn't know what to do. I couldn't stop them," I cried.

Siön Baptiste brushed my hair out of my face. "My little storm, they could not kill me. Not after finding you could they ever tear me from this earth." He laughed.

Sevastian walked into the room His eyebrows lifted at the sight before him. "You have fed well tonight." He smirked.

Siön Baptiste sat up and rolled off the opposite side of the bed. Every wound had disappeared and he appeared to be in better shape than before the incident. "She has tasted my blood." He sighed, walking to my dresser.

Sevastian laughed a soothing melody over my skin. "I know. She is our little protégé." He chuckled again, walking towards Siön Baptiste. He slapped the man across the back. "You have also done as our father…" he paused, "As Nicholi wished."

Siön Baptiste's eyebrow rose as he smiled. Both men stared, eyes wide open. "What are you saying, Sevastian?" He shook his head as his brother spoke quietly in French.

I couldn't make out a word they were saying, but I knew I had to get a French book and start learning the language if they were going to use it against me. "Cut it out, the both of you. I don't appreciate all the whispering and mumbling behind my back," I growled. "What did you do that Nicholi wanted?" I asked.

Siön Baptiste walked over to me, and took my hands in his. "We were not talking behind your back, my sweet. We were very much right in front of you," he teased, eyes shining brightly. A light that hadn't been there minutes ago now flamed in those gorgeous eyes.

I sent my power over him but he only grinned. He had placed an impenetrable wall up around himself. I couldn't pierce the lock he had in place but it didn't hurt to try. "You have learned so much in such a short time," he confided. "But I have had years of practice, my sweet, and you will not break my guard."

Turning to Sevastian, he asked, "What shall we do, brother?"

"You cocky son of a…," I growled. "You feel a little better and already you're giving me tude."

Both men stared at me, amusement in their eyes. "Tude?" Sevastian asked.

"Yes, attitude. I am tired and grouchy and can't take your double talk anymore."

"It is you who speaks double talk, my sweet. Tude?" he accused.

A bright light entered my mind. Something or someone clawed desperately at my own wall. I attempted to mimic Siön Baptiste's blockade, but the invading energy broke down my mental hedge, and called to me. I sent my power out beyond and saw a figure hunched over, tied to a stake. Ty crumbled to the ground as a man stood over him, beating him.

Ty looked to the sky, seeing my eyes. *"Samantha!"* he cried as his head slumped.

The man beating him turned to me, eyes amber. *"Adeem!"* I screamed. *"You will pay for this."*

He waved his hand in the air. He heard my voice in his head. For a brief moment, fear ran across his face, which soon turned to anger. *"Samantha, you will be ours or you will die. Come to your love and face me."*

I fell off the bed screaming. Siön Baptiste and Sevastian rushed to my side, eyes wide with astonishment. They sniffed the air. "This can't be." Sevastian paced the room. "We got there before they…" His words trailed off. "I didn't smell this scent earlier. She has been marked." He twisted around quickly to face Siön Baptiste. "If she does not drift with this creature, she will die." He clenched his hands into fists.

Siön Baptiste stood in front of me, peered down, hand held out to mine. "So it is true. You are infected with the Lycanthrope disease. I could not smell it in my weakened state." His eyes were emotionless as he dropped his hand to his side. "I thought I sensed it in your blood but passion clouded my judgment." He turned, and walked to the wall leaning against it before he raised his fist and punched the wall with such force it sent his fist straight through the drywall. "NO!" he screamed. "They will all die for this."

"If they kill him, I will die too." I heard my voice but what I said seemed so far away.

Siön Baptiste hit the wall once more, plunging his fist deeper into the drywall. "We must save him. I will not lose you Samantha or…" He knelt down on the floor, head leaning against the bed. "We have come too far to lose this battle, to lose you."

Is that all he cared about, the battle? I thought to myself.

Sevastian strode across the room, his leather pants making a soft creaking sound as he walked. Drawing my attention to his long legs and lean waist, I hastily forced my gaze elsewhere. I knew he could feel my desire as red stained my cheek.

He stopped dead in his tracks. "Can you connect with this creature?" He growled.

I had no doubt I could find him again. He'd reached out to me to warn me. I needed to help him to help me. "Yes."

Siön Baptiste stood and walked to the door, his hand rested on the frame, head bent. "We leave tonight." He paused before heading out the room, and shutting the door behind him.

Sevastian turned to follow. "Please don't go," I whispered. "What is happening to me? Please tell me who the Drackontz are?" He fell silent. I couldn't even see him breathe.

He faced me. The smell of leather and lilacs stroked my senses. A cold wind flowed over us. "We must find them and destroy them all." He turned away from me and walked from the room.

I fell to the ground, crying. My life was in shambles. I placed my hands over my face and gave way to the torrent of tears. If there was a God out there, I needed him now. I needed direction, knowledge, and power to defeat my enemies. Instead, hatred filled my lungs, my sobs. Hatred filled the hole in my heart, causing me to send my power searching for him. I found Adeem at the werewolf fortress. I followed the hallway down below the house where Ty was tied to a stake. Two werewolves surrounded him while he lay naked, swimming in his stench. *"I am coming."*

He glanced up at the ceiling. *"It is a trap."* Then his head fell motionless. His mind spoke when his body could not."

"Wait, we have time. Surprise will be your best ally," he whispered. *"Do not come now, it is a full moon and they will be most powerful. You will find help at the Wolves Den. You have until the next moon."* His voice faded as the connection dissipated.

Trap or not, I either attempted to save him and live, or forget him and die anyway. Disgust and the need for revenge made me irrational, throwing caution to the wind. Only five hours until dusk, then we would move. I wanted them all dead.

Chapter 30

I took a quick shower and returned to my bed. Crawling comfortably under the warm sheets, I sighed, thankful I was finally home. The bedroom door opened and then clicked shut. I pulled the shades close earlier and my room was dark. The person slipped into bed, sliding over, gently kissing and holding me in his arms. It was Trevor. I could smell him.

"Sam, you should have never taken this job."

Placing my hand in his, I managed a faint smile. "It was six figures. Do you really think I could have resisted?" I laughed. "I am so sorry, Trevor. I had no idea it would lead to this."

He slid his arm around my waist and tugged me to him. "We can't go tonight. We have to gather some troops."

I struggled to pull away from him. "Did they send you in here to tell me?"

He gathered me tightly in his long arms, strong from the new vampire blood coursing through his veins. "They thought it would be better coming from a friend."

"Samantha, I only want what is best for you…," he stopped. "We can be a family together forever."

I grabbed his arm and squeezed. "Trevor, what are you trying to say?"

I could feel his warm breath on my back, snuggled into my hair. Something had changed in him--he was different somehow. It wasn't just that he was a vampire. His whole being felt different. I waited for him to speak. "I want you to be mine." His hand slid up my arm and a cold chill ran down my back.

I shot up out of bed. "What do you mean?" I stood glaring at him while his honey-brown eyes pleaded with me. "You're my friend, my brother."

He sat up. "Samantha, you are beautiful and caring. I can make you my lover."

"Trevor, snap out of it." I watched him, as his gaze grew dim.

"Sam, I'm sorry, not sure what came over me. I had this desire to…" He shook his head and stood up. I could tell he was fighting against my power. Vampires had less control, and were attracted to power itself. I shut down and tried to block my power from saturating him.

"I don't know what happened." He turned away, sitting on the other side of the bed, leaning his head in his hands. "I know you slept with him." He got up and walked to the door.

"Trevor, please," I croaked, tears running down my face.

"You belong to Siön Baptiste. He made that very clear to us all. I'm afraid to lose you, sis." The venom in his voice stung my skin.

"I don't belong to anyone," I growled.

"You slept with him, Sam. What do you think that means to him? He claimed you for his own and will fight to keep you. I am not willing to sit in the next room while your.. while you.." He didn't finish but I knew what he was saying. "I care for you too much to see you used like this," he snarled.

"We cannot continue our friendship. He is too jealous of our closeness. I can't be a part of this and see you with him." He left the room, leaving the door open.

His words hurt and I knew he was lying, I could taste it in the air. Why did I feel hatred pouring from his veins? Did he hate what I had become or what I did? I sat on the bed, watching the clock, waiting to make our next move. I was impatient and if I thought it possible, I would have left on my own. But I waited in the dark, alone. Revenge was just around the corner.

Chapter 31

It felt like the last few days I had done nothing but sleep, kill, feed and sleep some more. Oh, and get chased by half- crazed werewolves out to kill me, oh, and become a vampire slash werewolf in less than three days. I looked at the alarm clock. It was 12:00 a.m. I must have dozed off brooding alone in the dark. *Damn!*

Dressed in a comfy pair of gray sweats and a t-shirt, I grabbed some white socks and sneakers and headed downstairs. Sevastian and Siön Baptiste were sleeping comfortably on the couches. Both were covered in blankets and guns were sprawled out over their chests. Voices talked quietly in the kitchen and I recognized Trevor. I entered the kitchen where Shadow and Trevor sat at the table drinking coffee.

I laughed. "You boys drink coffee?"

Trevor coughed on his drink, standing up. "Yes, Sam. Why? Do you find that funny?" He was angry and his voice could barely hide the fact that I upset him.

I walked over to him, wrapping my arms around his waist, placing my head in the swell of his back. He stiffened. I nuzzled my nose into his back and he let out a deep breath.

"I am sorry, Trevor. I didn't mean to be a smart ass."

He took a step forward, filling an empty cup. "Good to know you can still be a pain in the ass, Sam." He filled the cup with coffee, two creams, one sugar. A deep voice spread through the kitchen. "I don't think the master would appreciate you touching what is his," he said.

I turned swiftly, staring Shadow in the face. He was lighter than he had been at the fortress. His eyes were colorful against his tanned skin. I couldn't decide what color. He was taller than Trevor and bulkier.

"Just whose girl do you think you're talking about here? I am my own woman, not anyone's property." I could feel my skin burn with fury. *How dare he presume!*

"She is so right, my friend. Samantha is definitely her own woman. She belongs to no one." Laughter filled the room, sending fire burning through my body. Siön Baptiste floated in; he wore a long red silk robe. It parted, exposing his strong perfect legs and a smooth muscled chest. His eyes flickered, his smile took my breath away. I don't remember when I first realized I had been holding my breath, but was quickly rushed back into reality when he took my cup of coffee and began to drink. *You don't mess with a girl's coffee.*

I reached for the cup and he held it away. "That is the last cup," I growled.

His eyebrow lifted as his smile widened. "I am sure Trevor would be more than willing to make some more for us," he said, looking up over his cup in Trevor's direction.

"Sure, why the hell not?" Trevor mumbled.

I shook my head, and stepped past Siön Baptiste to the coffee pot. "You are all a bunch of babies. I will make the damn coffee. Trevor makes it too strong anyway." His coffee was always too strong, but I drank it to please him.

He looked surprised as if he had been thinking the same thought. "I thought you liked my coffee?" he asked.

I tried to erase the frown as I contemplated his hurt expression. "I never liked the coffee. But you make one hell of a breakfast." I smiled, erasing all emotion from my face. Nothing I could say or do would ever change the wounded look in his face.

He stomped out of the room like a hurt child, but I couldn't blame him. In only five short days, his life had been turned upside down. He couldn't still be a cop as a vampire. His life had changed and I was to blame.

"My sweet, Trevor's choice was his own." Siön Baptiste walked toward me, and handed me back the cup of coffee. He wouldn't meet my gaze.

"I know." I plopped down in the chair, folding my head on my arms. "What should I do?" I sighed.

No one answered. Siön Baptiste just sat silently beside me. I heard Shadow exit the kitchen, leaving us alone. Siön Baptiste hands moved over mine. His thumb caressed my wrist, sending heat coiling in my stomach as he spoke, "We need to seek council. The elders will help."

I raised my head, watching his face. He wasn't trying to read my mind but he had no idea what I was talking about. "I mean about Trevor."

He sighed. "There are things that are beyond my control. Trevor has made his choice and now he lives. He told Sevastian he would have chosen death over not being with you." He shrugged his shoulders. "I do not know what to say to appease you."

I felt empty. I pulled my gaze from Siön Baptiste and stared at the table. "We need to get Ty. What do you suggest?" I asked, attempting to change the subject.

He stood behind me, placing his hands on my shoulders. "We must contact the elders. We need backup."

I lifted my head, and leaned back into the chair as his hands massaged my shoulders. "I want all of you, Samantha. Your heart, your body and your love. I need to tell you something…," he paused and we both turned as Sevastian walked through the kitchen door.

Sevastian's robe was black velvet and it flowed to the floor. His long auburn hair was tied neatly behind his head. The black of the robe brought out the green in his eyes so that they appeared to be real emeralds. His chest peeked out from the ruffles at the top of the robe.

Surrounded by gorgeous vampires, what the heck was a woman to do…. RUN!

"Tazmaine is coming tonight." He looked at me, smiling. "We should prepare. If she senses any weakness, we will fail." He waved his hand at me.

"Who is Tazmaine?" I asked curios at the silent looks they exchanged.

"She is our queen." Is all they offered as they spoke in unison.

Sevastian nodded in my direction. "No matter what happens, we need to get her ready. She is too weak."

I knew the comment was meant for me. I stood abruptly, pushing Siön Baptiste into the counter. I stalked over to Sevastian, standing before him. "Weakness? Say that to my face." My blood boiled as my power exploded in the room. The coffee pot exploded and the dishes rattled. I was pissed.

He took a step closer, and bent his face directly over mine. "You are weak in your present state." He added, "You have no control over your emotions or your power. You are a ticking time bomb, Samantha. You emanate sexuality and have no way to control it."

I pushed my finger into his hard chest, and hit him with all my might. "You pompous butthead." My power glided through the room, mingling with both men. As my power coursed over them, I fell to the ground. My legs gave out, as my body began to convulse in pain. Something bit back at my power and it was coming from the monster inside me. I felt my skin begin to break and seep as my bones began to move. "GOD!" I screamed.

Siön Baptiste and Sevastian held me between them, sending their power through me, calming the beast. The pain ceased as warmth crept through my skin.

"What was that?" My breathing was still rapid as the last remnants of pain left me.

"Weakness, my sweet," Siön Baptiste whispered.

Sevastian grabbed my shoulders. "Can you stand?"

"Yes, what was that?" I held onto his arms as he anchored me.

"You were attacked by a Lycanthrope. His blood is in you." He looked at Siön Baptiste as we all stood.

I scowled, shaking my head. "No kidding. Really?" I asked sarcastically. Then it hit me. "Hold on. You're telling me I am going to turn furry like those creatures?" They turned, both facing me, eyes foretelling my future. "Oh god, no, they are awful." This was the worst news all night. "No way. How can I stop it?" My anger flared its ugly head as I walked out of the room, leaving the men to follow me. "I will kill myself before I become a monster." I ran up the stairs and walked into my bedroom. I searched the room and found my twin Berettas lying on a chair beside the bed. Tears ran down my face as I remembered the transformation of the werewolf. The way they tore Carl apart without any conscious. They were demonic creatures and I wanted them dead. I grabbed a gun, checked the clip and took the safety off.

A hand reached across me and grabbed the gun before I could move. Two hands held my shoulder as the gun flew, hitting the wall. Siön Baptiste shook me, jerking me close. "No, Samantha. I cannot allow any harm to come to you. Not now, not ever," he ordered, his anger evident.

I had to close my eyes, because I suddenly felt dizzy. "We need to meet Tazmaine tonight. She will know what to do," he whispered in my ear. "I am sorry if we upset you, my sweet."

"I am not weak." I stepped back, watching Siön Baptiste's handsome face. "I want them all dead. I've seen what they can do. They are pure evil."

He ran his finger down my face. "They will pay for what they have done. I promise you that much." He pushed me to the dresser, and made me look into the mirror. "You are most powerful for a baby vampire." He laughed.

I smiled. "A baby vampire, my bum. I am one bad mojo." I winked.

He walked to the door and brought back something in his hand. "An outfit, my dear, fitting for my queen." He slapped me on the butt and strutted out of the room. He quickly returned, walking to my chair, and took my guns. "Until I know you're sane I will be holding these till the fighting begins." He smiled that dazzling flawless face my way, making me grab the dresser to steady my legs.

"Get out, Siön Baptiste, I can't think when you're around."

He grinned, and shut the door behind him.

I opened the bag Siön Baptiste had brought me. *Of course*, I thought to myself. Black leather pants, vest and jacket. He seemed to like me in leather. Wearing leather had its positive points too. Leather was more durable when being ripped to shreds by a werewolf. It also protects from the normal scraps and bruises someone might get when running from werewolves, too.

* * * *

I walked down the stairs and sat on the couch across from Shadow and Trevor. "Where are Sevastian and Siön Baptiste?" I asked.

Trevor shrugged his shoulders while Shadow answered, "They are preparing for Tazmaine. She will be here shortly."

I nodded. "Who is Tazmaine?"

He laughed. I didn't think Shadow could laugh but it was a friendly laugh. "You have gotten yourself into a predicament, haven't you?" He smiled as he got up off the couch and walked into the kitchen.

Did he just say predicament? I decided to ignore the comment and wait patiently. Trevor looked miserable, and I hastily averting my gaze from him. I was nervous while I sat waiting for what seemed an eternity. Twiddling my thumbs for at least ten minutes, I eventually gathered my legs up under me and sat Indian style on the soft sofa.

Siön Baptiste and Sevastian entered the room and the two of them were enough to make a woman cry. The masculinity and testosterone in the room just about blew me away.

"I do not want the elders to know where I live," I said, watching them both for a reaction. The thought of having these elders knowing where I lived upset me. I had an uneasy feeling about the elders and their motives.

Siön Baptiste put a hand on my shoulder, looking earnestly at Sevastian. "We cannot refuse the elders. Their word is law. We must accommodate Tazmaine."

A deep voice bellowed through the room. "I agree with the woman." Shadow appeared in the doorway, nodding his agreement. "Tazmaine is not to be trusted. You know as well as I do they will betray us all," he growled.

I watched Shadow carefully. He was a good inch taller than Siön Baptiste and every bit as powerful. His shoulders were broader and overall he was a larger, more intimidating man. The aura that surrounded him was of many colors swirling in a prism of radiant light. I couldn't seem to focus clearly enough to determine just what color his aura projected most. When I first met Shadow, his skin was pitch black but now he was flashing multiple colors all at once. *Amazing!* His long hair was held back against his neck in a ponytail. His eyes were the same colors of his aura, shimmering and swirling with anger.

I approached him slowly. This man was a predator and I had an overwhelming feeling there was more to him than everyone let on.

"Listen, I appreciate the vote of confidence but I don't need your help," I said calmly, facing him.

He leaned against the doorframe, frowning. "Siön Baptiste, keep your woman on a leash," he growled.

Your woman? I could feel my anger swell as I said, "You cocky son of a…" I paused turning to Siön Baptiste. His face was void of emotion. "I am not his woman." I waved my hands towards Siön Baptiste irritably.

Siön Baptiste stood motionless, looking from me to Shadow and back to me. He rubbed his chin thoughtfully, attempting and failing miserably to hide his amusement.

Trevor coughed, laughing from across the room. I glared at him, trying to wipe the smug expression off his face. "*Smug bastard!*" he said.

"*Shut up, Trevor,*" I said, tapping my foot nervously.

"*You heard me?*" he asked.

"*Yes, now quiet,*" I answered.

"*Samantha, you are talking in my mind.*"

I glanced at Trevor again and we both were astonished. My powers were increasing. Even as we sat arguing, I discovered a new hidden talent. I smirked, wondering if I could speak to everyone that way.

Shadow broke the silence. "You are his. He has made his claim on you."

Trevor moved towards him. He had played this protective role before and had no problems, but Shadow was a force to be reckoned with. He stood his ground, not afraid of the menacing look in Trevor's eyes. "Siön Baptiste has no claim on her. She is a free woman to choose whom she wants," he hissed.

That silenced the room immediately. Trevor continued, now turning to Siön Baptiste. "I don't give a damn what you say."

I couldn't believe my ears. What was Trevor thinking? Get a little vampire blood in you and you go nuts.

Shadow moved in a blur of inhuman speed, tackling Trevor. He grabbed him by the neck, squeezing the life out of him. Shadow's skin, once a multi-color, was now a midnight blue. "You will do no such thing," Shadow threatened.

Standing eyes wide-open, my mouth gaped as Trevor clutched Shadow's neck, rolling and growling as they fought. Everyone was going mad. Something inside of me broke, fueling my power. The air in the room grew warm.

"STOP!" My voice and energy crashed into Shadow and Trevor, lifting them both off the floor.

The power boiled under my skin as I felt something creep within me. A creature of the night moved inside, trying to break free. Its eyes glowed demonic red. I could feel its desire to consume me, turning me to the dark side. I screamed, falling to the ground, shaking my head at the beast. The power receded dropping my hold on Shadow and Trevor. White lights flashed before me as I moved to the window. Everything moved in slow motion as the desire to jump out into the darkness overcame me. I could feel the desire to hunt and run through the woods seeking prey.

Siön Baptiste's whisper floated through my mind, calming my anger. "You are okay, my sweet. Push the monster back. No one is hurt, control your anger." He wrapped his arms around me, pulling me to his chest. I could hear his heartbeat slowing and mine matched its soothing pulse.

"I don't think I can take this anymore," I muttered. My world was crashing around me, changing by the minute and all I wanted to do was kill the people responsible.

Sevastian traipsed across the room, shaking his head. "We will take our chances and meet them at the Silver Fang"

"We have to go now," I said.

Everyone left the room but Siön Baptiste who still held me comfortably in his arms. "My beau l'orage, what am I to do with you?" He paused, running his fingers through my hair. "You are very stubborn." He turned me so that I faced him.

Keeping my eyes on his chest, I tried to avoid his loving look. "I am not stubborn," I whispered, fire already burning inside from his closeness.

He laughed and it touched my face as he bent closer. His warm inviting breath purred tenderly in my ear. "I love you, Samantha Houston."

The words shot through me like a bullet while my knees buckled. My heart beat rapidly in my chest as butterflies swarmed my stomach. "I can't." The only words I could say.

He lowered his mouth over my lips, rubbing gently against mine. He kissed me, stealing my breath as an eruption of desire consumed us both. My hands moved to his back, pulling him closer. I only wanted to smell him, taste him, and feel him. Every doubt in my mind was erased as he probed deeper, devouring my mouth as if it was the last kiss we would ever share.

I pulled back, looking up at his beautiful face. "I have to work this out before we…" I stopped as the thought of ever losing this wonderful man caused a pain in my heart like never before. "You have to give me time, Siön Baptiste. I feel like we hardly know each other." I sighed, dropping my hands to my side. I couldn't look into those eyes and not feel something. I cared for him deeply but love. Love was such a strong word.

He released his hold on me and walked to the mantle, leaning against the wall, folding his arms over his chest. "I can wait. I have waited an eternity for you and can wait longer if need be. I have no intention of walking away, not now, not ever." His accent was thick as he mumbled under his breath, "We must go."

Frozen in shock at the words he spoke, I just stared at the handsome man before me. He was the epitome of sexual masculinity. How could anyone resist?

"You have resisted quite well, I must say." He laughed, sending a shudder down my spine.

"You can read my mind? You have to stop doing that, Siön Baptiste."

Gliding back to my side, he held his hand out. I took it reluctantly and his eyebrows rose at my hesitation. "I will not bite. At least not without permission." He chuckled low and soft. I dropped my gaze as the memory of our encounter sent tingling sensations between my thighs.

God, he could still affect me hours later.

"You have the same effect, Samantha. You are a drug. I cannot have enough of you to satisfy my thirst." He chuckled in my mind, amused with me.

"GET OUT of my MIND!" I yelled, releasing his hand, walking to the front door. "They are all waiting, let's go."

"Are you forgetting something, my little firefly?" He flew by me in a blur of speed. I was pleased that I saw him move at all.

He stood motionless holding me with his stare. A seductive grin swept across his face as he pushed me against the door. "We have been here before, have we not?" He laughed. "You almost forgot your precious weapons." He smirked, holding the Berettas and gun straps out as he pushed his legs against my hips.

"You will never change, Siön Baptiste. You will always be a cocky son of a bitch," I growled.

He laughed almost hitting his head on the door. He stepped away laughing as he leaned one hand against the wall to steady himself.

"What is so funny?" I screamed.

"You, my dear, are wonderful. I will never tire of your antics." He flashed me a dazzling mind blowing smile.

He could take his antics and shove them where the sun doesn't shine for all I care.

"Oh, my dear, I would love to...."

I didn't give him a chance to finish. I grabbed the guns from his outstretched hands and left him while I marched into the cool night breeze, his laughter trailing off in my head. The breeze had a cooling effect on the flames of desire floating across my skin. I could still hear Siön Baptiste's soft whispers as I stomped to the limo.

Ralph stood stationary as I approached the vehicle. He didn't smile. Guess our last meeting had left a bad impression on him. "How you doing, Ralphie?" I asked.

He didn't answer, just glared at me. I reached for the car door and Siön Baptiste's hand moved me away, opening it for me. "You must let me treat you like the lady you are."

Ralph coughed, drawing our attention. He smirked at me but when Siön Baptiste noticed the attitude, Ralph shuffled away.

I slid into the limo and over to the opposite side, allowing Siön Baptiste room beside me. Shadow, Sevastian and Trevor sat across from us all watching Siön Baptiste. Trevor fidgeted with his shirt, looking uncomfortable wedged between the two powerful vampires. He was powerful in his own right but the two that sandwiched him were ancients. I watched all the men in the limo carefully scrutinizing their auras. The auras were now stronger than ever and each man had their own strength.

Siön Baptiste's aura astonished me. There was always a colorful aura around him but now it was nearly blinding my eyes. I focused on our surroundings outside the window, not fully understanding everything that had happened in the last few days. I would get my answers if I had to pull someone's teeth or fangs out to do it.

Chapter 32

The night was cloudless and the stars dotted the midnight sky. I could feel the call of the demon deep within begging for release. I took a deep breath and realized everyone in the car was watching me intently.

"Don't you all have anything better to do? You're making me nervous," I said, shaking my head.

Nobody answered. They stared blankly in my direction. It must be a vampire trick to be so still. I peered into the dimly lit limo and couldn't even tell if they were breathing. They sat utterly still.

Creepy!

New Orleans had been my home for 29 years. The buzz of traffic and people on the roads brought joy to my heart. The city had been a long time attraction for thrill seekers. In the quiet neighborhoods, normal people and vampires lived together in harmony, for the most part. What they didn't know wouldn't hurt them. A war was coming, and they were going to be smack dab in the middle.

I broke the silence. "So who are the elders?"

"You must keep her quiet," Shadow glared at me while he spoke.

"You know, I don't think I like your attitude," I snarled.

"See." He pointed at me. "She has no control, Siön Baptiste, how do you expect Tazmaine to react. You will taunt her with this child."

Child? "Shut up, bat boy," I responded adamantly.

Siön Baptiste clutched my hand and squeezed lightly. His look was a warning not to push Shadow. *"I cannot control him when he is angry. Do not upset him. He is a very powerful ally and we need him."*

"Ally schmally, I don't give a hoot. He is a pain in the arse." I snatched my hand from Siön Baptiste and smiled wickedly at Shadow.

"I can play your game, Shadow, but know this, you mess with me or mine and I will make you regret ever meeting me." I turned my gaze to Trevor and Shadow and growled. *"Siön Baptiste will not be able to hold me back."*

"I will put up with only so much, young one. You do not know with whom you mess." His laughter filled my mind, blurring my sight. For a moment, I only saw colorful lights enveloping my senses and thoughts. *"Siön Baptiste must tame you and if he does not, I will."* He sent another wave of spine-tingling energy over my body.

I jerked back in the seat as his power crept over me.

"What is he doing to her?" Trevor asked, eyes blazing with rage.

"No more," Sevastian demanded, reaching across grabbing Shadows arm. "Enough for tonight. We have a tough task ahead of us and we must concentrate."

Enough for tonight? What the hell does that mean?

Shadow growled and Sevastian released his grip. I could feel him touch the beast within me. He fondled it with his power, stroking the monster inside. He pulled away, leaving an empty void in my body.

"Don't think I won't use these," I threatened, removing both guns from my holster.

In all the commotion, I hadn't realized the limo stopped moving. Ralph opened the door before I could shoot. *Perfect timing.*

We all exited the vehicle and headed towards the now abandoned club. Everyone seemed a little on edge. I placed the guns securely in my shoulder holster so I could reach them easily. Strapping the leg wraps on, I tested my ability to reload. I counted how long it took to remove the clip and how long to replace it. When I was satisfied with my gun situation, I proceeded to the entrance.

Siön Baptiste grabbed my arm, stopping me before I could go any further. "If something should go wrong tonight, you get out. Do not worry for any of us. Your safety and well being is all that matters."

I searched for his true feelings but his mind and face were blank. "Why is everyone walking on eggshells? What haven't you told me?" I paused. *"Be HONEST with me, Siön Baptiste, or I will never forgive you."*

"Tazmaine must accept you. The elders must accept you as one of us or…" He didn't finish the statement but I knew what he was going to say. When he sensed me probing his mind, he shut me out completely. "We must not keep her waiting."

"I am not going anywhere until I get my answer," I demanded.

Trevor walked over with a black bag. A sudden dread came over me. "Do they have to accept Trevor as well?" I asked.

"Yes," Sevastian answered. "You must be careful tonight, we walk a thin line. The elders must approve all new vampires. It is how we keep our race strong and healthy."

"Give me more weapons," I barked.

Siön Baptiste nodded at Sevastian and he reluctantly handed me throwing stars. "I don't know if this is a good idea," he whispered.

Siön Baptiste shrugged. "I will not have her go unarmed against such odds."

I wasn't happy about the whole idea but the stars were my favorite weapon. "What the hell are these?" I held out the stars, looking at the intricate pattern in the metal. They were silver, but they were also thick. "They are rounded, no pointed edges, how will this help."

Sevastian took one from my hand. "Be careful." He then pushed a hidden button in the middle of the star and six blades shot out each holding a syringe like needle that ejected a fluid from the blades. "This is filled with holy water. It can either kill or maim a full blooded vampire and it will kill a Drackontz." He pushed the button again and they blades retracted.

Handing the stars back to me, I tested the mechanism. "Cool," I said, placing them in the pocket of my leather jacket. "Let's get this over with." I stepped past everyone and headed for the entrance. I remember that night just a few days ago, when I thought, Trevor was lost to me forever. What had I done? I had ruined his life and mine with my stubborn I can do all attitude.

Trevor walked up beside me and took my hand. "Its okay, Samantha."

We both knew something had changed forever between us. I wondered if we would ever be the same. But before I had the time to worry about it, the stench of evil floated through the evening sky into the building beyond or was the evil emanating from the Silver Fang?

* * * *

The club was well lit, unlike the party scene from the other night. There were burn marks on the floor and water dripped from the ceilings in a few locations. It looked like a bomb had gone off. The smell of charred flesh permeated the building. Siön Baptiste led us all to a door. He opened it and we entered a room behind the club. It was untouched by the fire and water damage.

There were four chairs in the room. One ornately decorated chair with gold and satin was set on a pedestal above the rest. The room was elegantly decorated with red and black draperies covering the walls. The only pieces of furniture in the room were the chairs.

A cool breeze coated the area as a woman floated into the room. She evolved out of thin air. She looked tall but that could have been from the floating effect. She had long auburn hair with streaks of black. She wasn't alone. Three men stood below her as she levitated above us.

"Welcome." Her voice shimmered with sensuality, causing every muscle in my body to twinge. "I have waited so long to see you again, Siön Baptiste." She rolled his name off her tongue as if she was making love to him. I watched Siön Baptiste, but he showed no visible evidence it affected him. *Good.*

"You must be Tazmaine," I interrupted.

The silence in the room was deafening as she floated back to earth and strolled towards me. Her hips swayed a seductive dance. Even I couldn't keep my eyes off her.

"Don't look her in the eye." It was a warning from Siön Baptiste.

As soon as the words entered my mind, I looked up. I don't know why when people warn you not to do something, it always makes you want to do just that. I faced what had to be the most beautiful creature on earth. Her eyes black sparkling globes that captured my gaze in hers. I was being swallowed into her darkness as the heat of her power filled me. I knew she was standing in front of me yet I felt she was inside my head, touching me softly. She was offering me the world with one look. *"I can give you so much more than these creatures. I can give you power and pleasure you have never experienced before."* Her voice echoed in every nerve, sending a jolt of yearning through my body. I wanted her to touch me. I needed her to touch me.

She towered over me, brushed my face with her pale lean hands. I couldn't break away from her beauty. She held me with her power and my desire. I was on the edge of a dark abyss as her mind pressed against mine. She smelled wild like honey and forest.

"NO!" A voice bellowed over us, sending an ice-cold power through our veins. I jerked away, shaking my head, trying to regain control. "You will not have her." Siön Baptiste's voice saturated the room. "It is not your right."

Tazmaine laughed slowly, licking her lips. "Oh, her mind and power tastes so delicious." She turned, walking towards Siön Baptiste. "I remember a time when you would have died to taste me, my love." She had a stronger older accent than either Sevastian or Siön Baptiste.

"I no longer desire that love," he said, watching me carefully.

"Oh, but Siön, you hurt me so." She laughed. "What about her? It is my right to claim whoever I deem as a gift. She is one of us, I can feel her power. You must honor my request as your queen."

I shook my head and stepped between her and Siön Baptiste. I had enough. "Listen Taz, I don't ride both sides of the road."

"Careful, my love. She sets a trap." I heard his voice but ignored his warning.

"What do we need with her, Siön Baptiste? I don't understand this meeting." I sighed. "I don't need permission to kill those who attacked me."

Tazmaine's eyes grew darker. "You will address me with respect, young one."

Sevastian moved closer, drawing Tazmaine's attention away from me. "My queen, you requested this meeting. As your humble servants, we can only oblige but we're confused about your wishes." His voice curled around us all, comforting and calming everyone in the room.

"Nicholi is dead. Why do you think I come? I want to know what happened. The elders need to know that the city will stay in the control of our own kind. A rumor of werewolves seeking new territory has everyone apprehensive about our future. And he was your father. Have you no respect?" she asked.

"He was not my father. He was a deceitful, hateful creature who used everyone around him." Sevastian glided towards Tazmaine, hips strutting seductively.

"He was your master," she hissed. "I do not understand your blatant disregard for our laws. You have no gift for your queen, and yet you dare to insult me." She sashayed in my direction, holding out her hand.

I felt compelled to touch her. Siön Baptiste held me in place, keeping me tucked against him. He wrapped himself around my waist, holding me to his chest. *"You will not go to her. If you accept her offer, you will be lost to me."*

"Release her. I chose my gift." Her eyes flashed wickedly between Sevastian and Siön Baptiste.

With all the hubbub going on, I hadn't notice Trevor slowly walking past our group. "If you need a gift, take me," he said.

Sevastian and Siön Baptiste exchanged glances and then guardedly watched Tazmaine, waiting for her response.

Forget this, I wasn't about to let her have Trevor either. I shifted out from under Siön Baptiste's arms and walked towards Trevor, catching him by the arm. "The hell you will," I said hastily.

"Let me go, Sam." Trevor swung around, angry at my interruption. *"I won't let her hurt you. Damn you, Sam, just leave it be."*

Everything was spinning out of control. This was crazy. *A Gift!* Where the hell did these people come from?

Tazmaine was standing directly in front of us. She appeared out of thin air. Her long pale fingers stroked Trevor's arm. He swiveled to face her, putting his back at me. I stood directly behind him, praying for a miracle. Something wasn't quite right.

Tazmaine leaned up and kissed Trevor. I stepped around him to face them both and cringed as their mouths moved. She released her hold on his chin. "Oh yes, I will take this one. He is young and strong, fit for a queen." She pulled his hand, and he followed blindly. Trevor was in a trance as he leisurely followed her sitting in the chair nearest to her.

"Siön Baptiste, you have some explaining to do. The elders will not be happy with what has happened here tonight." Her voice echoed throughout the room.

"Something is wrong here. I can feel a presence and I can't put my

finger on it." I sent my thought to Siön Baptiste.

"*She is right, I feel it too.*" Shadow repeated in our minds.

I wanted to grab my gun and start shooting but I wasn't sure if that would help. Just as the thought crossed my mind, someone appeared from the far corner of the room.

"Oh, my God," I cried, retreating until my back met the cold hard wall. Everyone in the room stared at me, not noticing the man in the corner. He smiled, sending a quake of fear rushing through me. "It's not possible." Covering my face, I hoped and prayed what I saw was a figment of my imagination. When I peeked again, the figure had joined Tazmaine next to Trevor.

"What is wrong?" Sevastian, standing near me, reached out for my arm.

I stepped back, only to stumble, losing my footing and falling to the ground. "Don't touch me," I screamed. The images of the man and the memories of what he'd done came pouring back in a stream of hate and revenge.

The man's laughter filled the room. "We meet again, my sweet."

"Alastair!" Siön Baptiste whispered.

Everyone watched as he played with Trevor's hair. Trevor was a motionless zombie. "You remember me." Alastair sent his words straight into my heart. "Thought you killed me, did you? Your own father. I am an elder, child. It takes much more than a knife to put me down."

"What is wrong?" Sevastian appeared torn between supporting me or taking his side by Alastair.

I remembered that fateful day. I had done something horrible and would forever be ashamed even if the act meant my survival. The vivid memories of being tied to the bed and the flashback of slicing his throat caused me to scream. "You should be dead," I cried, tears running down my face.

Alastair grinned. "I claim retribution for the wrong that was done to me." He turned towards Siön Baptiste. "You must give me a gift and I claim Samantha." His hideous laughter made us all cringe.

"What is wrong?" Sevastian asked, looking me straight in the eyes.

Alastair interrupted the silence. "The woman." He pointed at me. "She killed Nicholi, leaving me to clean up the mess. As a witness to the murder, I can choose the punishment. I brought her to my home and thoroughly reproved her," he sneered.

Siön Baptiste had been moving quietly forward, inching his way towards Alastair. "What did you do, Alastair?" "*Why didn't you tell me? What did he do to you?*" he asked in my mind.

"He raped me," I answered, head bowed, eyes tightly shut, trying to forget the vivid images.

Everyone stopped breathing all at once. The whole room stood motionless watching me.

"What?" Trevor who had once sat quiet now stood.

Tazmaine pushed him down, placing her hand firmly on his shoulder. "Sit, my pet." She paused, watching me warily. "There is no such thing as rape when it comes to our own kind. Elders can have who they choose, you silly girl." She laughed.

Sevastian interrupted her laughter. "She was not one of us, Tazmaine. He had no right."

Tazmaine stopped laughing, glaring at Alastair. "She was not of our people when you took her?" she growled.

Alastair shrugged, smiling cruelly. "I did not rape her. She offered herself freely and then tried to kill me."

I could feel my anger and power building to a point of no return. I wasn't going to let this creep control my feelings. He had no hold over me or any claim over my life. I got up off the floor and headed straight for him, only stopping inches from him.

He was pleased with my reaction. "My sweet enjoyed it as much as I did." He stroked my face with his knuckles, pulling me into his arms.

I fought the overwhelming desire to kill him on the spot and decided to play his game. I had to make it count when I attacked. "You're right," I replied.

Siön Baptiste's breath caught in his throat and a soft moan escaped his lips. I tried to talk to him but somehow he prevented me from speaking to his mind. Everyone's minds were cut off to my thoughts.

"I enjoyed being tied to your bed and painfully cut. I enjoyed you forcing your power and strength to bend me to your will. I especially enjoyed your threat on my life if I didn't obey you." I returned his caress, taking his face in my hand. "As a mere human I couldn't resist you." I reached up pulling his mouth to mine. He shuddered, closing his eyes. I rubbed my lips over his and he leaned into me.

Siön Baptiste reached us, grabbing Alastair with such force he nearly threw me to the ground. "No." I took his hand in mine, gently shoving it away. "It's okay." I smiled, trying to hide the fear I felt.

He just stared into my eyes and then stepped back. Alastair laughed. "So you want me, little fire." He enfolded me in his arms, hovering over my mouth. "I will enjoy your sweet taste for eternity. You will serve me like the dog you are." His mouth crashed into mine, spreading my lips with his tongue. I fought every cell in my body to remain in control as his aura mingled with mine, sending sensations of fire and ice through my body. He moved his mouth to my neck, licking my pulse. "Such sweet blood," he whispered. He flicked his tongue again and then sunk his teeth into my neck taking my blood. Molten lava exploded as white light danced through me. I could hardly stand as he held me to him. I maneuvered my hand inside my jacket while I caressed his neck, pulling him closer.

"Stop! You will kill her," Sevastian screamed.

I could feel myself giving in and when I thought there was no return, revenge fueled me. I clenched my fist, digging my nails into the palm of my hand. The nails cutting into flesh sent pain shooting up my arm. The pain woke me from Alistair's trance, enabling me to concentrate on getting my gun. I shifted, allowing me easy access and moving with inhuman speed, I placed the gun on Alistair's temple. "Get the fuck off me," I whispered.

Alastair released my neck but didn't release his hold over my body. "You will be dead by the time you pull the trigger. You insolent fool. I will snap you in half." His hideous laughter grated my every nerve.

"At least I will die happy." I fired three shots into his skull as he screeched, flying backwards. He had no time to react because he didn't think I had it in me. *Surprise!*

I swiveled around, dipping to the ground, already feeling Tazmaine's power, seething with anger.

Siön Baptiste moved with lightning speed as he rushed the men who stepped forward. He killed the two vampires without losing a stride. They fell to the ground in a whirlwind of dust.

I circled around, leaping in the air, tossing two stars at the third vampire who just reached Siön Baptiste. The first star hit the vampire in the chest and the second star embedded deep into his skull, directly between the eyes. Once the stars hit flesh, the six blades protracted, shooting the holy water directly into the victim. I had never heard such horrible screaming as the vampire's body bubbled, finally exploding in a rush of blood and bones, spraying everything within walking distance.

I removed the second Beretta from my holster, pointing them both at Tazmaine. "Just give me an excuse, bitch," I taunted.

She stood, watching it all unfold with a wicked smile beaming on her face. "Siön Baptiste, you have made a grave mistake tonight."

He shrugged his shoulders. "It is you who have made a mistake, Tazmaine. You have broken our covenant. Do you not honor the ways of our people?" He sighed, walking casually to my side. "Taking a human who has been claimed is a penalty of death."

"How was I supposed to know she was a human at the time Alastair claimed her." She was retreating and Siön Baptiste used this opportunity to ruffle her feathers. "He lied to me. It was his right to take her." Her eyes now wide with fear. "I did not know, I swear."

It's funny after everything that had happened, I almost pitied her. *Almost!* "Siön Baptiste, what does your law say about conniving bitches?"

She hissed, taking a step in my direction. "I would stay put if you don't want a bullet in your ass," I sneered, finally feeling a bit more in control. "What are we going to do?" I asked Siön Baptiste.

"She is to be taken to the elders. It is their problem not ours," Sevastian answered.

"Wait! You mean she walks out of here tonight?" I watched her as she smiled. "No gift. She doesn't get Trevor." I would kill her if she tried. *Just try please. Give me an excuse.* I thought to myself.

I didn't like the idea of her walking out of here alive. For some reason I had a sneaking suspicion she would get her own revenge.

"Shadow, take her," Siön Baptiste commanded.

Shadow strolled over to the she-devil and started to escort her out of the room. Sevastian followed on their heels, only to steal a look back and then leave. He was trying to say something to me but I didn't understand.

Siön Baptiste wrapped his arms around me. "It is over."

Trevor walked toward us, stopping to look at us both. His eyes were hurt tremendously as I peeked past Siön Baptiste to see him watching. I reluctantly drew away, and that was when I felt it. Something was terribly wrong. I stepped by Siön Baptiste and stood a few feet from Trevor. Out of the corner of my eye, I saw a flash and turned to see. Then I heard Trevor gasp. I swiveled back to him and saw a hand through his chest, holding his heart. The heart disintegrated as Trevor slowly turned to ashes. His eyes were wide with fear and pain as he crumbled before me.

Alastair stood behind Trevor's now decaying body. His head and skull blown open from my attack. His voice was slurred as he spoke. "You thought you could kill me with a gun! You will die and everyone you love will die. I have made a pact with the werewolves and we will rule the world. You had your chance to join me." He launched his attack, racing towards me.

I got three more shots off before Siön Baptiste hit him in mid air. Both men flew through the room, plummeting into the drapes and walls. I heard an inhuman scream as they rolled slashing at each other. A loud rip and tear screeched into the air as Siön Baptiste stood holding Alastair's still beating heart. Fire appeared out of no-where, leaping into his hand, devouring the heart. Alistair's body crumbled as it fell to the ground.

"No!" I cried. "No, this can't be happening." I collapsed, falling into darkness, only hearing Siön Baptiste's soothing voice speaking in my head.

* * * *

Siön Baptiste held me, searching my mind. I could feel him probing for answers. *"Will you ever forgive me, my love?"*

Trevor's decaying face would be imprinted in my nightmares for all eternity. Could I ever forgive Siön Baptiste for barging into my life? Only time would tell. I only knew my life could never be the same. The love of my life was gone forever as so many others and nothing I could do would bring him back. The hurt in his eyes would haunt me for the rest of my days.

Nothing could change the fact that I was responsible for Trevor's death. I wasn't sure if I wanted to go on living with the guilt. The only thing that spurred me on was revenge. I would have Trevor's, Carl's, and my own revenge before I died. I promised myself that much.

Time grows short as the next full moon quickly approaches. I have to find Ty and drift to survive. Sevastian wants to work with me on strengthening my powers so that I can fight without the aid of weapons. I am all for his help. Even Shadow has agreed to help train me.

I've been avoiding Siön Baptiste for days. Sevastian told me he'd made peace with the elders, however fragile it was. I vented my frustration about vampire politics but only Shadow agreed with me. Sevastian ensured me we needed the elders in order to keep all the vampires in check. I somehow don't believe him.

"Without them the world would surely perish," he explained.

I didn't trust them as far as I could throw them. I would just as soon kill them all, that way I know I would be safe.

My love life is nonexistent for the time being. I care deeply for Siön Baptiste but the pain of losing Trevor has halted the natural progression of our relationship. He sends flowers every day and every day I send them back. I won't be bought. We will just have to see how things work out but for now, revenge was the only thing on my mind.

All hell will break loose in a few weeks and I am leading the way. Vampires and werewolves alike had better keep on the look-out because there's a new hunter in town.

The End

Printed in the United States
68440LVS00003B/103-126

9 781586 087258